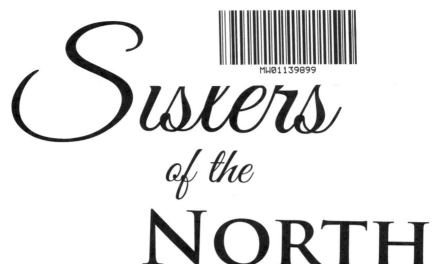

Sisters of the NORTH

A Modern Retelling of Sense & Sensibility

To Jodie

EMILY KIRKHAM

Emily Kirkham

DRAGON HILL

The Publisher: Dragon Hill Publishing Ltd.

Library and Archives Canada Cataloguing in Publication

Title: Sisters of the North / Emily Kirkham.

Names: Kirkham, Emily, author. | Adaptation of (work): Austen, Jane, 1775–1817. Sense and sensibility.

Identifiers: Canadiana (print) 2021028191X | Canadiana (ebook) 20210281928 | ISBN 9781896124803 (softcover) | ISBN 9781896124810 (PDF)

Classification: LCC PS8621.I7375 S57 2021 | DDC C813/.6—dc23

Project Director: Marina Michaelides
Layout & Production: Alesha Braitenbach
Cover Design: Tamara Hartson
Cover Image: From Getty Images: levkr, MCRMfotos

Produced with the assistance of the Government of Alberta

Alberta
Government

Printed in China
PC: 38-1

Dedication

To my mom and dad who taught me patience,
perseverance and how to poop in the woods.

Acknowledgments

First, thank you to Jaclyn for all the stories; without you I would be too boring to write a book. I would also like to thank my beta readers, Nicole Dhillon, Santana Laird and Pat Steffes who gave me the hope that people might actually like to read what I write. This book would also not be possible without the tireless work of my editor Faye Boer and kind consideration of my publisher Marina Michaelides.

CHAPTER
one

The day Ellie's Dad died was as boring and uneventful as any day in Sober, BC. Even though it was late, the northern sun glared into Ellie's eyes as she hoisted her hockey bag onto her back and made her way into the arena.

Ellie played hockey like she did everything in life, reserved and emotionless. If there is one thing growing up in a small Northern oil town will teach you is that you better be prepared to fit a stereotype, and if you don't, you better keep your mouth shut. Women don't play hockey. Not in small towns anyway. Figure skating, sure. Slow pitch, fine. But hockey, that was for the Y chromos.

Ellie may have been reserved and calm on the ice, but that didn't mean she wasn't good. She skated around the boys, scored goals and got shit done. Ellie didn't last long in the minor leagues. Eventually, the parents started making comments about "the appropriateness of a young impressionable girl on a team with teenage boys." They were "concerned about her." And it wasn't just the parents; her teammates resented her talent and wanted her off the team. She left without a fight. Ellie didn't play again until she was an adult in a local rec league.

The first time she played no one knew she was a woman. The general comment was, "Who is the small dude with the bad mullet and the wicked backhand?" But they figured it out in the dressing room afterwards, when she changed without showering, avoiding eye contact with the overweight men walking around with their dongs wagging in the air. It was amusing to Ellie that a group of tightly wound homophobes would be comfortable hanging out naked, snapping towels at each other's butts.

Ellie wasn't the only woman at pickup hockey. Carrie Braun, the gym teacher at Sober High School, played defense at least once a week. Happily embracing the stereotype of lesbian gym teachers the world over. When Ellie met Carrie, who had come to town from the city looking for work, she thought the town would eat her alive. The conservative moms of Sober whispered under their breath about Ms. Braun. But then she taught their pubescent sons to jump like Jordan and run track like FGJ, so a quiet truce emerged.

Carrie held back no punches (on the ice or in the dressing room), showering with the sausage-party men, shrugging her football-player shoulders at Ellie when she came out, her six-foot form dripping wet and naked, "I'm not going to work smelling like hockey-ass." Today's game was no different, as Carrie would come to Ellie's defense yet again on the ice.

A couple shifts into the second period, Ellie scored her third goal of the game. Snagging the top corner of the net after dangling around the defenseman and making him look like a fool for falling for the deke. The defenseman was overweight and slow, and he was at least a foot taller than Ellie on skates. He wore number 69 on his jersey, and like most adult male recreational players, he didn't wear a face cage, so you could see he was missing a few chicklets in his jaw.

Ellie didn't celebrate the goal but skated behind the net, giving Carrie a quick fist pump for her pass. She didn't see Number 69 coming with a sucker punch to the back of her head.

Ellie hit the ice hard, and her ears rang with a deafening squeal, echoing through her head like the sound of a hollow drum. Her mouth felt wet, and she saw a red spray on the ice. Ellie traced her tongue around her teeth. Good, none missing. She rolled to her back just in time to see Carrie shake her gloves to the ice, grab number 69 by the front of the jersey and punch him straight in his toothless mouth. Number 69 fell backwards on top of Ellie, the weight of his 250-pound body driving the air out of her lungs like the squeeze of an accordion. At that point her mind must have decided to play safe and check out for a while, as blackness crept across her eyes like spilling ink.

When Ellie came to, she was lying on the floor of the dressing room, looking up into Carrie's face, head pounding.

Great, another concussion, Ellie thought.

"Ellie, your phone has been ringing like crazy, so I answered it. There's bad news." Carrie said.

"What?" Ellie sat up, watching the room spin.

"Your dad passed away from a heart attack an hour ago. Your sister Val just called from the hospital."

CHAPTER
two

Valerie Dashwood grew up a dancer. Ballet, hip-hop, jazz—she even tried Highland for a brief period but was weirded out when the instructor tied her hands to her sides to prevent them from moving. Of all the dances, ballet was her greatest love. Her plan was to get out of this hick town and get into the National Ballet School in Toronto, then get chosen for a company.

She was talented and had the perfect ballet body to match—long legs, graceful neck and toe muscles that would make a body builder jealous. Her marks in high school weren't great, and each time she applied to ballet school with her audition video and transcripts, she got a simple rejection letter: "Perfect form and skill; improve your grades and apply again." But Val had run out of time; she was done high school now, ending up with a permanent low B average (to be honest, there were a few more Cs than Bs). The only way she could improve her grades was to go to the local college for upgrading.

At least that was the plan, until her dad passed away. On the day she heard the news, it was early July. Val worked as a server at the local gentlemen's clubs, The Northern Bush. Val wondered why they called strip joints "gentlemen's clubs"; the patrons were definitely not gentlemen. But it was the best paid serving job in town, so she put up with it.

Val was finishing up her shift when she noticed a few of the strippers gathered around in the corner. The club was nearly empty as the stragglers were being ushered out the door by the bouncers. As a rule, most bars didn't have good lighting, but strip clubs took low lighting to a new extreme. No one wanted to see the giant mole on the stripper's inner thigh or the crow's feet around her eyes. So, the atmosphere was hazy, even though smoking wasn't allowed, so when Val peered over at the girls, she just barely saw a stout man sitting on the couch.

"You want us to kick you in the balls?" Candy asked. She was the tallest of the girls and naked to her nipple pasties and thong.

"Yeah, four hundred. And I wanna feel it," the man said as his tongue flicked out over his lips like a snake's.

Val came closer to the group as this looked to be an interesting deal. Strip club patrons tend to be a mixture of unwashed people talking to themselves and boisterous bro-type alpha males attempting to prove their heterosexuality in front of their friends. This middle-aged man was definitely in the former category. He wore small Harry Potter–style glasses and sported a bald spot that perspired like an orange left out in the sun. Val suspected he lived in his mother's basement and trolled on a dangerous amount of porn online.

A round of giggles erupted from the group of strippers. "I'll do it," Candy said. "Four hundred for sure?" Candy was a good foot and a half taller than the other strippers, partly because of the five-inch stilettos she wore.

"You better do it right, or I'm not paying," the man replied as he readied himself, spreading his legs slightly wider than his hips, a look of excitement passing his beady eyes.

"Alrighty," Candy said.

Val put down her tray of empty glasses to get a better view of the action.

Candy put one knee on the couch next to the man and swung her other knee directly into his crotch, her arms braced on either side of him. It was more a lover's tap than a real kick in the balls. If that was all she had, she would never survive a mugging.

The man didn't call out or move, he just sighed, and shook his head. "No way, that's not what I asked for. I want you to step on my balls!"

Candy rose off the couch. "Freak," she said as she rolled her eyes at the other strippers, "Someone else can look after you. This isn't worth the cash. He smells like my grandmother's closet."

Val stepped into the circle, facing the man on the couch. "I'll do it," she said.

The man eyed Val up and down, taking in her five-foot one-inch body. She was tiny, mostly legs and boobs. No one would think Val could pack any punch.

"No way," the man mocked. "I want a stripper, not some girly girl."

"Look, I know you're probably used to luring young girls into a white panel van," Val walked closer to the couch, "but I can certainly kick the sand out of your pussy if that's what you want." The man raised his eyebrows at this comment and licked his lips, obviously turned on by her feistiness.

"Great! Let the little server girl try," Candy said. "Come on gals, let's get outta here. I need to close up with the DJ, and this freak show is boring."

The other strippers knew who the Queen Bee was around the place and made to follow Candy, but they were moving slowly, looking over their shoulders to see what Val would do.

"Come on, little girl," the man taunted, which filled Val with memories of every pervert who'd ever hit on her or grabbed her ass. And there were many. She got the feeling this guy might like it if she were underage and not actually 19.

Val stepped up onto the couch next to the man. She wasn't going to fuck around. This guy was going to get what he asked for and more. As Val lifted her high heeled foot in the air, using her long-trained ballet muscles to balance, she thought about every asshole douchebag from her past and slammed the point of her high heel directly into his ball sack.

The man took in a breath but didn't let out a sound. His eyes stared up at Val with a disgusted look that could only be predatory. Val felt a fire in her head and smashed her heel down into his crotch again. This time, the guy actually shuddered, like he had eaten some of Hannibal Lecter's fava beans.

Val climbed down off the couch, breathing slightly from the exertion but feeling rather cathartic. *I really should do this more often,* she thought. The man panted like a dog in heat. He reached into his pocket and pulled out a roll of cash, flipped out four hundred-dollar bills and handed them to Val.

"Here's one more," he said, as he pulled another hundred from his wad. As he passed the last bill to Val, he grabbed her arm and pulled her close, putting his mouth next to her ear. The smell of stale burritos and beer on his breath nearly knocked her out.

"That was the best I ever had," he said. "I'll be back." He released Val's arm, and she pulled away, feeling a sticky warmth from where his damp hands had gripped her arm.

Val took the money and turned to walk away. It was the easiest five hundred she had ever made, but the money felt hot and dirty in her hand. She quickly slid it into her pocket with the rest of her tips from the night. A heavy pocket always made her feel good, but that feeling was about to be smashed apart.

As she turned to leave, Joey, one of the bouncers approached her, his face not his usual "fuck off" that he had for the bar patrons. He looked like he would be a great, big teddy bear, if it wasn't for the sleeve tattoos of snakes eating bunny rabbits. Or bunny rabbits eating snakes? Val could never tell which one was first.

"There was a call from the hospital," he said. "Your dad has had a heart attack." Val felt the room go silent, her head ringing.

"Is he okay?" she asked, her voice cracking.

"No, he didn't make it," Joey said. He grabbed Val into a rib-crushing hug, and she broke apart, sobbing into his chest like a lost child.

three

Dave Dashwood spent most of his time loitering around the local pub of Sober (the name ironically bestowed before it became the town with the highest pub per capita in British Columbia), looking for new and innovative ways to blow his money. He was constantly searching for the next great pyramid scheme or sure thing bet that would launch his forever fading bank account into the stratosphere and out of this back-end hole of a town.

On this particular Sunday afternoon, Dave met up with his eldest son, John. Dave was an affectionate sort and did love his son; however, this regard doubled when John married Fanny Price, the great granddaughter of George Price, who held the original stake on the oilfield claim nine kilometres south of town. John had married into money, somewhat by accident, having knocked-up Fanny when she was twenty-two and so securing the marriage. Dave couldn't be more proud.

Today, Dave wanted John to invest in his newest venture: selling face rejuvenation cream. He needed five grand to buy stock of the cream. He would begin to pull in the profits as he built his sales team of local stay-at-home moms selling the product to other stay-at-home moms. Given this was an oil town and the ratio of men to women was about ten to one, this latest venture would fail about as fast as you can say "wrinkle-free," but nothing would deter Dave when he had a scheme in mind.

"John, you know this will be good for you and Fanny," Dave claimed, slurping from his pale yellow, slightly warm beer. "Fanny could do some sales of Juvy-Cream too; it would give her something to do while she's at home with Michael." Michael was Fanny and John's eighteen-month-old child, who was set to inherit the Price family fortune.

John was wary of any propositions his dad made. Even though he was raised by his mother, who had rarely let John set foot inside the house of Dave and his daughters, he was well versed in the relative ease with which his dad could lose his money. The last time Dave had tried to get money out of his son, it was to pay back a loan he took out to buy llamas. He was going to bring them up north to Sober with the plan to sell their wool online. The llamas had in fact made it to Sober, but no one had mentioned to Dave that he didn't need to butcher and skin them to sell their wool. He had found a friend on the local reserve who was experienced in looking after animals and had paid Dave for the lama meat, although he declared later that it wasn't nearly as good as moose or bear and was only fit for dogfood.

No one would buy the lama skins, and Dave was left with five hides he didn't know what to do with. They became permanent rugs on their floor, adding a certain musty farm smell to the house every time it was humid outside.

"Dad, you know Fanny and I would love to lend you some money, but we have to think about Michael. He is going south for his education, and that won't be cheap." John had ordered a Shirley Temple, his drink of choice, and he sipped from the straw like a hummingbird at a feeder.

"Of course. Have to look after the boy. Good kid that Michael," Dave said. "But John, this could be an opportunity of a lifetime! Think of the return you'll get once we have five salespeople hocking the Juvy-Cream around town. You don't even have to do any work once that happens; you just take a skim from the sales."

"What about Ellie? She's welding at the site, probably making a killing. You should ask her." John leaned back, looking confident about his suggestion.

"Asked her. She said no." Dave's head was drooping. He was feeling the effects of his fourth watery beer. It was Sunday afternoon at two, and he was almost behind his usual intake. Dave felt his opportunity with John slipping.

"John, there is something else I wanted to ask you about." Dave leaned in. He had put this off for too long, and he knew he had to get this one request out before it was too late. Somewhere in the back of his half-drunk mind, Dave knew that he would never be rich or even comfortable. Even though he had also worked as a welder at the Sober Oilfields for over twenty-five years, and he had a comfortable salary, the money never seemed to stick around. It disappeared on him, leaving his account nearly the minute it came in as if dropping into a black hole.

John's eyes rolled back. He didn't know what was coming, but the serious look on his dad's meaty face made his stomach turn. This couldn't be good.

"I need you to promise me you'll look after your sisters when I'm gone," Dave said, and in an unexpected way, he looked into his son's eyes. John sensed that Dave's words were more a command than a request.

This, he hadn't expected. He liked his half-sisters, Ellie and Val, but what did his dad mean by "look after them"? He hadn't really been thinking about his father's longevity, but when he looked into his dad's watery eyes, he finally saw an old man. One who had kept his liver properly pickled for as long as John had been alive, as well as a man who worked a hard labour job (when he showed up for work) in an unforgiving climate. Maybe his dad didn't have that much longer?

"Of course, Dad, I'll look after Ellie and Val," John said, forcing an awkward smile and thinking about how he would break the news to Fanny. Of course, he wouldn't say anything until his dad actually kicked it, but the thought of telling Fanny she would be parting with any money filled John with a sense of unease.

Dave sighed, his body sagging back into his chair with relief, mentally thinking that he no longer had the pressure of putting money away for Ellie and Val, should something happen to him. That he hadn't made any payments on his life insurance policy (which had already expired) would no longer burden his mind. After Dave got his son to shake on the arrangement, John made a quick exit, lest his dad try to extract any other promises, or squeeze him for a loan he didn't want to give.

John didn't find out about his father's death until later that evening. He got a call at home from the hospital, informing him that Dave Dashwood had passed away of a heart attack after being told by the pub owner that unless he paid his overdue tab, he wouldn't be allowed back in. Even though the bar owner liked Dave, he found it annoying that Dave should find a way to avoid his overdue bill by dying right there on the spot.

John sighed as he put the phone down, thinking of how he would tell Fanny about the debt he now had to his half-sisters.

CHAPTER
four

Ellie was used to getting her sister out of bed in the morning. Today was no different. She had been dragging her sister from her room since pre-school. Her tactics had always been the same. Come by, knock twice hard on the door. Ten minutes later, crack the door and yell at the comatose figure twisted up in the sheets on the bed, her form like a crime scene body outline, arms askew. Who could sleep that way? Val's room matched her personality, slightly below hoarder's hollow but above a simple untidy with the distinct smell of damp wood chips mixed with decaying fruit. The former attributed to her long-since-deceased rabbit, Batman, whose cage remained in the room like a solemn tribute. The last time Ellie had attempted to remove the cage, Val had broken down in tears, saying it was "too soon" even though the rabbit had been dead some three years.

Ellie spotted a plate with molding apple slices on Val's bedside table, having brought them to Val a few weeks ago when she was on a hunger strike, and obviously she had refused to eat them. She sighed as she shoved the door past forty-five degrees because of the piles of clothes on the floor and grabbed the plate of apples.

She gave Val's shoulder a shake, "Fanny and John are going to be here any minute, Kiddo." An audible groan issued from the figure on the bed.

"Vultures," Val said, her eyes still closed and body motionless.

"They're coming to help us organize Dad's stuff." Ellie was guessing at the object of her brother and sister-in-law's visit as they hadn't told her why they were dropping by. She stepped on a curling iron buried beneath the clothes on the floor and had to grab the door jamb to keep from falling on Val's bed.

Val sat up, her covers dropping off. She slept naked and never felt much reason to hide her body from anyone, including her sister. "That bitch Fanny wants to come and take anything we have of value."

"There isn't much to take, Kiddo," Ellie said, as she turned to leave the room. "Might as well get it over with."

Ellie didn't want to deal with her half-brother and his wife today either. Since her Father's unexpected death, she had more on her plate than she could handle. All the financials were left up to her, and Dave Dashwood hadn't really left anything in what could be called an organized state. It felt like a losing game of monopoly, one where there were no Get Out of Jail Free cards, or jackpot in the middle, just endless debt with no chance to buy back any properties from the bank. Ellie always hated playing that game anyway. She'd always suspected her Dad of cheating.

It is not that Ellie thought that their family was ever well off. That much was obvious. She just never realized that his death would mean the creditors would come hunting for what meager possessions they had. The house was going to go, that was for sure. It was mortgaged beyond all possibilities (How had the banks allowed him to do that?) and represented the bulk of any value left in the estate. Dave had not made payments on his truck in over six months. But since he was buddies with the only car dealer in town, somehow, he'd managed to hold on to it. Until now, that is. Kenny, the car-dealer "friend" had come by to pick up the truck two days post mortem. He was nice enough to bring Ellie and Val a sympathy card and a tuna casserole his wife had made him bring over. Val had smashed the casserole into the garbage before Kenny had even left the house, embarrassing Ellie (only slightly).

The final kick in the teeth from all this was that Ellie had to make the hard decision not to go to university. She had finally saved up enough money welding that she had submitted her application to the nearest northern city equivalent of an educational institution. Her high school grades were excellent, so she wasn't surprised when she received her acceptance letter into general sciences. Her plan was to transition to engineering in a big city university once she had a few years under her belt. With an engineering degree she might end up back at the oilfields, but she wouldn't have to deal with the hard labour work of welding anymore. Not to mention the pay would be enough that she and Val wouldn't have to worry anymore.

With all the debt her dad had accumulated, there was no way she could take off to university, not this year, maybe not ever. Val wanted to go to ballet school, and who was going pay for that? Ellie's heart sank at the thought of telling Val about her withdrawal from school. Val would freak out. She always said Ellie was the "smart one," who was going to make the big bucks and get out of this hick town.

So why were John and Fanny coming by? To fight over the few possessions they had left? The lama rugs on the floor? Ellie hoped they would take those, as the animals' socket-less eyes were constant reminders of another of her father's life mistakes. Maybe they were coming to gloat? She wouldn't put that past Fanny; she was a Grade A bitch as her sister would routinely point out.

A second after the doorbell rang, their front door swung open and a small child burst into the hall, followed closely by a Filipino woman Ellie had never met. This must be the fourth nanny her sister-in-law had employed since her son Michael was born a year and a half ago. Michael ran into the living room and began doing laps across the furniture, like a tiny gymnast. His nanny followed him, arms outstretched as if for fall protection. Fanny strode in, dropped her Gucci bag on the living room table and flopped into the couch, her phone held tightly in her carefully manicured hands.

Fanny was put together like a puzzle missing a few pieces. It all snuggly fit, but the gaps in the picture were enough to make you wonder if Fanny had been dropped a few too many times as a child. She was pretty, there was no doubt about it. But her face changed every time Ellie saw her. A little cheek pull here, a small lip injection there. It was enough to make Ellie do a double take when she saw her sister-in-law, just to make sure she was looking at the same person. Fanny was also incredibly tiny; her small form could be mistaken for a child if not for the boob job and expensive handbags.

"Hi Fanny." Ellie was civil, but her voice carried an edge of her not-so-secret exasperation. "And you are?" Ellie asked, her comment directed to the nanny, who was attempting to keep Michael from impaling himself on the furniture.

"Oh, don't bother, Ellie," Fanny said. She didn't look up from her phone. "She doesn't speak English. I thought it best this time, as I had so much trouble with Isabella. I knew she was hitting on John, so that little bitch had to go."

Ellie slowly lowered the outstretched hand that she had offered to the nanny. The nanny's eyes looked from Ellie to Fanny in quick succession. Ellie wondered if her English wasn't nearly as bad as Fanny assumed.

"Doesn't that make it hard to…well…talk to her?" Ellie assumed that some sort of parenting would require communication between the parent and the caregiver, but as she had never been a parent herself or been exposed to what could be called good parenting, her perceptions may have been wrong.

Before Fanny could answer, surmising she cared to do so, being as she was engaged in a rapid text battle, Ellie's brother, John, entered the room, diaper bag on his shoulder.

John was pale-faced with a tall, lean body. He was not a bad-looking man; after all, he had managed to snare Fanny. Sadly, marriage and fatherhood had not been good to John as his once thick hair was thinning on top, and his insecurities shone through his complexion like a deep sea creature.

In an awkward gesture, John raised his arms to give Ellie a hug. She didn't usually hug her brother. They rarely saw each other, but Ellie suspected this show of affection must be because of their father's death. She hoped it would be short-lived.

Ellie gave in to her brother with what she thought would be a quick hug, but John held on and patted her back in a "there-there" sort of way.

"He will be missed, Ellie. He will be missed," John said. Was he attempting to cry? Ellie politely shrugged away from his embrace.

"Yes, he will, John. Thank you." Ellie turned and sat on the couch, avoiding Michael as he came round the room on his fourth or fifth lap.

"Where is Val?" John asked as he sat down.

"She will be out in a bit, I'm sure," Ellie said, hearing her sister-in-law snort as she stared at her phone. Fanny looked at her husband, opening her eyes in a meaningful way. Obviously, she wanted him to get on with the point of the visit.

"Ellie, Fanny and I wanted to talk to you about something." John leaned forward, his eyes conveying what might be considered empathy if you didn't know him. "Before Dad died, he asked me to look after you and Val."

Ellie gave a sharp intake of air, the shock of this statement causing her thoughts to jumble. Was there a possibility that her own family might be coming to help them out? Fanny had money; everyone knew that. Her father had a part of the original claim on the oilfields, but Ellie would bet her life there was no way Fanny would part with a penny of that money, especially for her husband's half-sisters. Perhaps John himself intended to help them out?

"I know you will lose this house, so I've found somewhere for you to go. Fanny has an aunt and uncle out in Hilcrest with an acreage. They have a trailer on the back of the lot, and they've agreed to let you stay there for a few hundred a month." John reached out and patted Ellie's knee as if she were a small child.

"Kids keep breaking into the damn thing, so they need someone in there to look after it. I think they were going to have the live-in nurse stay there, but she refused," Fanny chimed in.

"Also, in return, if you could let us take over the house property here, we'll pay off the debt to the bank." John said. He gave a nod to his wife and crossed his arms, looking like a dog who deserved a biscuit.

"You want to live here?" Ellie asked, still trying to wheedle out the motives behind this transaction.

"God, no!" Fanny said. She slammed her phone down in her lap, and as Michael came by, the boy attempted to climb up on his mom. He must have assumed a break from her device meant he had an open invitation to climb onto her lap. She brushed him away and snapped her fingers at the nanny, pointing at her son in a "look after this" fashion.

"No, Ellie" John said. "The Price Family just wants the land the house is on. The neighbourhood block is to be converted into condos."

Bingo, thought Ellie. The Price Family business was constantly looking for the next big development. The houses on this block were not in the greatest shape. They provided somewhat affordable housing in an oil-rich town where developers were always looking to claw back from the people in the form of alcohol, housing and Tim Hortons coffee. Stuffing people into overpriced condos was a profitable endeavor.

"You assholes!" Val stormed into the room, still in her PJs and bare feet. She looked like she was ready to take names.

"Val! Language!" John said, "I know you are distraught over Dad's passing, but we have Michael here." He looked at his wife proudly as if he was expecting approval of his intervention, but Fanny was concentrating deeply on her phone's screen as if it held all the answers to the universe.

"Dad isn't even buried yet, and you're already thinking about making money off his place!" Val crossed her arms, her teeth gritted like she was holding back more.

"Val, sweetheart, this house isn't yours anymore. Didn't Ellie tell you? The bank owns it, so you might as well let us take care of it for you. John and I are doing you a favor." Fanny's swollen lips were pursed in a half smile. Clearly she was enjoying the situation.

Val shot a dirty look at her sister. Ellie hadn't told Val they were losing the house.

Ellie sighed, "Sorry, Kiddo, I didn't tell you yet, but John and Fanny are right. The house is going. We might as well look at this trailer they have for us. A few hundred a month is pretty affordable."

"Affordable? You're worried about what we can pay at a time like this?! Dad would never have let this happen to us!" Val said with an edge of desperation as she held back tears.

The tension was sharp in the room now. Michael had stopped his furniture cruising and decided that all the yelling drew attention away from what was really important—him. He started to wail.

"Now look what you've done!" Fanny said. "Michael is upset, and he probably won't go down for his nap, and I might have to miss my mani-pedi this afternoon!" Fanny grabbed her bag and waved at the nanny to pick up her sobbing son. She motioned to the door.

Ellie was impressed at how easily Fanny used hand gestures to communicate with her nanny. She wondered if there was a command for "diaper change" or "spank my child," and what if they got confused?

"Yes! Leave!" If Fanny's command wasn't enough for John to get out, Val's fierce look as if she was ready to claw his eyes out was enough. He stood, gave a half-smile to Ellie and scurried after his wife and child like an obedient pet.

Ellie was soon alone in the living room. In quick succession, the front door slammed, marking the exit of her half-brother and family, followed by Val storming out of the room, slamming her bedroom door and audibly sobbing into her pillow.

In contrast to all the emotional hullabaloo of the meeting, Ellie felt an eerie calm inside her. She hadn't always been this reserved. Life had thrown her so many curve balls that she had learned to bat them away with the calm patience of a monk. This was just another of life's train wrecks that Ellie would have to steer through.

CHAPTER
five

Ellie's memories of her mom were fuzzy, misty around the edges. She remembered sleeping in her mother's lap, feeling the rise and fall of her chest as she blew cigarette smoke from her lips. She could remember her smell, a mix of Chanel Number 5 with its sweet undercurrent of berries. Sometimes it was strong enough to make Ellie's eyes water, but it didn't matter, she'd felt safe then and cared for.

Ellie never saw her mom much. She left when Ellie was four. "Time this kid learns to feed herself," her mom had declared as she walked out the door, while her dad, Dave Dashwood, was sobbing on the couch. After that there was a lot of crying from her dad. Sometimes Ellie would try crying louder, just to see if he would pay attention to her, but it didn't go anywhere.

Ellie did learn to feed herself. It was pretty much a necessity. For a while, some of the neighbors would come by, but they were just a hassle. She had to pretend like they were helping. But Ellie had already figured out how to boil water for noodles and pour her own milk. Why did she need some half-drunk guy from next door coming by to tell her he would make grilled cheese, only to pass out on the couch halfway through, meaning Ellie had to rescue it and scrape all the burned bits into the garbage?

Life wasn't perfect, Ellie knew in her heart that one day her mom would come back, and she would have a normal family. Three days before her sixth birthday, Ellie's world was rocked. Not in a sit-com-happy-ending sort of way but more in a Jerry Springer fashion.

When Ellie opened the door, her mom, Joanne, stood before her. On her arm hung a car seat with a tiny squalling baby strapped in like it was ready to be launched into space.

"Where's your dad?" she asked.

Ellie's mother brushed past and plunked the car seat down on the floor. Ellie watched her go by, as she marched off into the living room with the determination only seen from skinny, short women with something to prove. Ellie felt a warmth inside her despite the –30°C chilled air that had flooded the entryway from the open door. Was her mom finally coming home? Or maybe the warm feeling was a fever? She brought the back of her hand to her forehead. Nope, no fever.

Ellie stayed in the doorway and looked at the baby, the tiny face screwed up and wrinkled like a turtle's. Were these things supposed to be cute? Her thoughts were interrupted by the loud voices of her parents from the living room.

"What do you mean, it's not my baby?" her dad bellowed, emotion surging out like an overflowing toilet.

"Well, Dave, how am I supposed to know? You think I keep track of that shit? Doesn't matter. I'm leaving for good, going to the city. I'm tired of looking after the mess you make. Ellie could use a sister, anyway. It's not like she ever has anyone around here." Joanne's tiny form paced back and forth as Ellie peered down the hall into the living room. Her dad was planted on the couch, his form partially obscured by the sprawl of empty beer bottles on the table.

Sister? she thought. Ellie felt a lingering hope and wondered if her mom was going to come back for real, and Ellie would have a sibling to add to the family. The little baby continued to squawk; her tiny arms pumped the air like she understood the injustice of being strapped into the contraption. Ellie decided to free her. It took a bit of twisting to get the belts off from around her little arms, but as soon as she pulled them free, the baby's wails began to quiet.

Ellie put her hands under the baby's arms and lifted. The baby felt light, like a doll made of jelly. She pulled the wiggling form into the crook of her arm and planted her butt on the floor. Ellie knew if she stood up, the weight of the baby would likely make her fall over because she wasn't used to holding an object almost a third of her own weight. The baby fussed, although much less. Ellie saw a soother in the car seat.

No wonder she's cranky, Ellie thought, *the baby must have been lying on top of it.* Ellie plugged the soother into the baby's open mouth and watched as she immediately clamped down and began sucking, her mouth making a quiet smacking noise.

The baby had giant brown eyes, like the deer you see on the highway. She stared up at Ellie, unblinking. Ellie hoped this kid wasn't as dumb and inbred as the deer around town.

"Joanne, you can't leave me again," Dave said. "I don't know how to look after a baby."

"Whatever. I'm done. These are your mistakes; you can deal with them." Joanne pulled her jacket back on. Ellie felt her throat close up, as if she'd swallowed a bite of sandwich that wasn't going down.

"But the baby might not even be mine!" Dave cried, his voice cracking like a prepubescent boy.

"Look, Dave," Joanne stopped to look at him, "Ellie needs someone because she sure as hell doesn't have you or me, and there ain't no way I'm staying in this fuck hole anymore! Having a sister will be good for her."

Her mom stomped back to the front door and yanked it open, letting the cold air whip around. Ellie looked down at the baby again. Any hopes she had of her mom coming back were being sucked out that door. In that moment, she knew that she would keep this baby safe. It felt like a weight on her body, pushing her into the floor. Ellie pulled the baby closer to keep the cold air from her bare cheeks.

"Mom, wait!" Ellie called, her voice a whisper.

Joanne stopped and looked down. A flash of what looked almost like sadness hit her face, but the moment was gone before Ellie knew if she had really seen it.

"What's her name?"

"Val," she said, "short for Valerie. But whatever. Call her anything you want, Ellie. I'm out of this shithole." Her mom knew an exit moment when she had one. She stepped out into the wind and slammed the door.

CHAPTER
six

After the encounter with Fanny and John that morning, Val had a difficult time getting ready for work. Her head swirled with emotions. One minute she was angry at Ellie for not telling her how bad things were and that they were going to lose the house, and the next minute she would burst into tears, believing in her heart that both of them would be stuck in this town forever.

It was a well-known fact when growing up in a small town, you either got out successfully after high school and made your way in the city (after which point it was acceptable to return to the small town to do a sensible thing like raising a family), or you never left. Usually pregnancy was the cause, or money reasons, or both.

In Val's mind, dance was her ticket out of Sober. Dave Dashwood, despite all his deficiencies, had supported Val and her ballet all along. Likely that support was to the detriment of saving for other important items, such as paying the mortgage or contributing to your other daughter's education savings. But now that he was gone and the true mess of what he'd left behind was revealed, Val knew she had to make a change. Bussing tables at the local strip club made enough money to buy makeup and shoes, but it wouldn't get her out of Sober, not anytime this century.

Val tried to straighten her dark hair, but the little flyaways always kept shooting up, making her head look more like Crusty the Clown's.

"Fuck!" she wailed, as she threw her brush at the mirror in frustration and fought back tears for the hundredth time.

Despite her messy locks, Val was still beautiful. Her olive-toned skin was in stark contrast to Ellie's pale complexion, highlighting that they obviously had different fathers (even though Dave proclaimed both girls had to be his). Val always wished she was more like Ellie, who was pretty in an uncomplicated way. Val's looks attracted the wrong type of men, the kind who would grab her ass when she walked by or offer to take her to dinner and then be pissed off when she didn't want to go back to their place on a first date.

Val looked at her reflection, her hair falling around her shoulders in soft waves. A dramatic thought passed through her mind, and she decided to leave her hair down. She picked up her darkest lipstick and passed it over the pale pink she had already donned. She then went to work on her eyes, adding a striking eyeliner and some sparkly blue eyeshadow that she had bought for Halloween a few years ago when she had dressed as Carmen Miranda. When she was finished, Val was pleased with her appearance. She looked sexy. She usually avoided anything that brought attention to her looks, but today she had another plan.

She quickly packed up her bag and headed out the door, jumping into the 1985 Ford Escort her dad had bought for her as a graduation present. It was black with faux red leather interior. Because of an unfortunate issue with the carburetor, the engine often stalled and she would be stuck somewhere waiting until it cooled down so she could get the little shitbox going again.

Despite the inconvenience, Val was just happy to have her own wheels. Getting around Sober on transit was pretty much impossible. The transit system was set up under a political promise from the province to help small communities. But when ninety percent of the town's population worked in the oilfields, and the other ten percent worked to service oilfield employees, the upshot was poor transit coverage in too many parts of town. Taxis were no better because they didn't make any money so had resorted to becoming the drug network for the town. So, calling a cab and not buying drugs from the driver meant he was losing money and often resulted in the passenger getting dropped off in the cold at some random location and having to walk home.

Thankfully, the little Escort gurgled to life on the first try, and Val made her way to the Northern Bush Club (affectionately called The Bush) for her shift. It was a Wednesday evening, so the club would be relatively quiet until about eight, when a lot of the guys would rumble in, being done work and having made an appearance at home before squeezing out the door to spend a few bucks watching the peelers.

A good portion of oilfield workers didn't even live in town. They did a three-week shift at the site and then sped down the highway in their pickup trucks to the city to visit their families for a week or two before repeating the whole cycle again.

As Val walked into the club, the contrast between the outside late northern sun and the dingy lighting made her blink to adjust her eyes. She nearly ran into the bulky form of Joey, who was standing in the entryway, checking the club patrons on their way in. Joey Dawson was built like a mailbox, as wide as he was tall. He had known Val for as long as she could remember because Joey was the same age as Ellie, so they had hung out together growing up. Even though Joey was from the rez, all the kids in the downtown went to the same school.

Joey often said he thought Val was from the same tribe. "You don't get skin like that unless you are some part Indian," he would tell her. "Plus, your butt is as flat as my ma's."

Sometimes it was annoying to be treated like the little sister at your place of work, but most of the time it was comforting.

When they were kids, Ellie would have to bring Val along when she hung out with her friends because either their dad wasn't around, or he was off drinking at the pub. Val remembered the time when she was seven years old. When you're that young and get to be around a bunch of teenagers, you feel like a superstar. During northern summers, kids wander around the town until all hours because the constant sun gives them a sense of invincibility. After walking for hours, Val felt like her legs had turned to Jell-O, and she just wanted to go home. She began to whine. Without saying anything, Joey scooped her up and placed her on his wide shoulders. Val felt like a queen, towering over everyone with her chin resting on Joey's dark hair.

"Hey Val, whatcha doing here today?" Joey said. "Didn't think you had a shift today."

"Got something to talk to Frank about. Is he in?" Val asked.

"Yah. He's in his office," Joey said. "You got a sec, Val? I got something I wanna show you." His face had a look of anticipation and stress, which was a strange contrast to his usual bouncer ass-kicking look.

"Sure, buddy," said Val. The club barely had any customers, and no one was coming in the door, so Joey and Val had the entryway to themselves. Val noticed that Joey had a Tupperware container sitting behind him on the check-in table. It looked circa 1960s, the kind that was baby-shit yellow with a ribbed fan impression on the lid. Val figured Joey must have inherited his mother's set. Mrs. Dawson was known for her baking.

Joey pulled out the Tupperware and opened it for Val. Inside the plastic rectangle was more than a dozen sugar cookies, each one carefully decorated with intricate designs of daisies, tulips and roses, all in matching pastel hues.

"Did you make these?" Val asked, her eyes wide in awe.

Joey nodded, an expression of absolute pride on his round face. "Yah. My ma's recipe, but the icing is my design. Have one!" He held the container out to Val, watching her closely with anticipation.

Val grabbed a cookie that was covered in neat tiny violet lilies, her favourite flower. Joey watched Val as she took a bite. He appeared to be holding his breath, like a man waiting for his jury verdict.

"Joey, these are so good," Val said between bites.

"You really think so? Ma thinks I should start a catering business. I figured I would test them out on my friends first."

"You should do that," Val agreed.

"I'm going to call it 'The Three Bisquiteers,'" he said, his small brown eyes lighting up with excitement.

"Nice one," Val said. "Okay, I'd better go. Wanna catch Frank before it gets busy."

Val munched on her sugar cookie as she made her way to the back of the club. She hoped that Joey would find success with his cookie catering, but Sober was a hard town to make a go with any small business, especially one that relied on catering for events. When she reached the office door, she knocked with more confidence than she actually felt.

Val heard a muffled "come in," so she let herself into the office. Frank Miller was the owner and operator of the Northern Bush Club. A middle-aged man with a slight belly, Frank Miller had a full head of grey hair and wore a button-down collared shirt that looked like it had seen the inside of a washing machine about a thousand times.

"Valerie Dashwood, to what do I owe the pleasure?" Frank asked as he motioned for Val to sit in a small folding chair in front of his desk that was cluttered with papers and empty coffee cups. Val liked Frank; he always treated everyone at the club fairly and never hit on anyone. The strippers gossiped that Frank was a closet gay. They were always suspicious of any man that treated them with civility and looked into their eyes instead of ogling their surgically augmented body parts.

Val sat in the folding chair, which gave a small squeak and tipped to the side. She had to angle her legs to one side to keep from tipping over.

"I think you have something on your face." Frank pointed to the corner of his mouth. Val brushed her face with her hand, finding a large chuck of cookie icing stuck to her lips.

Great, thought Val, *trying to talk to the boss with food on my face.*

"Mr. Miller," Val wasn't sure where to begin. She hadn't planned any of this. Suddenly her mouth went dry, and she felt an immediate dampness in her armpits.

"You want some time off because of your dad passing? I'm really sorry about that, Val and, of course you can take some time off. Not a problem. And please call me Frank." Frank folded his hands on his desk, his eyes displaying genuine sympathy. Val suspected that Frank understood what it felt like to lose a parent or someone close.

"No, that's not why I'm here, but thanks anyways. I wanted to ask you about a new position at the club." Val was nervous, and she hoped it didn't show.

"What do you have in mind?" Frank asked.

"Well...I want to try dancing."

Dancing was a stripper's euphemism for what they did on stage. Girls that took their clothes off for money didn't call themselves strippers or peelers; they preferred the term "dancers" or maybe "exotic dancers" to avoid confusion. Val found it ironic that the career she had dreamed of having from the time she first put on a tutu when she was four years old could have the same name as stripping down to your hoohaw for money in front of a bunch of horny middle-aged men.

"Oh, I see," Frank said, as he shuffled some papers around on his desk, apparently looking for a particular document. "Val, how old are you?"

"I'm 19. You have to be of age to work here."

"Okay, good. Sometimes we get girls with fake IDs, and to be honest, you look really young."

Val had thought that her added makeup and hairstyle would take away some of her young girl look, but obviously it didn't work on Frank. He paused and stopped shuffling papers around to look straight into Val's eyes.

"You know, it is one thing for the girls like Candy out there to do this work. I mean, that girl is a straight hard-ass bitch, but you Val, you look like if some guy looked at you the wrong way while you were on stage you might break down and cry. I can't have that happen. Dancing is no joke. You have to look like a Barbie Doll but have the skin of an elephant seal. You have the looks down, that's for sure, but I'm not so sure about the rest."

"I'm tougher than I look Frank," Val said.

"What about the sales part of the job? You know you'll have a nightly quota to fill for private dances?" Val was aware that the strippers had to sell private dances. They always bickered about who was stealing the best customers, the ones that would buy ten dances in a row and top out their quota.

"I can do that." Val was less sure about selling dances than she was about the actual stripping part of the job. But she needed Frank to know she could do all parts of the job. Somehow being on stage felt like it fit her personality. But the part where she would have to wander around the club and get the patrons to buy a dance filled her with dread.

Frank sighed. "I'm willing to give you a chance to see what you can do. You won't have your serving job anymore, and you'll have to take stage times at the start that aren't the greatest. That's just how it works around here. You won't get the good times until you prove you can pull in customers. If it doesn't work out, then I'm sorry, but I won't be calling you in. As luck would have it, one of the girls split town this week. She was supposed to be on, so you can start as early as Thursday night for the 7:00 PM show. You'll need to work your shift tonight because I don't have anyone on call for waiting tables, but I'll figure that out for the rest of the week."

Frank pulled a sheet of paper from his messy pile and handed it to Val.

"Fill out this paperwork and get it back to me. If you want Thursday's spot, I'll need your stage name right now."

"Stage name?" Val asked.

"What you want us to call you. We aren't going to have a stripper named Valerie Dashwood. You know, like Candy or Charlie."

Val hadn't thought to consider a stage name. What popped into her mind immediately was the old schoolyard game where you took your mother's maiden name plus the street name where you grew up and that would be your stripper name. But all the streets in Sober were named after trees, so that wasn't going to work. Nobody would get turned on by a name like Wilson Oak? It sounded like the name of a furniture manufacturer.

For some reason a memory surfaced in her mind from when she was a small child. Val and Ellie were being given a bath by a babysitter named Stacy. They were all blowing bubbles together and laughing. Stacy was known to have a pocketful of M&Ms, and she let Ellie and Val dip their fingers in anytime they wanted. Like most of their babysitters, Stacy didn't last because Ellie became the primary caregiver pretty quickly when their dad wasn't around, which was a lot.

"Stacy Bubbles," Val said. Not sure if this was a good name, but she didn't want to miss an opportunity to get her first shift. She figured it was as good a name as any.

Frank nodded and stood up, reaching out his hand, "Welcome to The Bush, Stacy Bubbles," he said. Val shook his hand and found that her palm was sweating; she must have been clenching her fists in her lap. She was nervous and excited, but as she left Frank's office and put on her serving apron for the night's work, a sudden dread filled her mind. How would she ever tell Ellie?

CHAPTER
seven

Life has a way of trucking on after tragedies, whether your mind is ready to accept it or not. As Ellie headed out for work the next morning, the sun was barely hitting the horizon, lighting the fog and illuminating the line of trucks on the highway headed to the oilfields. She thought it poetic that she should just fall into the same line so soon after her father died. Before, work had been a means for her to go to school. Now it felt like a prison sentence.

Her dually truck was cold this morning. It was ten years old and a pig on diesel, but no self-respecting welder could work without a truck. Plus, when winter really hit, driving the highway in some tiny import car just wasn't safe. She needed to be at least as big as all the other vehicles on the road. She swung the truck around and into the Tim Hortons parking lot, avoiding the five-block-long lineup for the drive-through.

This phenomena was something Ellie's rational brain could never sort out. Why sit in your idling truck for forty minutes to get your coffee when you could just park and walk inside? The inside of the coffee shop was always nearly empty, so she got her coffee and was back on the road to work before the waiting idiots had advanced to the order window.

Today, though, Ellie was not alone in the café. A flash of irritation crossed her mind as she saw a tall man ahead of her in the line. He turned and smiled as she joined him. It was strange to see a man in this town who wasn't wearing work boots and overalls for work. Ellie suspected his straightforward business attire meant he was one of the white-collar workers in town, maybe a lawyer or an accountant.

"Come here often?" he queried, still smiling. She wondered if he was being sarcastic. Everyone in a northern town went to Tim's every day.

"Uhm, yah," Ellie eyed him. Was he fucking with her?

"Quite the drive-through lineup, eh?"

"You know Soberites. Won't get out of their truck even if it's on fire."

There was a true story in town of a guy whose truck had caught on fire when he drove off the highway during a snowstorm. He had jerry cans full of gas in the back, and because it was minus thirty and snowing like a motherfucker, he thought it was best to stay inside the truck and wait for help. After the jerry cans exploded, and the local fire department put out the flames the only remains the investigators found were a few of the guy's teeth inside his coffee mug. They deduced he was probably still sipping his coffee, waiting to be rescued as his truck burned around him.

"Hah! Is that so?" the man said, his eyebrows raised.

Okay, that settled it. The guy was definitely an outsider.

"Can I help who's next?" The teenage girl behind the till was attempting a Goth look, which contrasted strangely with her beige uniform, like graffiti on a library wall.

"You go ahead. You look like you're on your way to work," the man said.

Ellie wasn't about to deny this guy the opportunity to be nice.

"Sure, thanks," she said, as she walked up to the till.

"You know, you can't help 'who's next.' That's a question. You could, however, help the next person in line," Ellie commented. She hated the reputation small towns had of being filled with uneducated boobs, and because the girl looked like she was old enough to have a few pickles in the jar, despite the fact that her eyebrows looked like they were drawn on with a Sharpie, she felt the need to say something.

"Sure, whatever. I just say what they tell me to say. Do you want something or not?" the till girl replied, rolling her eyes so far back that Ellie thought she looked like she would pass out.

"Double-double and a cheese Danish," Ellie replied.

As she waited for her coffee, she noticed the tall man smiling at her. Did she have something in her teeth? She turned away and ran her tongue around her mouth. What was the deal with this guy? He was good looking and seemed nice, but that put Ellie on edge. She was used to most men in town treating her either like a sex object or as one of the guys. No one gave "friendly smiles" anymore. Especially since the oilfields were under threat of takeover, and there was a risk they might be cutting more than half the jobs. So, there was a sense of unease everywhere and a worker-against-worker attitude.

Ellie picked up her coffee and turned to walk out. She returned a half smile to the man as she left, wondering if she might ever see him again. As she got into her truck and got the engine warming up, she heard a tap on her window. It was him.

Her truck still had manual wind-down windows, and the handle was stiff, so she slowly began to roll down her window using both hands as the man patiently waited, a brown Tim's bag in his hand. It was cold outside, and he wasn't wearing a jacket over his pressed dress shirt. It was always windy in Sober, and today was no exception. The wind was also causing chaos for the man's neatly coiffed hair.

By the time she got the window down, the man's hair looked like he had just rolled out of bed, and he was shivering. Strangely he was even more attractive to Ellie in his disheveled state.

"Sorry," Ellie said, blushing, partly from the effort of opening the window but also for making this decent guy wait out in the cold for her.

"No worries; here you go," he replied, as he passed the bag with her Danish through the window.

Ellie took her Danish and murmured a quick "thanks" before starting the slow process of winding up the window. She thought that next time, the more prudent approach would be to just open the damn door. The man stayed at her window, watching the progress.

Now, this was really getting awkward.

"You should get that fixed," he said. "I know a good mechanic who could fix that for you."

Ellie stared at the man for a moment, confused about how this guy who was obviously an out-of-towner could know a local mechanic.

"If your truck ever went into a lake you would need to be able to exit the windows quickly."

"Yeah, I guess that's right." She hadn't thought of that. No one had ever given her practical advice, her father being far from a practical kind of man. But it was kind of weird that this guy was thinking about her truck going under water with her in it.

The man was really shivering now. "Here, let me get your number, and I'll send you my mechanic's info." He passed her a receipt from his pocket. Ellie quickly wrote down her name and phone number.

"I'm Edward, by the way," he said and offered his hand through the window.

"Ellie," she said as she reached out and shook his hand. It was ice cold, but he still gave a firm handshake. Ellie hated men that shook her hand like she was some delicate creature. "You'd better get back inside before you freeze."

Ellie watched as Edward walked back into the café. He had a nice ass for an office worker. As she drove to the work site, Ellie wondered what his story was.

Sunday morning Ellie got a call at just after 8:00 AM. She didn't work weekends, but she was already awake, lying in bed and dreading getting up. She had an onerous day of packing boxes to look forward to. They had a few days to pack everything up before the house was transferred to the Price family. Ellie didn't recognize the number on her cell. Normally, she would have dismissed the call as a telemarketer, but lately she'd received numerous calls from the bank and lawyers regarding her father's estate, so she decided to answer and get it over with.

"Hello?" she said. Her voice sounded like Axel Rose on helium.

"Uhm, is this Ellie Dashwood?"

"Yes, this is Ellie."

"Hi. It's Edward. From Tim Hortons."

Ellie sat up in bed and fumbled for her covers, dropping her phone as she did so. As she rapidly attempted to find her phone in the mess of covers, she could hear Edward's muffled voice.

"Hello? Hello?"

Ellie found the phone hiding under her right butt cheek. Like Val, she slept in the nude (northerners learn to sleep hot to keep from freezing to death in the winter months), and she didn't realize that her butt had pressed on the video call button, When she brought the phone up to her face she gave Edward a full view of her bare chest. (Thankfully, her bottom half was still under the covers.)

Ellie gave a quiet gasp when she saw the small picture-in-picture on the screen. She could see Edward's face on the phone, his eyebrows raised and a small smile on his lips.

She quickly turned off the video call and put the cell to her ear.

"Hi." She felt less like Janet Jackson and more like a crazy streaker.

"I hope you don't mind that I made an appointment for your truck window," Edward said, obviously taking the high road as his voice showed no signs of amusement or shock, having just witnessed Ellie's inadvertent wardrobe malfunction.

"Oh right…er…yes…thanks," Ellie said, still trying to calm the red blush from her face.

"Are you able to meet me at Fas Gas on 5th at 11:00? My mechanic has the back bay of the shop there. He said he could squeeze you in."

Ellie knew how difficult it was to find a good mechanic in this town, and it was near impossible to get an appointment on such short notice. Considering her window wasn't really a major issue and money was tight right now, she wasn't sure this was something she needed to do.

"Edward, I really appreciate the offer, but I'm not sure I need to get the window fixed right now." She was conflicted because part of her wanted to see Edward again. The guy was attractive and resourceful, and you don't come across men like that in Sober very often (if ever).

"Look, you don't need to do the repair right away. My guy will give you an estimate for free, and then you can decide later."

Ellie paused for a moment, but then figured, why not? "Okay. I'll be there at 11:00."

"Great!" Edward sounded more enthusiastic than one would expect this early in the morning.

They hung up. Ellie sighed, pulling herself out of bed. She needed to get some packing done before going to the mechanic today, and she was sure that Val wouldn't be out of bed until after she left.

Ellie spent the rest of the morning sorting through her father's room. He was a borderline hoarder just like Val, which was one of the reasons he claimed parentage on her. Ellie assumed that was one of the "nurture" traits that Dave had successfully passed along. Ellie had finished packing up his sock collection (he never threw a pair away, even when they were so thin and worn that they could be used as cheesecloth) and started on his clothes. She pushed through the piles on the floor, deciding to start on the closet, but when she opened the doors, she found it stacked to the ceiling with boxes of Juvy-Cream.

Ellie had not heard of her father's latest venture, but nothing would surprise her now. She pulled a box down and opened it, finding it filled with cylindrical glass bottles, each equipped with a small hand pump. The Juvy-Cream container looked more like a bicycle pump than your usual fancy face cream container. Ellie grabbed the handle with one hand and had to pump it up and down a few times before the tip of the bottle spurted out a small amount of semi-translucent gel that had the consistency of snot. She gave a small shudder, wondering what housewife would want to "jack off" their hand cream every morning, only having to spread what looked more like cum on their face. But hey, if it got rid of the wrinkles, anything was possible.

Ellie smelled the small dollop of goo that she now had on the tips of her fingers and was instantly reminded of spawning salmon. She decided to give the Juvy-Cream a pass for daytime, but she might keep a bottle to try at bedtime.

"Wow, what smells like fish?" Ellie was surprised to see Val as she poked her head into their dad's room.

"Oh, you'll love this. It's some face cream Dad must have been selling." Ellie gave the bottle in her hands a few more jerks, but this time the goo launched onto the floor a foot in front of her.

"Oh my God! That is awesome!" Val said.

Ellie smiled, realizing she hadn't seen her sister happy since Dad had passed away, and it eased a tension in her she hadn't realized was there.

"You're awake early," Ellie said. She used her sock-covered foot to wipe the Juvy-Cream goo off the floor only to find it spread in a translucent smear, like she had wiped the nose of a snotty child.

"It's not early," Val said as she turned away from the door. "It's almost 11:00."

"Fuck!" Ellie had not realized how much time she had spent organizing her father's things.

"What?" Val yelled from the kitchen.

"I've got an appointment with a mechanic at 11:00. I have to go."

Ellie raced out of the room. She grabbed her purse from the kitchen table, where Val was sitting and drinking coffee.

"A mechanic?" Val said, "I need a mechanic! There are literally none available in this town. Where did you find one?"

"I don't have time to explain. I'm going to be late."

"I'm coming with you!" Val said, getting up from the table. She was in her My Little Pony jammies. They covered her from neck to ankle in flannel with smiling pictures of

Pinkie Pie. A small "crap flap" over her ass was held closed with two buttons.

"I don't have time for you to change," Ellie said, heading towards the door.

"No problem," Val said, as she stuffed her feet into a pair of pink crocs and shuffled out the door, looking part trailer trash and part toddler.

On the drive there, Ellie filled Val in on meeting Edward and their impromptu truck window maintenance conversation. She had to be brief because the drive was short. Unless you were driving exactly at the moment when everyone else was trying to get on the highway in the morning (or into the Tim Hortons drive-through) you could get anywhere in town in 10 minutes or less.

"This is interesting. Mysterious Handsome Man Helps Lonely Desperate Spinster." Val emphasized each word with her hands like she was reading a playbill.

"Spinster. Nice." Ellie frowned. Her sister liked to rub in Ellie's singledom at any chance she got. It was not that Ellie never went out with anyone, but most didn't last past the first date. Some of them she had even tried sleeping with just to see if things improved by having sex, but it only made things worse.

Ellie characterized the men in Sober into two categories: Desperate Dongs (DeeDees) or Pompous Pricks (PeePees). DeeDees came across the best at first. They dressed nicely, offered to pay for the meal but graciously accepted going

Dutch. The conversation was relatively unboring and went outside of oilfields gossip or the latest "insert-professional-sports-team-name-here" game. The problem was, if you made the mistake of sleeping with a DeeDee, they were likely to fall in love with you and call you repeatedly from the morning after until you permanently blocked their number from your phone.

One time Ellie had slept with this guy Jason Kelly, who worked as a local insurance broker. Ellie and Jason had gone to school together, and during the evening, he admitted to having a crush on Ellie all through high school. At first glance it appeared sweet and endearing, and Ellie had been smitten (or maybe it was the three glasses of Zinfandel?) enough that she brought him home. The sex was boring and (worse) awkward, a sure sign it wasn't meant to be. When Ellie didn't call him back right away the next morning, he started texting her pictures of Ellie from back in high school, and not fun pictures of happy moments—pictures of Ellie in a bathroom stall or adjusting her bra when she thought no one was looking.

When the Jason incident happened, Val was ready to file a police report against him and try to get a restraining order, but Ellie figured it wasn't worth the bother. After she blocked his number, the problem appeared to go away. What Ellie didn't know was that Val had secretly snuck into Jason's insurance broker office, hid in the bathroom and took a few pictures of him taking a dump from the next stall, which she texted him from a blocked number later on. The guy was freaked out enough that he left town later that day on an extended "holiday."

The other type, the Pompous Prick or PeePee, were Ellie's least favourite. A small northern town filled with trade workers was overflowing with PeePees. They were like a toxic masculinity cake iced with insecurities with an underlying flavour of homophobia. Many of them were pretty to look at on the outside—nice bodies. The sex was often worthwhile as well, more so than with the DeeDees (they had enough confidence to preclude the awkwardness). However, if Ellie managed to get by the first date without falling asleep to the sound of them talking about themselves, she often scared them away with her inability to accept their "man-splaining" of some particular aspect of her life. Her particular favourites were those who liked to try and tell her how to weld, like she wasn't already a journeyman, when the guy was a truck driver, shit scooper, tree cutter and so on. Or when they found out she liked to go to the gym or play hockey, they would begin to name how much they could bench press or how many Gordy Howe hat tricks they had—a Goal, an Assist and a Fight.

"So, what is this guy, Pompous Prick or Desperate Dong?" Val asked. She was well aware of Ellie's categorization.

"I don't know. I guess we'll find out!" She responded as she turned her truck into the Fas Gas station and pulled to a stop.

The gas station had old-style pumps where the numbers clicked over like an odometer. People didn't gas up there because you actually had to go inside to pay, rather than just flash your credit card at the panel reader. Dave Dashwood used to like gas stations like this one. He told the girls he was supporting a business that had to employ a gas attendant, instead of a computerized system that took jobs away from the "little people." The reality was that Dave's credit cards rarely worked, so he was stuck getting gas only when he had cash in his pocket.

Behind the pumps were a series of garage bays, one of which was open. Ellie could hear classical piano music coming from the open bay. Two men stood behind the hoist in conversation. She recognized one as Edward. He wore a pressed dress shirt again, but his khaki pants were dressed down enough that he might be going for a casual Friday look. The other man was obviously the mechanic in the shop. He was shorter than Edward by almost a foot but just as broad, if not more so, in the shoulders. His close-cut beard and dark hair made him look a bit like a 1950s greaser, all that was missing was the pack of cigarettes tucked into the folded sleeve of his white t-shirt. The mechanic looked like he was in his late thirties, but Ellie could be off by a decade because hard-labour jobs tended to add age to guys' faces like computer programmers added mass to their butts. Edward looked up and saw Ellie and Val. He waved for them to come in.

As they entered the garage bay, the volume of the piano music escalated, and Val must have recognized a part of the piece from her ballet years. She raised up onto the tips of her pink crocs, lifted her leg to the side and gracefully spun around on one toe, hands delicately arched. Despite her hair tied messily into a bun and her baggie jammies, she looked every inch the dancer she was.

"Wow! Bravo!" Edward said. "That was beautiful." Val mouthed "DeeDee" silently at Ellie and raised her eyebrows.

Ellie pursed her lips to avoid laughing. Maybe Val was right, and this guy was a Desperate Dong; he sure had many of the characteristics.

Val's little performance would have embarrassed or annoyed most siblings, but for Ellie it reminded her of what her sister was capable of and how much she deserved to succeed. She envied Val's indifference to what people thought of her. Ellie was trapped in her body of sensibility, plus she had about as much grace as an elephant in heat. In contrast to Val's easy elegance, she always felt like the ugly stepsister.

"This is my sister, Val."

Val gave a little curtsey at Ellie's introduction, her hand gracefully extended. To her surprise, the mechanic reached for her hand and feigned bringing his lips to her knuckles.

"Brandon Turner," he announced, as he bowed slightly.

Val pulled her hand away but smiled. "Charmed," she said, keeping with the formality of the introduction.

Brandon's eyes didn't leave Val for a second. Even as Edward turned to introduce Ellie.

"This is Ellie. She is the one with the window problem I was telling you about." Edward turned to Brandon to get his attention, but he appeared to be in a kind of reverie. Ellie could see Val was getting uncomfortable under the stare of the mechanic, so she decided to keep things moving.

"My sister also has some car problems, so she wanted to come along to meet you."

Brandon seemed to come back to his senses. "What kind of car do you have?"

"A Ford Escort. It has carburetor problems."

Brandon whistled. "Carburetor problems? Must be an oldie. '87?"

"Yeah, it's old," Val responded, not really remembering exactly how old her little Ford was.

"Maybe you can take a look at Ellie's truck since she brought that in today," Edward said, trying to bring the conversation back around to the matter at hand.

"For sure. Let me take a look," Brandon responded. He took Ellie's keys and walked out to Ellie's truck, leaving Edward, Val and Ellie alone in the garage.

"Thanks again for helping with this," Ellie said.

"No problem. Happy to help." Edward paused, looking intently at Ellie. "Maybe afterwards we could go for a coffee? You know, avoid the drive-through lineup again?"

Val noticed the close conversation between her sister and Edward, so she pretended to be looking at some of the random car parts scattered on top of a workbench.

"Your sister, too, of course," Edward added, gesturing to Val.

"Uhm, thanks Edward, but Val and I really have to get home. We are moving in a couple days, and we've got a ton of packing to get done."

Ellie was disappointed. This guy was trying hard, and she still didn't know what the deal was with him. It was a bit like an unsolved mystery, and she wanted to get to the bottom of his story.

"Your window problem is an easy fix. I can get it done this afternoon if you want to leave the truck with me," Brandon said as he walked back into the garage. "Won't take any parts, so just an hour of labour. Around fifty dollars for the job."

Ellie couldn't say no to a deal like that, especially if the guy was good. Maybe he could fix Val's car, too. She suspected the low price had something to do with his association with Edward, but she didn't really care.

"That would be awesome. Thanks, Brandon. My sister and I didn't bring the other car though, I didn't think I would be leaving the truck here."

"I'll drive you both home," Edward said. "Not a problem."

"Thanks!" said Val before Ellie could disagree. Ellie didn't want to owe this guy anything more. She gave her sister a scolding look. Val was oblivious.

"You should bring that Escort in. Carburetor problems can be serious," Brandon said. She didn't seem to notice the intent look on his face as she wandered out of the garage without looking back at Brandon.

"Thanks, Brandon. I'll get Val to bring it in. Let me know when you have some time," Ellie responded.

"Anytime," he said as he got Ellie to fill out some paperwork. "I'll call you when the truck is finished."

Ellie left the garage with Edward, meeting Val outside. He led them toward a navy-blue BMW 5 series that was parked on the side of the lot. Val gave Ellie a look behind Edward's back like a kid who was sneaking a cookie from the cookie jar. This guy obviously had money. Ellie might be tempted to ignore the obvious DeeDee characteristics that were oozing out of the guy's nostrils.

"Sorry, the car is a bit of a mess," Edward said, as he grabbed the one bag that was on the floor in the back.

It didn't compare to the way Val kept her Ford. You had to sweep a pile of empty coffee cups off the seat just to sit down. Ellie, on the other hand, kept her truck neat. She figured if she didn't have a nice vehicle to drive, at least she wasn't going to sit surrounded by garbage.

Edward started the engine, and they were immediately blasted by "My Heart Will Go On," which Edward fumbled to switch off. Val gave a snicker from the back seat and covered her mouth with her hand to keep from laughing. Ellie was not a fan of love ballads; they didn't suit her practical nature, and Val knew it.

"Sooooo, Edward, what brings you to town?" Val asked as they sped out of the garage's parking lot.

"Oh, a few things," Edward replied. "I'm working on a business deal, plus I have some family in town."

Val rolled her eyes. This was not enough of a juicy tidbit to satisfy her. "What kind of deal?"

"I can't really get into the details. Plus, are you really interested in some boring business crap?" Edward smiled at Val in the rearview mirror.

"I'm sure Ellie would be. Maybe you guys should have dinner sometime so you can talk about it?" Val grinned, looking every bit the conniving matchmaker she was.

Ellie turned and gave her sister a "shut up" look.

"Yes! I would love that," Edward said. "What about later tonight?" This guy was persistent.

"Val, you know we have to keep packing. We're already behind. Sorry, Edward."

"How about this? I'll pick up some pizza and come over to help put things in boxes."

"Great! Around 6:00 then?" Val said eagerly, her already tangled bun flopping to the side as she stuck her head between the two seats to grin at Ellie. "I have to go to work, so Ellie could really use some help!"

Ellie sighed. There was no fighting Val when she had a plan in her head. It would be like trying to stop the buffet line at a Weight Watchers convention.

"This is us," Ellie said, pointing to their small white rancher on the left.

Edward pulled the Beemer to a stop in the driveway, and Ellie and Val climbed out.

"See you later," Val waved to Edward as he drove away. Ellie thought she heard the muffled voice of Cecile Dion as the sedan took off down the street.

"You could act a little more interested, you know," Val said as they went into the house. "The guy is hot, rich and obviously into you, and you keep turning him down with the lamest of excuses."

"I like him, but I don't really know anything about him," Ellie said, pulling off her shoes and pushing away Val's crocs that she'd kicked off in the middle of the entryway. "He could be a Grade A Desperate Dong for all we know, or at best, just an entitled rich boy. Neither of which I'm interested in. Also, I can't believe you invited him over, and then you're going to ditch me and go to work."

"I think you could just use a good fuck is all. And he has a nice ass, so why not? That certainly couldn't work with a little sister hanging around."

Val sat down in the middle of the living room floor and pulled a cardboard box towards her, casually throwing in random nick knacks. She held up a white porcelain figurine of a naked cupid, his hands pulling back on a tiny bow. Val had dropped the figure when she was around four years old, and his little penis had snapped off, making the angelic expression on its face appear more pained than before.

"Keep?" Val asked, looking up at Ellie.

"Val sometimes I think your idea of dating is border-line medieval. Toss." Ellie added the last comment to indicate where Val should put the cupid figure. Val chucked the cupid into another box on the other side of the room marked "FUCK OFF," where it gave a satisfying shattering sound, meeting its untimely end with other such useless crap that Dave Dashwood had wasted his money on over the years.

"I haven't dated anyone seriously since high school," Val said. She picked up a pile of coasters off the table, each one adorned with a cat wearing various costumes and their respective names, showing Ellie one dressed as a furry Chinese dictator named Chairman Meow. "Keep?" she asked. "When I meet the right guy, I will know."

"Toss! How will you know?" Ellie pulled out a stack of record albums and began to put them into boxes. She smiled at the Smurfs album that lay on top but reluctantly put it into the "Donate" box.

"No! I love the kittens. And you can't give away the Smurfs album!" Val said. "A guy that I fall for will be passionate, cultured, educated and rich."

"In that order? And no, we aren't keeping either. We won't have room for the record player in the trailer anyway." Ellie decisively stacked the albums into the box.

"If I can't have the Smurfs, I'm keeping the kittens. They don't take up any room. How can you throw away little Captain Cat Sparrow?" Val held up the coaster with a grey shorthair wearing a pirate patch and bandana, looking like Johnny Depp coming off a bender. "In no particular order, and despite what you think of me, they don't even have to have money."

"Sure." Ellie knew her sister. She may be a romantic at heart, but the relationship wouldn't go far if the guy couldn't afford to pay for dinner. Val placed the coasters into one of their "Keep" boxes.

"This guy Edward wouldn't work for me; he is way too reserved. But you need to give him a chance," Val said. She held up a letter opener with a translucent pink dildo handle.

"I guess we'll see soon enough," Ellie said, as she turned to see the dildo in Val's hand they both yelled "Toss" at the same time as Val chucked the pink phallus into the "FUCK OFF" box.

CHAPTER
eight

Edward arrived as planned at six, with two large pizza boxes in his hands that smelled deliciously of cheese and garlic. Val had already packed her bags and was on her way out the door. She snuck back into the kitchen, dipped her hand into one of the boxes and grabbed a floppy slab of pepperoni.

"Thanks for the pizza, Edward!" Val said with her mouth full as she waved her hand back at her sister, who had venom in her eyes.

"Anytime," Edward said, as he took off his coat and hung it on the back of a kitchen chair. He had switched his dress shirt for a tight-fitting tee that had the word BACON spelled out using elements from the periodic table. Ellie's eyes were involuntarily drawn to his well-defined arms that nicely matched the classically chiseled features of his face. Val noticed where Ellie was staring from the hallway and caught Ellie's eyes for a moment, conveying with a slight eyebrow raise her knowledge of her sister's impure thoughts.

"Let me know if you are going to be late," Ellie called down the hallway.

"Oh yeah, Frank asked me to work a double tonight, so don't wait up." Val left the house with a decisive door slam. Ellie thought it strange that Val would be working a double shift on a Thursday, but she wasn't going to dwell on it. Double shift meant she would get double pay, and they could use the money.

"Should we have some pizza first before we get started?" Edward asked, scanning around the small kitchen. Boxes littered the floor, and most of the cupboards were empty, doors hanging open, their insides yawning into the room, sporting their 1960s flowered paper lining.

"I'm afraid I don't have any plates left out, but I do have paper towel," Ellie said as she peeled off a few sheets for Edward and herself. "Would you like a beer?"

"Sure," Edward sat down, pulling the top pizza box toward him and grabbing a couple of slices.

Ellie pulled two beers from the fridge. They were still working through her dad's supply of Coors Light, which he had started drinking earlier that year in an effort to go on a diet. Ellie had tried to explain to him that the "light" part of the beer name didn't imply that he wouldn't still get a beer belly if you drank six of them a day, but that kind of talk to Dave Dashwood was like trying to educate a monkey on why he shouldn't eat bananas.

"What does Val do for work?" Edward asked as he bit into his first slice. Ellie was surprised to find that he was still good looking while eating pizza. She was reminded of the scene in *Crazy Stupid Love* where Ryan Gosling casually leans on a glass railing, a floppy buck slab in his hand, looking as yummy as always. Ellie and Val could watch that a hundred times and never get bored.

"Swerver," Ellie said with a mouth full of pizza.

"A what?"

"Sorry, a server," Ellie blushed, embarrassed at her behavior. She hadn't exactly been raised in a family that observed high levels of etiquette. Ellie remembered going to dinner at a friend's house, only to have the well-dressed stay-at-home mom of the family smile at her in a condescending way and say, "Ellie dear, what if you were going to have dinner with the queen? Would she be tolerant of your large elbows resting on the table, hmmm?"

"She works at the Northern Bush Club downtown. Not the greatest place to work for a nineteen-year-old, but she makes really good tips there."

Ellie took a swig of beer. She almost wiped her hand across her mouth before she remembered to use a paper towel.

"I know the place," Edward said.

Ellie wondered how Edward knew about the only strip club in town. Perhaps, like most men, he frequented the establishment. Edward must have seen a look cross Ellie's eyes.

"I don't go there or anything, but I've certainly heard people talk about it," he said quickly.

Ellie relaxed. She didn't want to be a prude, but guys who blew their money on strippers in this town were definitely Pompous Pricks. She felt Edward's eyes on her arms, which she had propped up on the table holding her pizza slice. Ellie quickly dropped her elbows off the table, wondering if this guy was more of a prude than she'd originally thought.

"I was just admiring your arms. You must work out." Edward put his elbows on the table to match Ellie.

"Oh, thanks." She was used to people commenting on her arms. She did work out, but a lot of her muscle definition came from a combination of good genetics and having a physical job. "I do work out a few times a week. Your arms are, uhm, really nice, too." Ellie felt immediately embarrassed with her compliment.

Edward smiled, "I know what it takes to get definition like that. What gym do you go to?"

"Just the rec centre."

The rec centre gym was both cheap and relatively free of fire-breathing, vein-popping man-splainers that you would find at your Gold's or other large gym chain. Even still, she had to withstand relatively frequent comments from men who looked like they couldn't bench her weight, telling her if she swung her back while doing bicep curls she would double her "PR" (totally false, and pretty much definitely way to throw your back out).

Her other pet peeve was guys who took over a certain apparatus at the gym, basically setting up camp for what seemed like hours, only to spend most of the time staring at their phones. She sincerely hoped that Edward didn't fit into either of those categories.

"Nice. Rec centres are decent. I'm just going to the hotel gym right now."

"I thought you had some family here," Ellie wondered why anyone would choose to stay in one of the Sober hotels, that is, if you were lucky enough to get a room. Many of the contract workers for the oilfields stayed at the hotels, so they were often booked up for months.

"Oh yuck, family, no I can't stay with them," Edward said, shaking his head. "We get along as long as we don't have to live in close quarters. Family can be annoying, right?"

"Yeah, I get it," Ellie said.

Edward paused, wiping his hands and sipping his beer. "So how come you are moving? Want to be closer to the gym?"

"Oh, our dad passed away a few weeks ago. Val and I have to get rid of the house." Ellie tried to convey a sense of ease in her tone, but her voice cracked as the words came out of her mouth. She didn't want to put a downer on the night.

"Oh...I'm really sorry Ellie. I didn't know." Edward's face sagged; he was obviously upset at making light of his own family situation.

Ellie felt a surge well up inside her. She was always reserved and sensible, but the long day of going through her dad's things and dealing with all the money had worn down her hard facade. She pursed her lips, trying hold back tears, but it must have been obvious to Edward because he got up from the chair and came around to Ellie, squatted down beside her chair and grabbed her in a hug.

As Edward's strong arms held her, Ellie felt something inside her release, her face buried in his neck. He smelled sweet, like vanilla and lavender, and her mind left the sadness of her dad's death to ponder what soap he used.

"I lost my dad a few years ago. It was really tough, a lot harder than I thought it would be," Edward said into the back of Ellie's hair. Ellie pulled away, her face composed. She could always push her emotions down when she needed to, but something about Edward's presence had caused a slight lapse in her self-control. She wouldn't let that happen again.

Edward's face was inches away from Ellie's. She was suddenly aware of her pizza and beer breath.

"I need to brush my teeth," she said out loud.

"So do I," Edward responded, as he moved his hands to the back of her neck and pulled her into a kiss. Ellie couldn't resist even if she wanted to; this was everything her mind and body needed right now. She didn't care that Edward tasted like pepperoni and Coors Light, and as they progressed from the kitchen to the bedroom, rapidly removing pieces of clothing and dropping them onto the floor, she figured Edward didn't care either.

Once Ellie was topless, Edward paused and looked down at her breasts and smiled. "They're better in person." "Shut up," Ellie responded as she grabbed him and pushed him into the bedroom.

CHAPTER
nine

Val was disappointed to leave Edward and Ellie; she wanted to witness the flirting. It would be like watching a bad romcom. It gave her joy to see someone else flailing about with courtship. Val was more outgoing, so she never had much trouble getting boyfriends, but she definitely had trouble keeping them. Where Ellie tended to find an even split with her men on the DeeDee and PeePee scale, Val tended to attract just the latter variety. She had Pompous Pricks salivating all over her, like dogs in heat, only to find that once they got what they wanted, they tended to split with lightning speed. Perhaps it was her busty appearance and tiny frame that gave men the wrong idea, or maybe it was her outgoing nature. Whatever it was, Val was tired and fed up with the men in Sober.

Val felt guilty lying to Ellie about her double shift that evening. The two sisters had a strict "no lying" policy between them, but in this case, she knew that if Ellie found out about her plan to strip, she would throw a John McEnroe on Val's ass. Val planned to work at it for a while and have a big wad of cash to show for it when she told Ellie what was going on, hoping that the money would prevent Ellie from losing it.

She didn't start at the club until 7:00, so she had some time to get ready. These days, strippers couldn't just go up on stage, swing around the pole a few times while peeling their clothes off and expect big tips. There were standards. At some point a creative stripper had raised the bar by adding theatrics to her routine. No longer would sewing Velcro into leather pants suffice; you had to have a theme, a routine and a costume good enough to get you on a float in Louisiana during Mardi Gras.

The parking lot was already half full when she pulled her small, sputtering ford into her usual spot. She yanked a Hefty garbage bag out of the trunk and slung it over her shoulder, making her way to the side entrance of The Bush. Instead of heading to the bar to gather her serving apron, she turned down the hall to the dancers' change rooms. On the way she passed Joey, who stood at the entryway to the hall. He looked scary and ominous, which prevented any patrons from trying to follow a stripper into the wrong part of the club.

"Val! Whatcha doing down here?" Joey asked in his soft voice. For a guy as large as he was, it always surprised Val how soft spoken he was. Even when he was grabbing some asshole off the floor who was attempting to grab a girl's Va-Jay-Jay, he would speak softly and calmly. Val figured the paradox that was Joey's demeanor confused the subpar brains of the club patrons.

"Hey, Joey," Val said, pausing to heft the heavy black garbage bag she had slung over her shoulder onto the floor for a rest. "I'm dancing tonight."

"Shit girl, why? You don't need to do that crap."

"Money, Joey. Isn't that always the reason?"

"I guess, man, you gotta do what you gotta do." Joey's quiet voice had a calming effect on Val's nerves. She hadn't realized how worked up and nervous she was about tonight. Her routine was different, and she didn't know how it would come across.

"Okay, I better get ready." Val hoisted her large bag back onto her shoulder.

"Babe," Joey said, "don't let the bitches get you down, eh?" He smiled and gave Val a quick punch on the shoulder, almost knocking her off her feet, owing to the weight of the large bag she carried.

"Thanks, man." She knew Joey was genuine. Val was no wilting flower, but there was a hierarchy among the strippers, and they weren't going to take nicely to a new girl in their midst.

Val turned and walked through a door into the strippers' change room. In the year that she had been working as a server in the club, Val had never set eyes on the inside of this room. It was a Strippers-Only area; not even the club owners would venture in without risk of castration. Even though Val was a self-professed slob, she found this room chaotic. There wasn't an inch of space on the floor that wasn't filled with suitcases bursting with feather boas or leather wear. One side of the room was lined with mirrors that looked like they hadn't been cleaned in years. Someone had written in lipstick, "Misty sucks cock" on the far left side. Beneath the mirrors, a cluttered countertop was flooded with makeup, and flat irons jutted out of the wall. A ring of dusty half-lit light bulbs circled the mirrors like the gaping mouth of an aged boxer.

Candy stood on the far side of the room, one long leg up on top of the counter, wearing only a tiny pair of red lacy underwear. She appeared to be shaving the inside of her thigh with a small razor. Candy wasn't the only other stripper in the room. Katrina LaRue, a small woman with thin blonde hair and a mousey face, sat next to Candy's outstretched leg. Unlike Candy, Val knew Katrina's real name as Sarah. They'd chatted a few times, and Val had found out that Sarah was a single mom who also worked as a checkout attendant at a local grocery store. She had taken up stripping in the evenings to pay the bills, lucky enough to have an elderly lady neighbour who watched over her daughter when she was working. Sarah was applying glitter to her cheekbones with what looked like a glue stick.

Candy looked up from shaving when Val entered. "Aww, how cute. They're letting little girls strip now." Candy's condescending comment filled Val with a quiet rage.

Sarah looked up briefly from her glitter application and smiled at Val. "I'll make some space for you, Val. Come on." She pushed some bottles across the counter, clearing a space for Val to use to get ready. One of the bottles rolled off the counter and bounced on the floor in front of Candy.

"Hey, watch it, bitch!" Candy screeched, plopping her foot on the floor and standing over Sarah. "That cream is five hundred bucks a pop, and I doubt your skanky bod can pull that kind of cash in a month." She was pointing to the bottle that had fallen onto the floor, which Val noticed looked strikingly similar to her dad's Juvy-Cream bottles that were plugging up the closet at home. She wondered if her dad had been hawking his wares here at the club. Val felt a strange surge of pride for her dad. If he had actually sold some bottles of that shit to dumb strippers for five hundred bucks a bottle, maybe he had done something right.

Sarah stood up, her eyes barely above Candy's nipples, which were pointedly bouncing in Sarah's face. Despite her smaller stature, Sarah looked like she was a chick with some balls (any woman who had pushed a baby out their vagina had some cred in Val's books).

"Candy, I know for a fact that you got that shit for free from some guy who came in here the other week. And you know why I know?" Sarah grabbed a bottle from her stand and waved it in front of Candy's breasts. "Because I got one, too. And it smells like fish."

Candy pursed her lips. She must have known she was beaten because she turned and plucked her Juvy-Cream bottle off the floor and pranced off to a suitcase in the corner.

Val was happy someone was standing up to Candy but disappointed that her dad must have come to the club and handed out the cream for free to the strippers. He probably couldn't pay for dances any other way and had somehow convinced Candy that it was worth five hundred bucks. She had to give him credit for that.

Sarah sat down and motioned for Val to take the seat next to her. "Don't mind her, she's on the rag this week, as you can tell," Sarah said under her breath. "She isn't as bad as you might think."

"Really?" Val said as she plopped her garbage bag down on the floor and pulled out her makeup kit. She was doubtful about Candy. The woman could pass for a Valkyrie.

"You've gotta have a thick skin to do this work, and for some of us, we can't ever take it off," Sarah replied as she turned back to the mirror, continuing to apply glitter to her cheeks.

Val sighed and thought, *Maybe Sarah is right.* Val knew she had thick skin already; she just hoped this work wasn't going to change her for good.

Sarah must have heard her sigh as she turned back, "Don't worry. Keep your other life separate from stripping, and you'll be fine."

The rest of Val's prep went by in a panic. She hadn't realized how much time she would need to get ready, and the fact that she hadn't done it before on a practice run at home meant that the whole process was completely new. She was just finishing pinning her hair up for the final touch of her costume when a loud knock came on the door.

Joey's quiet voice was barely audible over the thud of the club music, "Five minutes for Stacy Bubbles."

"Shit!" Val said as she scrambled to throw her makeup back into her bag.

"Don't worry about this stuff," Sarah said. "Just leave it. Get out there and knock 'em dead. You look amazing!"

Just as Val was leaving the change room, she heard Candy call out, "Hey, new girl." Val turned back to see Candy smiling at her with what looked like a friendly expression.

"Don't fuck up, okay?" Candy said, still smiling. "Some of us have to go on after you, and I don't want all the pussies in the room to be as dry as dirt."

Val sighed and left the room, having to duck to get her costume through the doorway. As she walked down the hall she heard the DJ announcing her show.

"Alrightly! Ladies and gentlemen, for the first time ever, for your viewing pleasure, LIVE at the Northern Bush Club, I give you, the sensuous, the sexiest, *the* STACY BUBBLES!"

CHAPTER
ten

When Val stepped onto the stage, she was enveloped in complete darkness. Every aspect of her costume was black, and her face was turned to the side to give the impression of a silhouette. An unusual hush came over the room, as the club patrons breathlessly anticipated the show. Val was no stranger to performing. Growing up she often performed on stage as a ballet dancer, so she channeled that experience to keep her mind calm and poised. The DJ started her music set, which began with Tchaikovsky's Swan Lake, the symphonic tones bouncing around the club walls like a helium balloon in a morgue. Val raised up on her dyed-black point shoes and gracefully tiptoed out into the middle of the stage, arms arched like her strict teachers had pounded into her from the time she was five years old.

The stage lights came on and centred on Val, highlighting the tall dark wings extending from Val's back. She was the Black Swan. When the lights came on, the silence broke in the club like a glass smashing on a concrete floor; the club patrons began to shout and whistle. Val danced like she meant it, floating around the stage. She did a pirouette and came to a stop, grabbing the stripper pole. At that moment, a guy's voice called out over the din.

"Hey, if I wanted to see this shit, I would have gone to the ballet with my wife!"

"Yeah, Tinkerbell, show us your titties, or get the fuck off the stage!" came another call. Soon the whistles and hoots were replaced with boos and more heckling.

Val wasn't an idiot; she knew that ballet wasn't going to bring in the tips. At that moment (possibly a little later than she'd planned), the DJ switched the music from Tchaikovsky to a techno beat that was reminiscent of a symphony on crack. Val had timed the music, using this moment to switch from ballet dancer to stripper, as her arm on the pole lifted her body from the floor. Her long legs spun around as she descended the pole, toes delicately pointed. Quickly, the heckles from the audience swelled into catcalls again, and Val's heart rate calmed. *Give them what they want,* she thought as she stepped away from the pole and yanked her body suit off in one fluid movement, the Velcro sides she had carefully sewn in giving way with little effort. Instantly, she went from graceful swan to dirty dancer, her breasts exposed, leaving only a tiny black G-string.

Next, the wings came off, making her descent into sluttiness complete. The lights in her eyes made it difficult to see the people on the floor, but as a performer she could feel the vibe in the club. A large group of men close to the stage seemed to be making the most noise. As she danced closer to the group, she saw the money start to land on the floor around her. One of the men came up to the stage, holding a twenty in his hand. Val knew the drill, and she went down onto her hands and knees, walking her nearly bare ass close to him.

She heard his friends cheer him on from the sidelines. "Come on, Murph!"

The guy stuck the twenty into the string of Val's underwear and turned back to his buddies for a round of high fives.

Val heard the song shift again, and she knew her set was winding down, the DJ notifying her that she had another minute to finish up. In a flourish, she ripped off her G-string, (ensuring she had grabbed the twenty) and did another circuit of the floor naked, with a few pole turns to end it off. Her mind drifted as she spun around the pole, wondering if they sanitized the poles and stage at the end of the night. She hoped this job wasn't going to give her herpes, or something worse.

The music ended, and encouraged by the DJ, many other club patrons moved closer to the stage to drop money for her.

"Give it up for Stacy Bubbles! If you want her back, make sure you show your love on stage! Don't worry ladies and gentlemen, Stacy will be touring the floor after her show for private dances! So, keep the cash flowing!"

Val waved to the applauding audience and stepped down from the stage, still wearing her black pointe shoes. Her heart was pounding, and exhilaration tore through her like she hadn't felt since the last time she danced for real.

"Nice one, Val!" Joey came to escort her to the change room and patted her on the back like she was a pet. It was fitting, given he towered over Val by at least two feet.

"You liked it?" Val asked, as she made her way to the backroom.

"Yeah! You killed it. I actually wanted more of the real ballet stuff. I've never been to the ballet," Joey said.

"Ballet is awesome. We should go sometime."

"You would go with me?" Joey asked, his teddy-bear face looking almost childlike.

"Of course, I would!"

"You're a sweetie. Hey, I brought some cookies in today. Should be a container in the dressing room. I tweaked the recipe a bit, so they're a bit softer. Lemme know if you like 'em!"

"Oh man, I could really use a cookie right now. Thanks, Joey." Val said. A sugar hit would be just the thing before she went out on the floor again.

They got to the change room just in time to see Candy coming out. She was dressed as Minnie Mouse, but not one you would ever see walking around Disneyland. It was Candy's classic routine, and it worked well.

"Nice routine, newbie," Candy said as she passed. "Dry as a fucking popcorn fart, but I didn't expect anything less from a baby like you."

Val didn't care. She was happy, and the bucket she had on stage to pick up her tips was filled to the brim.

"Don't pay any attention to her," Joey said as Val headed into the change room.

"I'm tougher than I look Joey," Val replied, smiling.

"I know!" Joey said, and he turned to walk back out to the floor with Candy.

"Dickwad! Are you coming or what? I'm not walking out there on my own, or did someone not fill your dinosaur-sized brain in on what your job actually is?" Candy was shouting at Joey from the end of the hall.

Joey grinned at Val like a small kid and sauntered back toward Candy, obviously unfazed by the razzing.

The change room was thankfully empty when Val entered. Sarah must have cut out back for a smoke before her set, and the other girls who were on later hadn't arrived. She quickly dropped her tip bucket into her garbage bag along with the giant swan wings and tied it in a double knot. Looking around the change room, she saw that the other girls all had locking suitcases, and now she understood why. Way easier to carry all your crap around and safer once you had your tips. No one was allowed in here, but she didn't trust Candy not to rip her off.

Tucked in on the edge of the cluttered countertop, Val found Joey's green Tupperware container sitting open. She was happy that only a few cookies were left. It must have meant that people were eating and enjoying them. When you take your clothes off for a living, you only put calories in your body when it is really worth it, and Joey's sugar cookies were as addictive as crack but with the taste of home. Joey had catered to the crowd, making the cookie icing stripper themed. Val picked up one with a carefully drawn bra and panties on it. She wondered how these would go down at the local PTA meetings.

Dancing in the strip show was one thing, but now Val had to do the hard part, sell private dances. She had to make her quota every night, or she'd have to pay the club back what she didn't sell. It was quite the racket for the club. They paid the girls around a thousand bucks a week for the shows, but the private dances could end up killing you. If a stripper didn't sell her quota, she still owed the club its portion of the sales. So, girls who didn't make quota ended up eating into their show pay. Of course, there were the tips, but those were totally dependent on the night. On a slow night you might not make any more on tips than a server. Plus, you also had to tip the DJ and bouncers every night. Val had gone through the money in her head a few times. She could see that the dumb strippers who didn't sell their dances could actually be losing money and not even know it. Despite the fact that Val never did well in math at school, this kind of money stuff always made crystal clear sense to her.

Val walked out into the club, wearing her G-string, a dark lace bra and pointe shoes. At least they were more comfortable than the stilettos most of the girls wore. So now, she had the rest of the night to sell ten dances, and she had no idea how to even start.

Right away, Val noticed the group of guys that had approached the stage when she was doing her show. That was probably as good a place to start as any, so she wandered over to their table. Now that she was away from the stage lights, she could see that they were a stag party. The guy that had put the twenty in her G-string was wearing a T-shirt that said, "I only support gay marriage if both chicks are hot." He was built like a linebacker, stocky but with a slight beer belly. Val assumed he was the groom, as he had a studded collar around his neck that was linked by a chain to a large, black ball in the middle of the table. The group was cheering him on as he chugged back a beer.

"Look, Murph! It's the little ballet dancer!" said one of the men closest to Val. He reminded her of a drunken Paul Bunyan with his red flannel shirt anchored around his waist with a belt. The guy had a sway to him, like a tree on a windy day.

Val approached the table; her heart was thumping in her chest. What was she supposed to do? She figured going with the basic approach was probably best.

"Any of you guys want a dance?" She asked, trying to keep her voice sounding strong and sexy and not like a scared little kid.

"Oh! Little Dancer wants some more Murph, eh?" The groom, who appeared to be referring to himself in the third person, stood up from the table and eyed Val greedily. "Buy me a dance, boys!" Murphy said, as he slammed his glass down on the table.

"We gotcha covered buddy. Go have some fun!" Paul Bunyan slid a couple twenties over to Val. At least this would be one dance off her quota. As Val picked up the money, she noticed one of the men at the table looking directly at her. Unlike his friends, he was quiet, sitting with his arms crossed, his chair slightly pushed back from the fray as if he was attempting to distance himself. Even in the dim light of the bar, Val noticed his bright blue eyes staring intently at her as she slipped the twenties into the side of her bra. The man had blonde curly hair that framed his face, highlighting his square jaw.

"I'm gonna make this little dancer my bitch!" Murph called as he walked toward Val, the ball dragging off the table with a bang as it hung from his neck. He looked like one of those poles in the playgrounds with the tether ball you could whack around.

Suddenly the blonde guy stood up and placed a hand on Murph's chest. "Murph, take it easy, okay?"

"Hey! This is my stag, Will. I'll do whatever I damn well want." Murph tried to shove Will aside, but he was too drunk to be stable. The ball and chain around his neck swung to the side with the ineffectual shove, causing him to lose his balance. His head flopped down into the lap of Paul Bunyan, face first, giving the appearance of Murph going down on his friend. Val giggled and noticed that the tall, blonde guy was smiling as well.

Murph stood up fast, perhaps repelled by a nose full of lumberjack crotch. "What the hell?"

Paul Bunyan's face was confused; likely his impaired brain wasn't able to compute what was going on.

Val decided it was best to get this over with. She grabbed Murph by the hand to lead him to the private dancing room. As she walked away, she noticed that the tall, blonde man was still standing and watching her. He had a serious look on his face that contrasted sharply with the table of hooting stag followers like a speed bump in a drag race.

When Val entered the private dance room, she was immediately assailed by the smell of body odour, stale beer and cheap perfume. It reminded her of carnival fair lineups during hot summer nights. Several black couches lined the walls. In the dim light, the couches looked halfway decent, but Val knew the true state of the furniture, having gone into the room accidentally when the fluorescents were on one day. It was a mistake she never made again. As she guided Murph into the room, he sat down immediately, his ball and chain swinging to the side and yanking his neck on an angle like he was watching a bird fly overhead. There was no way that get-up was comfortable.

Val knew what was expected of her, but she was finding it difficult to get started. The song was playing, and she knew the drill; she had to strip and lap dance on this asshole for the length of the song. She just hoped it was a short one.

"Come on, sweetie. Let's go!" Murph said, smacking his lap with his hands. Val began to dance over his lap, peeling off her bra as she did so. Murph must have liked what she was doing, because she noticed something rising up in his pants. Val tried to swallow the bile she felt coming into her throat. How would she ever do nine more of these tonight?

As Val moved close to Murph, she raised her arms up to play with her hair. Murph quickly grabbed her ass and pulled her down onto him. Val was caught by surprise; she didn't think the men were allowed to touch the dancers, ever.

"Hey! What are you doing?" Val said, trying to pull herself free of his hands. He was holding her ass tightly and grinding his crotch into her.

"I know you girls like to make a few extra bucks, Just be quiet, and I'll make it worth your while." Murph slipped his hand into her G-string and yanked it off, the Velcro fastenings making it easy to remove. Val began to struggle.

"Hey! Get in here!" She yelled, knowing that the bouncers were supposed to be close by if anything happened.

"Oh, they won't be coming. They get a cut of the action, too."

"You fucking asshole!" She was fighting hard now, but Murph outweighed her by a good hundred pounds. She didn't stand a chance.

"You wouldn't deny a dude his last fuck before he gets hitched, would you?" he asked as he reached down to unzip his fly. Val struggled and pushed hard against him. She wasn't going to let this guy get the best of her. She felt his cock come loose from his pants, and she took the chance to pull her knee free and slam it into his lap. The shock of the hit caught Murph off guard, and he released his grip on her, allowing Val to scramble off his lap. But he caught her wrist hard before she could get away.

"You fucking bitch!" he said as he stood up. The grip on her arm was tight. "It's not like you won't get paid!"

At that moment the door swung open, and the guy named Will stormed into the room. He walked straight up to Murph and punched him in the face. The effect was like a sledgehammer hitting a birthday cake. Murph's body crumpled to the floor. He lay motionless, a pool of drool sliding from the corner of his mouth.

Val stared down at Murph's lifeless body. His dong was still sticking out of his pants at attention, proving to Val where a man's brains truly lie. The world began to swim around her as her body adjusted to the release of the stress of the last few minutes. She probably should have eaten more than a slice of pizza and a sugar cookie. She felt blackness creep into her eyes, and just before the world went dark, she saw Will's arms reach out to grab her.

When she opened her eyes, Val found herself pressed against a chest that smelled faintly of vanilla. She was cradled with strong arms wrapped around her shoulders and legs. She looked up at the square chin of that tall, blonde man named Will as he walked out of the club and into the fresh night air. She quickly came to her senses. The fall night was cold, and she was still naked. Val had not been carried like this since she was a little girl. Memories of her dad carrying her into the house when she fell asleep in the car flooded her mind. She felt a deep sadness creep into her mind like a fog, the emotions from the night overwhelming her senses.

"It's okay. I've got you now," Will said, his voice calm and quiet.

"Where are you taking me?"

"Home."

"I have to finish my shift. I'm working," Val was all too conscious of her job. Despite what she'd just been through, she couldn't afford to lose her only source of income right now.

"I've bought you out for the night," Will said as he strode across the parking lot.

Val was aware that a club patron could buy out the remainder of a dancer's quota and that would usually entail a night spent in the private dance room with the same lonely guy. But in this case, it appeared that this man had no intention of staying at the club.

He set her down in front of a bright red Dodge Charger and quickly took off his jacket, placing it around her bare shoulders. He opened the passenger door, and Val quickly sat down, not wanting to hang around in a parking lot half naked. The leather seat was cold on her bare ass. A flash of stranger danger jolted through Val's mind. But why would this guy go to all the effort of rescuing her from his asshole friend only to be an asshole himself?

"Wait. I have to go back in. I've left all my stuff and tips in there." Val said.

"No way," Will responded. "I'll go get it."

"You can't go in the change room. It's strippers only."

"I'm sure someone will be able to help me out." Will said, obviously not to be deterred.

"Okay," Val thought for a minute "Ask for Joey and tell him to get Katrina to give you my stuff. It's in a black garbage bag."

Will must have noticed that Val was shaking from the cold because he tossed her the keys and said, "Start the car and turn on the seat warmers." He closed the door and walked back towards the club.

Val started up the Charger, the engine roaring to life with a push of a button, and turned on the heat to the max. Within a couple minutes her ass was toasty warm from the seat heaters. She wished she could afford a car with such luxury. As she sat getting her body temperature back up, she thought back to the events of the evening. Was this what it was like all the time? Frank had told her she had to be tough, but having to endure near rape? She didn't have any other

shows lined up, so at least she could take some time to process. Whatever happened, she would have to sit down with
Frank and tell him she wasn't going to play the whore. It
wasn't long before Will returned, opening the driver's side
door and passing her large garbage bag over to her.

"Where to?" Will said, turning and smiling at Val.

"I'm in Pineview. You know where that is?" Will nodded as he maneuvered the car out of the club parking lot.

"Thanks," she said. Val realized she didn't know his
name. "What's your name by the way?"

"William Davis," he replied, holding his one hand out
from his steering wheel. "Call me Will."

"Val Dashwood," she shook his hand and smiled, holding his coat closed around her chest. Despite having spent the
night mostly naked, she felt self-conscious about her current
state of undress.

"Thanks for everything back there. That was quite the
punch."

Will sighed, "You don't have to thank me. Murph is an
asshole."

"How did you know, he was, you know…" Val trailed off,
not wanting to talk about what Murph had tried to do to her.

"I heard Murph talking to one of the bouncers. He said
something about not wanting to be disturbed. You didn't look
like the kind of girl that would be into that."

Val frowned. She knew Joey would never do that to her, but she didn't know the other bouncers that well. They didn't make that much, so the offer of a few extra bucks to look the other way might be appealing to some.

Val untied her garbage bag and pulled out the jogging pants and T-shirt she was wearing when she'd left the house. She quickly pulled the pants on while seated. She was thankful that Will's blue eyes stayed solidly on the road when she took off his jacket and pulled on her tee. The knot in her stomach was slowly releasing now that she was at least clothed.

"How do you know Murph?" Val asked, wondering why her rescuer would have been at the stag party to begin with.

"Old school friends. I don't know why he is getting married. The guy wouldn't know monogamy if it smacked him in the face."

Val hoped whoever Murph was marrying knew what she was in for. "Are you in the wedding party?" Val asked.

"Yeah, I am." Val glanced over at Will, the guilty look on his face was endearing.

"You must be a ballet dancer," Will said, obviously trying to change the subject away from his association with Murph.

"Yes. Oh, well, I was," Val responded, not able to keep the sound of regret from her voice.

"Anyone with your skill is always a dancer. I used to dance myself, you know." Will's eyes flashed from the road to Val's face and back again. He caught Val staring at him, so she looked away.

Val was shocked. Very few men in this small town would have the balls to admit to being a dancer. "Where did you dance?" she asked.

"In Fort George, but I had to stop when I was in high school. Achilles injury."

Val nodded. Achilles injuries were common among dancers. "Ballet?"

"Yeah, I had this teacher. Wow! Was she ever strict. She used to smack the back of my legs with a metre stick when I didn't hold my arabesque perfect."

Val laughed. She had been there. "Oh man, I know exactly what you mean. Ballet teachers are terrifying!"

"Right? I still have nightmares about Madame Pain."

"Her name was Pain? Are you kidding me?" Val said.

"Well, it's French, so it was pronounced like Pan, but we all called her Pain for obvious reasons." Will turned his Charger into Val's neighbourhood and slowed down to a crawl.

Val was enjoying talking to Will, but the ride was coming to an end.

"This is me," she said as they approached the small white rancher.

Edward's Beemer was parked in the driveway, and the house was dark and quiet. Val was happy for her sister; maybe she had got laid? She wasn't sure if she would continue to lie to her sister about her new job, especially after what happened tonight.

Will pulled the car to a stop in front of the driveway and turned to face Val.

"I know tonight was terrible for you. I'd like to come by sometime and see how you are doing, if that's okay with you?"

Will reached out a hand as if to touch her knee but thought better of it and pulled away at the last second. Even though Val's night had been filled with groping men, this was one touch she might have welcomed.

"Yeah, for sure. I'd like that," Val responded. She smiled at him, her eyes following down the nape of his neck, which was muscled and smooth. It was unfair that this attractive man had seen her naked and vulnerable.

Val pulled herself out of the low-slung Dodge, her garbage bag hanging awkwardly from her hands. She felt Will's eyes on her as she went up the walk to her door, so she turned and waved. As he pulled away and headed down the street, she wondered if his concern for her was genuine, or if she would never see him again.

eleven

Ellie woke up the next morning to find Edward gone from her bed. She immediately panicked, wondering if she had a "fuck and run" situation again. She sat up in bed and looked around the room. Edward's clothes were gone. She sighed and looked at the clock; it was nearly 6:00 AM. Thankfully, her internal clock had woken her at the right time to get ready for work. The night with Edward in her bed certainly had put all thought of work out of her mind. If Edward had run, at least she had some release. Her body and mind felt euphoric, even if somewhat sad at being ditched so soon. She was about to pull herself out of bed when Edward pushed in through the door, holding two coffees from Tim's in his hands and a brown bag hanging from his mouth.

"Cwaffey?" Edward said through a mouthful of bag.

Ellie laughed and stood up to grab a coffee out of his hand and the bag, which she found contained her favourite cheese Danish. She was still naked, and Edward grabbed her as soon as he had a hand free and pulled her to him for a deep kiss.

Wow, thought Ellie. She could almost have another round of this guy if only she didn't have to get to work.

"I had to run out for coffee. I didn't see anything in the kitchen. Double-double right?" he asked as he released her from the kiss. Ellie felt like she had no breath left to speak.

"Yeah," she said, not able to knock the goofy grin she had perma-plastered to her face. Edward looked as collected as always, his BACON T-shirt back on. Pressed up against him, she felt something below indicating that maybe he felt like another go as well.

"I have to go to work," Edward said.

"Yeah, so do I," Ellie admitted, although she was half willing to call in sick for the day if Edward even said the word.

"Although, because I don't have to stop for coffee I could spare ten more minutes?" Edward raised an eyebrow at Ellie, the expression melting her reserve (if she had any) on the spot.

Edward didn't need to ask twice.

Twenty minutes later, Ellie was in her truck on the way to work, humming to herself. For the first time in what seemed like forever she felt completely happy. Edward had asked if he could come by later and help with more "packing," saying that he would call her as soon as his meetings were over for the day. She thought that in all that had happened, she still didn't know what Edward did for work and why he had business meetings in Sober.

This morning the rolling boreal forest surrounding Sober was dusted with drifting fog. When Ellie was little, she thought fog like this looked almost alive or magical in some way, that if you walked into it your mouth would fill with the taste of marshmallows. Now it looked ominous, highlighting the clear-cut gaps in the forest like white paint on an old fence. In the past thirty years, the landscape had changed. It used to be that Ellie would see bears wandering through the town, lumbering along the streets like they owned the place, peeling the tops off locked garbage cans as if they were plastic pudding lids. But the bears had long since disappeared. The crows remained, the proverbial rats-with-wings creatures that would likely stick around past any apocalypse. When the oilfields were first claimed, residents were told this would be a boon for the town, like a coming gold rush. The gold was in the form of tar buried deep in the earth; it only had to be stripped from the ground, polished like old silver and then shipped south to the oil thirsty Americans. Boom! We'd all be rich.

When Ellie scanned in at work, she had a message waiting for her at the front desk. She was to report to the site manager before starting her shift. Ellie sighed. Nothing good ever came from talking to this guy. She quickly stuffed her bags into a locker and pulled on her welder's overalls. But, nothing was going to ruin her good mood today, not even a meeting with Wayne Smith.

She had met Wayne on her first day. After introducing himself, he claimed, "She was the prettiest welder he had ever met," while holding on to their handshake long enough that Ellie's palm began to sweat. After what felt like a lifetime, he had released her hand only to comment that most welders he likely knew had a lot more facial hair so the competition for prettiest was slim.

When she entered Wayne Smith's office, his back was facing away from Ellie, and he was loudly talking on his phone that was attached to an earpiece. He looked like a professor giving a lecture as he stood talking loudly to the back of his office, hands on his hips.

"Tell them we'll be ready for the meeting in half an hour," Wayne turned around and smiled at Ellie, motioning for her to come in and sit down. "I don't care if the union reps have their panties in a knot; the meeting is going to go ahead today, like it or not."

Wayne abruptly ended his call by touching his finger to the black protrusion sticking out of his ear. Ellie never understood why people saw these hands-free earpieces as a kind of status symbol, but for a manager type like Wayne Smith, it suited him perfectly.

"Ellie! My favourite Site C welder! Your face always lights up my day," Wayne said as he sat down at his desk and turned to face Ellie. "If only you would smile more, you'd be a beauty."

Wayne paused and looked expectantly at Ellie. She assumed this was some trigger for her to respond, so she raised the corners of her mouth like an elementary school kid at the class photo shoot.

"See? Pure radiance!" Wayne ran his hands through his dark hair, which was swooped back from his forehead with a considerable amount of gel. He was not a bad looking man, and he obviously worked out and liked to show it, since he wore dress shirts slightly too small for him, making his arms and pecks look like they were ready to bust the buttons and seams. Today was no exception. His shirt was a pale salmon colour and so tight that Ellie could see his barbell nipple piercings. Wayne must have noticed her looking at his chest, and he smirked, raising his eyebrows and looking down at her chest, which was thankfully covered by the top of her welder's overalls.

"So, you wanted to talk to me about something? I do have to get to shift start soon," Ellie said, trying to hide the blush on her face by turning her head sideways. This guy could possibly be God's perfect asshole, and she was mad at herself for looking at his nipple piercings. It really sent the wrong message. But how could she not? His chest reminded Ellie of saran wrap stretched too tightly over hors d'oeuvres where someone had left the toothpicks in.

"Yes, of course, you are always on time. I've noticed that about you." Wayne paused, like he was waiting for her to thank him for his platitudes, which were merely stating the facts about her punctuality. She wasn't going to bite.

He seemed to be caught in a sort of reverie, staring at her face with an intent expression. Was he having a stroke?

The last thing she wanted to deal with today was having to do CPR on this jerk.

Wayne shook his head, like he was coming out of a dream. "Right! Back to business. So, you may be aware that we have some very important guests coming to the site today for a tour. Given your exemplary behavior, we would like to come and view your work today. You won't have to do or say anything; however, we would like you to have your mask off and face visible for the guests."

Ellie was aware of the guests coming. Rumours had spread around the site weeks ago. The executives from Excon, the competing oil company, were coming to tour the site, preparing negotiations for the takeover bid. The discussion was that the board of directors of Sober Oil were split; half wanted to sell out, and half wanted to reject the offer.

"So, you're just going to come by, and I'll take my mask off when you're there?"

"Well, we would prefer it if we could bring them by while you are working, but we want them to be able to see your pretty face. So just make sure you already have your mask off."

"You are aware that I can't weld without my mask." Ellie responded, looking slightly distraught at this request.

"Yes, of course, don't do anything dangerous or against policy, but just make sure you are doing some of your work with your mask off."

"But my work is welding. What exactly am I supposed to do without my mask on?"

"Look, I'm not a welder. You'll have to figure that out. And I know what a smart cookie you are, so I'm sure it will be fine!" At that moment, it looked like the side of his head was vibrating, and his eyes got a distant look to them.

"I have to take this call. We'll see you around 1:00 this afternoon!" Wayne lifted his hand to his ear as he waved at Ellie to leave his office, turning in his chair away from her. "Benny, you fucking asshat, what time is tee off? Can we make it 5:00ish? I have some work shit to do. Make sure you come in hot because I'm going to get my drink on early."

Ellie got out of her chair and left the room, noting she was now 15 minutes late for shift start. She hated any demerits on her card. And now she had this weird request to put on a show for the execs. What the hell was this all about? Ellie didn't think of herself as pretty. She had a hardened look that came from working a physical job in cold weather. Between work, hockey and working out, her body didn't have an ounce of fat on it, and her biceps kept anyone from challenging her to an arm wrestle. But Val always said she was a classic sort of pretty, with pale skin that comes from living in a northern climate and blue eyes that were reminiscent of the eyes of husky sled dogs.

As Ellie was one of the few women that worked in the trades at the oilfields, she could only assume they were trying to put on a show that Sober Oilfields was a diversified workplace or some shit like that. Whatever happened later, she wasn't going to weld with her helmet off. Nothing was worth burning out her eye sockets.

The first half of the day went by quickly. She had a ton of work to catch up on, and with getting started late, she barely noticed that it was after lunchtime when she finally finished welding a joint on one of the new pipelines that was being constructed. She was just putting her rig aside to go for lunch when she spotted a group of suits walk into the work bay. Leading the pack was Wayne Smith, his hands waving dramatically, putting a considerable strain on his tight shirt, the salmon colour accentuating the dark pit stains as he pointed to the spider web of oil pipes branching over the ceiling.

Ellie still had her welding mask on, as she sized up the group of execs. One of them was Richard Branch, the CEO of Sober Oilfields. The Branch Family, along with the Prices, was one of the original founders of the site. Everyone thought that Richard would have retired years ago because he was almost seventy. But Richard Branch was a spry, wiry old guy, who continued to get up at 5:00 AM and come to the site to work a full day. He was never bothered by the constant reminders from the rest of the board about his impending retirement.

Richard was the kind of CEO who made a point of getting to know as many of the employees of Sober Oilfields as he could. As an employee, it made you feel pretty good when the CEO would come and ask you how your family was and remember what your kids' names were. It made you feel like your job had some security because it was a lot harder to fire someone when you knew they had kids at home to feed.

There were two others in the group that Ellie didn't recognize, so she assumed they must be from Excon, the company looking to make the takeover bid on the site. One was a tall woman with blonde hair pulled back into a bun so tight it looked like her face was being stretched by some kind of medieval torture device. She wore a beige power suit, and she was rapidly taking notes on her clipboard.

The other exec was facing away from Ellie, so she couldn't see what he looked like, but his back profile looked familiar. *Nice ass,* she thought. When the man turned around Ellie gave an audible gasp. It was Edward! He was wearing a full suit now, navy blue, that complimented his blue eyes. His hair was neatly disheveled, looking like he'd just got out of bed, which reminded Ellie of that morning. She felt a delicious feeling inside her as she remembered some of the activities of the last twenty-four hours.

Edward was looking around the bay, directed by Wayne's enthusiastic gestures. His eyes passed over Ellie, but she was still wearing her mask so there was no hint of recognition. She quickly turned to the side so he wouldn't see the name "Dashwood" on her overalls, but then realized how silly that was. She wasn't even sure she'd told Edward her last name.

For some reason, Ellie was filled with an inexplicable urge to hide. She quickly stepped away from her welding rig and cut in behind a giant electrical panel. She was already apprehensive about this parade, but now that she knew Edward was one of the Excon executives, she had no desire to be on display. As she moved behind the pillar, Ellie noticed Richard's eyes follow her, and his mouth curve in a small smile. She pretended to be fixing something on the panel to avoid her coworkers questioning her odd behavior.

"So here you see some welding work for the new infra-structure for the Site C development. I'd like you to meet one of our journeyman welders." Wayne turned to face the work area and scanned around, not seeing Ellie hiding behind the electrical panel. Wayne looked impatiently at his watch. "She should be here."

"She?" queried the woman with the tight bun. "You don't see many women welders," she commented without look-ing up from her clipboard.

"Yes, Sober Oilfields is proud of our hiring diversity. We have all sorts here; crippled, Asians, blacks, women and gays." Wayne ticked off fingers on his hand with a smug look on his face.

Edward looked slightly horrified, his eyebrows raised in disbelief. Even the tight-bun woman stopped writing for a moment and stared at Wayne.

"Do you mean 'persons with a disability'?" Edward said, looking pointedly at Wayne. "And is it safe to assume you have gender-neutral facilities as well?"

Wayne looked puzzled, "Yes, we have at least one women's washroom in every area of the site. Out on the rig, the porta potties are for men or women, doesn't matter. We did have them separated for a while, but the men would fill theirs up fast, and it was costing us double to get it drained and switched out, so we just took the signs off and that solved it." Wayne gave a self-satisfied smile. Edward sighed and shook his head.

"I think the important thing is that at Sober Oilfields we have always ensured a double-blind hiring process backed by our diversity policy." Richard was attempting to steer the conversation towards more politically correct ground.

"Yeah, what I said," Wayne said. "Where is she? She should still be on shift!" Wayne was anxiously looking around. Ellie was frozen in place, surprised by her own defiance. She didn't feel shame in her job, but she couldn't face Edward knowing now that he could possibly cost her this job.

Richard smiled, "Why don't we carry on to the laboratory area?" He gestured the group back towards the entrance.

Wayne shook his head and then reluctantly turned to leave with the rest of the group.

Ellie poked her head around the pillar as the group was exiting the work bay. Just before Richard left the bay he turned his head, looked straight at Ellie and smiled. She raised her hand in a wave of thanks. Sharing this little subterfuge with the company CEO somehow made her heart feel a little less heavy.

twelve

When Ellie finished her shift that day she noticed she had a voice mail on her phone. As she got into her truck and made the drive home, she listened to the message. It was Edward. As soon as she heard his voice, she felt a mixture of desire and anger swell up in her. How could he have hidden his real reason for being in town from her?

"Hey Ellie. It's Edward. Uhm, just wanted to see how you are doing. Hope work was fun. Where do you work anyway? I feel like we have a lot more to...uhm...talk about. Right. So, give me a call back, please. Oh shit! This sounds desperate. Fuck! I shouldn't have said that. Uhm, okay, how do I delete this thing...?"

Edward's voice trailed off as the sound of buttons being pressed and fumbling came over the message. There was a second message.

"Hey. Edward again. Sorry about that last message. I just wanted to say that...uhm...well, just give me a call when you get this, okay? Bye."

Ellie wasn't sure how to respond. She spent the rest of the drive home contemplating her night with Edward and the shock of seeing him with the Excon executives at work. *Why did every guy have to have some sort of problem? Man, the sex was so great, though. And he is damn hot.* Just thinking about him made her body tingle with anticipation. *No!* Ellie thought to herself. She couldn't be so desperate to date a guy who could ultimately ruin her. She needed this job more than anything right now. How could she look him in the eyes, knowing his company was planning on destroying this town's only economic resource?

Thankfully, Ellie had hockey tonight, so she decided not to call Edward. She would grab her gear and head straight to the rink, not letting her mind drift back to his washboard abs or his delicious neck or…No! Man, this was going to be harder than she realized.

Hockey was a great release for her. Thankfully, Number 69 wasn't playing tonight, so she didn't have to endure that jackass. She managed to keep her mind free from thoughts of Edward through most of the first period. After a shift she sat down on the bench next to Carrie. Her tall friend was grinning at her suspiciously as she drank from her sports bottle.

"What?" Ellie said, turning to face Carrie.

"Uhm, you haven't noticed?" Carrie responded.

"Noticed what?"

"There is this tall drink of water over on the sidelines, who is obviously here for you," Carrie said as she gestured over to the bleachers, which were empty except for Edward. When Ellie looked at him he waved enthusiastically.

"What the holy fuck," Ellie said under her breath.

"He obviously has a hard-on for you. I can't believe you didn't notice him staring at you on the ice. Not to mention the dorky waving. Who is he?" Carrie asked as she shifted down the bench. They would be getting on the ice again any minute.

"Long story," Ellie said, as the two of them got up and skated out onto the ice. Carrie would have to wait to find out.

The rest of the game went terribly for Ellie. She avoided Carrie on the bench, refusing to talk to her. Anytime Ellie looked at Carrie, she was making a new gesture, like she was offering suggestions. First it was the blow-job motion. Ellie responded by giving Carrie the finger. Then she attempted to demonstrate doggy-style using her hockey stick, which was made particularly awkward given the other linemate next to her was bending over and retying his skates. This time Ellie chucked her water bottle at Carrie's head, which appeared to silence the suggestions for a while.

This hockey game was supposed to be a distraction from the Edward problem, and here he was, following her around like a typical Desperate Dong. The conundrum was that all she wanted was to take this DeeDee back home and fuck him again. What was wrong with her?

When the game was over, Ellie could see out of the corner of her eye that Edward was cheering and yelling, "Go Ellie!" from the bleachers, which made Carrie laugh out loud and smack Ellie on the back.

"This guy is a winner. Let's go say "Hi," shall we?" Carrie started walking down the side of the rink, her skates making her six-foot form tower over Ellie.

"No! Carrie!" Ellie called after her, but it was no use. Ellie watched Carrie approach Edward, take off her helmet, which released her short pixie-cut brown hair in a sweaty mess, and held out a hand for Edward to shake. Ellie sighed and followed her over.

"Oh, so you just met Ellie, eh?" Carrie was saying, turning and smiling mischievously at Ellie as she approached.

"Ellie, you were awesome out there!" Edward said.

"Edward, what are you doing here?" Ellie demanded, her eyes glancing at Carrie as she spoke, trying to give her the "fuck-off" message.

"Ah, I'm sorry, I know I should have asked. But when you didn't call, I went by the house and Val said you were here, so I thought I would just come by. I love a good hockey game." Edward reached up and ran a hand through his dark hair, looking slightly embarrassed.

He should be embarrassed, thought Ellie.

"He's a hockey fan!" Carrie announced, pointing at Edward, an expression of mock surprise on her face. "How did you two meet?" She asked, pointedly looking at Ellie.

Ellie glared at Carrie. "Look, I have to go get changed. Edward, nice seeing you." She turned and started walking toward the change rooms. Ellie was conflicted. Seeing Edward again brought back all the memories of last night, making her already hot face flush. But she was still pissed at him for not being honest about his work.

She didn't look back at Edward, but she could feel his eyes on her as she walked away. *Whatever. Fuck him!* she thought.

Ellie was starting to take off her gear when Carrie came into the dressing room. "Man, you straight chicks are cold-ass bitches if you ask me," Carrie said, plunking down next to Ellie and in the process, shoving the guy who was changing too close to Ellie farther away.

"Carrie, that guy, Edward; he is an Excon exec."

"Oh, fuck," Carrie muttered, pulling her hockey pads off to reveal her broad, square shoulders.

"And I let him go down on me!" Ellie yelled this out unexpectedly, and the room full of almost naked hockey guys went instantly silent as they all turned to look at Ellie.

"Ah, none of your fucking business, assholes! Go back to stroking your dicks for each other or whatever," Carrie shouted at the staring men, most of whom looked like they were waiting to watch some co-eds in a sexy shower scene.

Slowly the talk and noise came back up in the dressing room again.

"So, you had a little fun with some dirty exec? What's the big deal? Even a big dyke like me can see that THAT asshole is sexy." Carrie put a large hand onto Ellie's shoulder, a considerate gesture given that Ellie's undershirt was dripping with sweat.

"I just don't need this kind of drama right now. What with Dad's funeral coming up, and the house and everything. Why do I keep making shitty decisions about men?" Ellie looked up at Carrie, an expression of disbelief on her face.

Carrie sighed. "I've told you time and again, your problem is that you need to switch brands and try some nice pussy for a change." Carrie's face was so straight she looked like she could be taking an oath in court.

Ellie stared back at her in a showdown, each one waiting for the other to break. Ellie never outlasted Carrie, and her face broke into a grin, and Carrie laughed out loud. It was an ongoing joke between them.

"Whatever. I'm not into fish, thanks," Ellie responded, feeling better already. She finished packing up her gear and got up to leave, being careful to avoid seeing the naked men walking out of the shower. She thought how repulsive naked men are when you are forced to see the ones you don't want to see. She was thankful that Edward was long gone when she left the change room. That was one guy she wanted to see naked but not actually talk to.

thirteen

The next few days went by in a blur. Val was quiet and reserved, which was unlike her. Ellie asked a few times what was going on, but Val just shrugged and went back to packing. Ellie didn't pursue it; she was wound up in her own issues, thinking about the house, money, and of course, Edward.

Since hockey, Edward had left two voicemails on her phone. One was apologetic, and the second was more abrupt. He put the ball in her court, saying he wouldn't bother her again, but felt like he at least deserved an explanation for the silent treatment. Ellie couldn't be bothered to let this guy stress her out. She didn't need anything else in her life right now, no matter how fun the sex was.

Strangely, Val didn't even bother Ellie about Edward either. Usually, Val was on her like a cat on catnip, but she seemed to have her own shit going on. Sisters know when to leave things alone.

Ellie took some days off work for the move and to get the last few things packed up. The two sisters loaded the cube van themselves. There wasn't much. They were selling most of their furniture because the trailer they were moving to was furnished. Ellie and Val climbed into the van to drive to their new home.

"Crazy, eh? That's the last time we'll be in that house," Ellie said as they pulled out of the driveway, the windows of the small house staring back at them like the eyes of a lonely child. She glanced over at Val only to see that she was crying silently, looking out the window.

"Hey kiddo, it's going to be okay. We're going to look after each other, right?" Ellie placed a hand on her sister's leg.

Val wiped her face with her sleeve in a gesture Ellie had seen her do many times when she was little. She'd sometimes woken up from a scary dream, and Ellie would lie down in bed with her and tell her she was safe.

Val turned and smiled at Ellie, her eyes red and puffy. "Yeah, I know."

They drove the van in silence, heading out of town to an area known as Hilcrest. It was where all the wealthy people in town owned large acreage properties. Many years ago, the government had given the land practically free to people who would use it for farming. Some ingenious rich businessman figured out early on that as long as you cut down a few trees on the property and grew a vegetable garden, you could be eligible for the grant. So, the properties in Hilcrest were hardly "farms." They had monster homes, immaculate gardens (with maybe a few zucchini plants during the summer months) and separate garages filled with ATVs and snowmobiles.

Ellie saw the ornate sign for Price Estates as she rounded the first corner in Hilcrest. The driveway was blocked by a large, elaborate metal gate, like something out of a Jane Austin novel.

Ellie rolled down her window and pushed a buzzer on a panel off to the side. No one answered the call, but suddenly, the gate began to swing open with a metallic clicking noise. Ellie slowly advanced the van onto the property.

"A bit of overkill if you ask me," Val smirked as they entered a meticulously manicured yard. The driveway rose up a small hill that was surrounded by neatly cut grass and ended in a circular roundabout. As they crested the hill, the Price family home rose up from the back of the property. It was a large mansion, for northern standards, with three floors and multiple large, south-facing windows. A well-designed flower garden lined the front yard. It was unusual to see so many blooming flowers this late in the season in Sober. Ellie wondered just how much the family paid for the upkeep of the yard alone, since for the majority of the year it was covered in snow.

Ellie pulled the van to a stop, and both the girls climbed out of the cab. As they walked toward the house a shrill cry rang across the yard.

"Hellloooo!"

Ellie and Val turned around to see a small middle-aged woman approaching from the back of the lot. Her short, curly hair was neatly styled giving her head the shape of a foam peanut. Following close behind her was a puffy older man, his face round and jowly, like a baby that had been forced to grow up too fast. Two small Corgi dogs ran up to Ellie and Val, yipping wildly at their feet. Their small legs barely allowed them to advance over the grass. Val dropped her hand for them to smell, she was always happy to greet animals before humans.

"You must be the Dashwood sisters, Ellie and Valerie! I told Jim we *had* to come out of the house and say hello. He thought it too cold for the walk, but I insisted. The doctor is always telling him he needs more fresh air, but does he listen? No! And aren't you both the prettiest little things!" The woman rushed up to Ellie and Val and immediately grabbed each of them in a quick hug. Ellie was assailed by the smell of mothballs and perfume, but the woman's embrace was genuine.

"Mrs. Price?" Ellie asked, once she was released. One of the Corgis jumped up on Ellie and began to enthusiastically hump her leg.

"Down, Herbert! Call me Betsy, please!" she responded, as she pushed the horny dog off Ellie. "And this is Jim. No misters and misses around here. Why, we are family after all! I mean, we should have seen you at Fanny and John's wedding, but what with the little baby incident they had, my sister-in-law had insisted it be a quiet affair. I can't tell you how disappointed Jim and I were, weren't we Jim?" Betsy looked at her husband briefly before continuing her monologue. Jim Price had a pained look on his face, like he was undergoing a colonoscopy.

"Come, come! Let's go inside and have some tea!" Betsy grabbed Ellie's hand and began to drag them towards the house.

"Mrs. Price," Ellie started, but she got such a glare from the woman that she quickly amended, "Betsy, I mean, Val and I have to get our van unloaded so we can return it by the end of the day. I'm so sorry; I don't think we can go inside just now. Could we see the trailer?"

"Oh, of course. You girls, so independent. I would have hired movers for you, but Fanny insisted you wanted to do it on your own. She said you wouldn't accept that."

Val glanced at Ellie, silently communicating how much they would have appreciated some help with the move, especially hired movers that they obviously couldn't afford.

"Come dear, the girls want to see the trailer," Jim finally spoke, his voice raspy like he had smoked most of his life. From the yellowing on his fingers, Ellie assumed this was likely the case. He whistled out of the side of his mouth as he began to walk towards the back of the property, calling the dogs to his feet. They clambered around him as if he had pockets full of bacon.

"You can drive the van up the side of the house, the trailer is at the back of the property. Jim will meet you there. I can't go. The ground is tricky for me, and my varicose veins are swelling." Betsy turned to toddle off towards the house. "Jim! Make sure the girls get settled. You two will have to come for dinner later. I insist!"

Val rolled her eyes at Ellie as they made their way back to the van. She was not a fan of overly pushy strangers, and Betsy Price felt like the type that had an empty schedule and a brain to match. Ellie started up the van and followed Jim Price and his dogs around to the back of the mansion. She had to drive slowly to stay behind the older man, who walked almost straight legged, like his large legs hadn't bent at the knee in years.

The property was huge, and it was a bit of a drive to the back of the lot where the lawn ended at a grove of trees. Tucked among a thicket of spruce was a partially hidden trailer. If you didn't know it belonged with the house, you might suspect a squatter had put it there. Green moss grew around the edges of the windows, the white paint having long since yellowed. Val glanced over at Ellie with a look of despair. She only hoped there was a good stove inside that would keep them warm.

Jim walked to the entrance, propping the screen door open with his foot and unlocking the main door. Like most trailers, it sat on raised wooden pallets at each end, keeping the structure from sinking into the forest floor. Ellie and Val scrambled out of the van and caught up to Jim, just as the screen door slammed shut on a spring catch, like a mousetrap.

Ellie and Val entered the trailer behind Jim and the dogs. The inside smelled of cat pee and mold. Underfoot was a mauve shag carpet that extended through the mini living room and down the hall. Each wall was adorned with a piece of 3-D religious art, including an ominous one over the kitchen sink depicting the Virgin Mary weeping blood.

"It is small, but the stove will keep you warm this winter. Sorry about the smell, our last housekeeper stayed here, and she had a few old cats."

Ellie was happy to see a small potbellied stove sitting in the middle of the living room, which must be the trailer's only source of heat.

"Okay, I'm going to head back. Here's the keys. You had better come to dinner, or Betsy will have a bird."

Jim handed Ellie a set of keys, smiling, his puffy face becoming warm and welcoming with the gesture. He turned to head out the door, whistling at the dogs who ran after him in a flurry of orange and white mini-legs.

"This place is a shithole!" Val groused as she trundled off down the hallway to check out the last few hundred square feet of their new home.

"It won't be so bad," Ellie wandered into the kitchen and dropped the keys on the counter only to hear a shriek from the hallway.

"Good God!" Val yelped as Ellie poked her head into the bathroom to find Val standing in what looked like 1980s hell. The mauve shag carpet extended all through the bathroom, including the toilet seat, like a mold that had spread across a piece of cheese. A small Barbie doll stood at attention on the back lid of the toilet, her dress matching the mauve shag and the smirk on her face tempting you to lift her dress and reveal...surprise! A roll of TP. The shower curtain was a spritely baby-shit brown checkered with vomit yellow, which made the small room appear darker than necessary.

"Maybe we can do some renos later, when we save up some money," Ellie said to Val, trying to sound reassuring.

"Renos? This place needs a hysterectomy, not renovations." Val pushed Ellie back down the hall and went to start unloading. Ellie sighed and went to help Val.

By the time they were done unpacking, the fall sun had dipped below the treeline, and Ellie had to drive the cube van back into town in twilight. She was tired, but she knew they had to partake of the dinner Betsy Price had planned for them this evening. As much as Ellie hated to think about it, the Price family had saved their butts by providing their little shitbox trailer to live in. Anything else in town would have been way more than they could afford.

Val refused to go to the Price mansion until Ellie returned. So, by the time the two of them had showered (Ellie had to rescue Val from a particularly large brown recluse spider that had taken up residence behind the shower curtain) and changed, it was nearly eight when they made their way across the gardens. As they approached the front door, they heard several low voices talking animatedly, filling both of them with dread. They were in no mood to make small talk.

They were greeted at the door by Jim Price, followed closely by his excited Corgis that had the effect of being swarmed by canine Danny DeVitos.

"I hope you girls got settled," Jim said as he took their coats. "Betsy has invited some friends and family over; we were just sitting down to dinner." Jim looked apologetic as he ushered them into the dining room.

The room was bulging with unexpected people, all seated around an ornate dining table that likely had been passed down through multiple layers of Prices. Ellie's eyes were immediately drawn to Edward, who sat at the end of the table across from Fanny and John. He looked like he was smirking, but somehow still managed to look hot in the process. Ellie felt like she must be in some sort of dream state, and she half expected to end up naked and holding a plate of meatballs (she often had dreams involving meatballs, and she never knew why), being forced to serve them to all the people from her recent troubles.

Ellie stood in quiet shock, but Val wasn't silent. "Edward? What are you doing here?"

"Edward, you bad boy, you didn't tell me you knew the Dashwoods!" Betsy said from her perch at the head of the table, holding a half-drunk glass of wine in her extended hand. She looked like she knew her way around a bottle of cabernet.

"Well, I thought it would be a surprise, Auntie," Edward responded. "Plus, I've only just met them a few days ago."

"She's your aunt?" Ellie had finally found her voice, her thoughts jumbling in her head.

"Wait, so that means...," Val was thinking out loud, her eyes scanning the ceiling like they always did when she was concentrating on something, "that you must be Fanny's brother!" Val looked happy with herself for having figured out the puzzle.

"Wow. Excellent detective work. Maybe you could get yourself a real job as a private eye," Fanny said sarcastically with a pinched look on her face.

"Come sit! You must be parched after your long day," Betsy waved at Ellie and Val to come to the table. There was an empty seat next to her half-brother, John, which Ellie moved toward, looking to avoid sitting near Edward. She was scolded almost immediately. "No, no, my dear, come sit next to Edward. That seat is for another guest. He will be a bit late, but he wants us to get started." Betsy motioned for Ellie to sit down next to Edward, and she couldn't help but notice Edward looking quite pleased with the arrangement.

"I want to hear everything about how you know these girls, Edward. Spare no details!" Betsy said, waving at her husband to fill all the glasses again with wine. Val took another seat across the table and gave Ellie an apologetic look.

"I guess we're family then!" Val remarked as she sat down.

"Well, not direct family," Edward said, looking meaningfully at Ellie. Ellie blushed, thinking about the night they'd spent together.

"Edward is in town working on a business deal," said Fanny. "He won't be here long; our mother needs him back in the city." Ellie could tell that Fanny was obviously the older sister, used to bossing everyone around. She wondered if Fanny might spill his true connection to the Sober Oilfields takeover. Maybe her sister-in-law could prove useful after all.

"So the Price family is involved in the takeover bid," Ellie said, looking at Edward with an arch expression she hoped would make him confess.

Before Edward could say anything, Fanny responded, "The Price family has long since needed to take back control of these oilfields. They have been running amok ever since Father passed away, and we had to sell our shares. Edward will bring back some sense into how things are run, stop wasting money on all these extras like benefits and sick time." Fanny looked proudly at her brother, who was staring down at his plate.

"Fanny, we can't talk about that right now," Edward replied, giving his sister a meaningful stare.

"You are right, Edward, especially since one of the Sober Oilfields employees is sitting right next to you," Fanny smirked at Ellie, thinking she should be ashamed of her welding occupation.

Edward looked at Ellie with a surprised expression, "You work at the oilfields?"

"Journeyman welder," Ellie said.

A wave of understanding crossed Edward's face like a shade drawn down a window. "Many women welders there?" he asked, feigning ignorance.

"Only one."

"Work-shermk! Why are we talking about this boring stuff?" Betsy said as she picked up a small bell that sat before her on the table and rang it two times. One of the Corgis must have taken this as an invitation for he hopped up onto her lap and began licking his back leg like a cat. "Time for dinner!"

At the bell call, a small, rotund woman appeared in the room dressed in a white apron, her face with a look of distress upon it that looked like it was imprinted from birth.

"Ah, Silvie, can you bring in the dinner please?" Betsy requested politely.

Ellie wondered if they had just gone back a century. She had never been in a household that had a cook, or a maid for that matter. Ellie wondered what Silvie's title was and how she came upon this particular vocation.

Silvie was fast on her feet for her size, and the table quickly filled with a classic English roast beef dinner. The guests began to fill their plates. Betsy was clearly adept at eating and keeping the conversation flowing around herself; it was an artful skill.

"Jim, tell everyone what we paid for this prime rib," Betsy said, her face glowing like an over-ripe cherry from her constantly refilled wine glass.

"Dear, you tell that story," Jim replied, his voice gurgling as if he needed to clear his throat.

"Oh well, Silvie and I went to the store together. You see, she is a wonderful cook and maid, but she can't be trusted to buy food...never watches for the deals," Betsy said the last bit quietly out of the side of her mouth. It was obvious from the disdainful look on Silvie's face that Betsy hadn't been quiet enough.

"You see, I saw the prime rib on sale in the flyer, and so I knew the price was ten dollars a pound." She paused for dramatic effect to take a sip of wine, tapping the glass with her finger, signalling Edward to pour her another glass.

"But when Silvie picked it up from the cooler it was marked at fifteen a pound!" She glanced around the table, obviously expecting everyone to be as shocked at the overpriced meat as she was, but the guests were all attending to their plates with pained looks on their faces.

"Well, I was not going to stand for that! I told Silvie right then and there to go and demand the ten dollar a pound roast. Isn't that right, dear?" Betsy looked pointedly at her husband for approval.

"Yes you did, dear," Jim nodded briskly, causing his jowls to oscillate.

"What happened?" Val asked, her voice edged with mock excitement that Ellie hoped she was the only one to detect.

"I had to talk directly to the meat counter manager," Betsy said, leaning back in her chair and looking very much like a child who has just won the spelling bee. "I find it very hard to deal with them, you know, the Orientals. They run all the local groceries and can hardly speak English."

"Auntie, you can't say that!" Edward said, looking pointedly at his aunt.

"Can't say what Edward, my dear? That they want to get every penny out of people like us? Oh, stop looking at me like that! I just mean the grocery store owners, not every Oriental in town. My dear friend Ester is Korean you know, on her mother's side, twice removed. She has the best skin and looks ten years younger than she is. I for one think it is all that bone broth she drinks. See, I'm not racist!" Betsy banged the table with her hand like a judge pounding a gavel.

Edward looked like he wanted to crawl away under the table, but he didn't continue arguing with his aunt.

Betsy took a gulp of wine and prepared to finish her story on a high note. "I was not going to pay full price. And what do you know, we paid ten dollars a pound for this very roast!" Betsy pointed a neatly manicured finger at the plate of sliced meat, like it was made of gold. The irony of the several large diamond encrusted rings on her fingers didn't fail to pass Ellie's mind. These people must be worth millions, and here they were haggling over the price of meat.

"Well, dear Auntie, you proved yourself very resource-ful in the situation," John spoke for the first time since Ellie and Val had arrived. He was quickly silenced by his wife, who gave him a look that said not to encourage her exuberant aunt.

Edward leaned in close to Ellie's ear and whispered, "There was a lot at 'steak' there." Ellie glanced over at Edward, a small grin plastered on his finely chiseled features. Ellie couldn't help but smile at Edward's awkward pun.

"I doubt anyone could 'meat' her expectations," Ellie whispered back, which made Edward's face light up.

Thankfully, the rest of the conversation drifted towards the state of the town's housing developments, something both Fanny and her uncle Jim could discuss at length. It was as boring as the discussion about meat, but at least Ellie felt like she could hide away and eat in peace. Just before the dessert course was served, the doorbell rang, causing the Corgis to turn into yelping fits of fur as they took off down the hall to greet the late guest.

"Ah, it's Brandon at last!" Betsy said, motioning for Jim to go and answer the door. Ellie figured they were to meet another one of the Price family, some rich cousin or whatnot, but she was about to be surprised.

Ellie almost didn't recognize the mechanic because his shop clothes were replaced with a well-fitted dress shirt and pants. Brandon Turner looked like the type of guy who could fit in anywhere. Ellie would have taken him to be a lawyer or other such paper pusher and not a guy whose hands were elbow deep in motor grease every day. Ellie checked herself; people likely thought the same about her. She stood out amongst the other welders like oil sits on water. Brandon's dark beard and hair were neatly styled, making him look younger than his age. Ellie thought him decently attractive, especially as his body was fit from his line of work.

Again, Val's mouth got the better of her as she commented out loud, "What's the mechanic doing here?"

"Oh my! You know our dear Brandon as well!" Betsy clapped with glee.

"Hello Val, Ellie," Brandon said, nodding at them both as he took a seat next to Fanny and John.

"Brandon has been good friends with Edward since they were kids. Shame he decided to take up a dirty occupation like fixing vehicles, but he can't be faulted!" Betsy smiled at Brandon with a pinched expression that highlighted her underhanded comment. "After your parents passed away…God rest their souls…and you received your inheritance, there was really no reason for you to keep working."

"Betsy, you know how I feel about my work. It means a lot to me." Brandon responded.

"Leave the poor man alone, dear," Jim said, his quiet raspy voice putting a final note on the discussion of Brandon's work.

Brandon turned to Val, who hadn't acknowledged his arrival. She appeared to be lost in thought, staring at the crystal bowl centrepiece filled with plastic fruit.

"You haven't got in touch about that Ford Escort of yours," he said, which pulled Val out of her reverie.

"Oh, yes, I will definitely do that," Val responded.

Ellie noticed that Brandon was looking at Val intently again. She thought he might be attracted to her sister, but she knew that was a lost cause. Val was never attracted to sensible men, and Brandon had sensibility written all over him like tattoos on a hipster.

By the end of dessert Ellie was looking for any reason to head home. She was bagged, and avoiding Edward's attempts at communicating with her was wearing her down. Val appeared to be noticing the attention that Brandon was paying her, and although he was polite and considerate, she did not look interested.

"Come, come! Let's all adjourn to the living room for some digestifs. I'm tired of all this boring business talk. I want to hear about everyone's love life!" Betsy rose from her seat but had to quickly sit down, the bottle of cabernet getting the better of her.

Ellie did not want this discussion to start. "I'm sorry Betsy, but Val and I really need to get back. Long day with the move and everything." Ellie got up, motioning to Val with her eyes that she really needed an exit. Val was happy to oblige.

"Sure, sure, so good to have you," Betsy appeared to have given in to the wine, like a child who finally accepts they have to go to bed. Jim came over to her and began to help her out of her chair, smiling apologetically at the girls.

"Thank you for coming. If you need anything with the trailer, just let me know," Jim assisted his wife out of her chair, motioning to John for help.

As Val and Ellie were putting their coats on, Edward showed up, followed by Brandon. "Can we walk you to the trailer?" Edward asked.

Val accepted the offer before Ellie could protest but not before she gave her sister an evil glare.

The night air was crisp and cold, and felt good in Ellie's lungs, like she was flushing all the stress out of her body with each breath. Edward kept pace with Ellie's strides, and Val suspiciously fell behind them, walking with Brandon. Ellie could hear Brandon start to discuss Val's car again and could hear Val's quiet and bored one-word responses. That guy would really have to up his game if he wanted to spark any interest from Val.

"Don't mind my aunt; she's not all that bad. She's just a bit sheltered is all," Edward said. "She doesn't get out of the house enough."

"It is good of them to let us stay here," Ellie responded, not able to come up with anything else positive to say about Edward's family. "Were you planning on telling me about your involvement in the takeover bid for the oilfields?"

Edward sighed, "I really can't talk about it. Plus, I didn't know you worked there."

Ellie thought he was avoiding the question again. "You know, a lot of good, hard-working people could lose their jobs," she said. Ellie glanced at Edward's face and thought she noticed a pained look.

"Look, it really isn't like that. I wish I could tell you more. Could you just trust me?" Edward took Ellie's hand. Ellie wanted to pull away, but his hand was warm, and she felt giddy at his touch. Val was always saying she was too reserved and untrusting with men. Maybe she could let go a bit with Edward and just trust him.

Ellie smiled at Edward and gave his hand a squeeze. "Do you want to come in and see our retro-trailer? If you miss the 1980s, you'll love this place!"

"Yes! Have I told you I'm a Duran Duran super fan?"

"No, and you shouldn't have," Ellie responded, laughing as they walked up to the trailer. She noticed Val was grinning at her when she turned to let Edward into the trailer, completely oblivious that Brandon had said his goodbyes and was turning to walk back to the main house.

CHAPTER
fourteen

When Val woke up the next morning, she was surprised to see that Edward's shoes were still at the front door. She'd left the two of them chatting on the paisley living room couch and gone to bed almost immediately after they got back. Given the paper-thin walls, she figured they must have spent the night playing chess or maybe kinky strip chess. She wouldn't put that past her nerdy sister. Either way, she was happy for Ellie. She needed an outlet, and Edward was the perfect type for her. Smart, good looking and sensible. The only problem was his connection to the oilfields takeover, but if Ellie could get over it, then it certainly didn't bother Val.

Val was dreading the day. She had to go back to the club and talk to Frank about what happened. Maybe she could get her old job back serving tables. She wasn't going to let herself get into a situation like that again. Her mind drifted to William. She was disappointed he'd never come by to check on her like he'd promised. Maybe he woke up the morning after embarrassed by the whole event. Val certainly was. Pretty fucked up that some asshole tried to rape her, and she was the one who felt embarrassed.

Val pulled her runners on and went out to the car, happy to have the fresh air to clear the smell of cat pee from her nose. She hoped the old Ford would start this morning.

It was dewy and cold out, a bad recipe for the engine's carburetor. She really needed to get the car to Brandon. He certainly had been pushy about working on it. For a guy who supposedly had a ton of money, she couldn't understand why he would want to work on her little shitbox Ford. The engine turned over on the second try, and she sputtered out of the property and past the giant Price mansion, where Edward's BMW was still parked. She glanced up at the windows as she passed and saw the peanut-shaped head of Betsy peering down.

Great, she thought, *that busybody was going to keep track of all their comings and goings. Probably would be the highlight of her day.*

The club was empty when Val arrived. It would be hours before the lunchtime patrons began to trickle in. This suited Val fine; she had no interest in running into any of the strippers, or even Joey. Val made her way through the empty club and knocked briskly on the back office door. When there was no reply, Val knocked again a little harder. She thought she heard the squeak of a chair moving inside, so she brazenly decided to walk in.

At Val's unexpected entrance, Frank Miller jumped in his chair, yanking out his hand that had been tucked into the waistband of his pants. He then grabbed the large, noise cancelling headphones off his head, dropping them on the desk. Val heard the distinctive noises of moans and bad jazz music before Frank was able to stop what was playing on his computer. If everything else wasn't obvious enough, there was a strategically placed box of tissues and bottle of pump Nivea lotion on the desk. Val wondered if tissues and lotion were sold as a two-pack in adult stores for convenience sake.

"Val! What can I do you for?" Frank queried, his round face blushing a bright pink as he scrambled to fiddle with some papers and shuffled the tissue box to the side.

Val wasn't going to let the awkwardness of the situation get in the way of what she came to say. She sat down in the chair opposite Frank but instantly regretted it. She could now see the reflection of Frank's computer screen in the glossy framed business license behind the desk; the image of two men dressed as Chinese geisha dancers was strangely alluring.

She pulled her eyes away and tried to focus on the task at hand. "Frank, I don't know if you are aware, but there was an incident last week when I had my first show."

"Ah, yes. I was going to talk to you about that. A young gentleman came into the club the next day to talk to me about that, but he didn't give me any details. He just wanted to find a way to get in touch with you. He was quite concerned for your well-being. Of course, we don't give out personal information of our staff, so I had to send him on his way."

"Will," Val said. He must have gone by the house after they moved and didn't know where to find her. Val felt a warmth in her chest at the thought that William had been looking for her.

"Yes, I think his name was Will, William Davis I think it was. What happened that night?"

Val was silent, trying to think about how best to describe the situation. Frank interjected before she could begin.

"You know, Val, your performance was one of the best I've ever seen. I've had customers coming in every day to ask when you'll be back. I knew you had some time off to move and everything, but we are very keen to have you back on stage. In fact, I'd like to propose that you enter the Ms. Northern Nude contest that's coming up next month. With your skills you have an excellent chance at winning the prize."

"Prize?" Val said, distracted by Frank's proposal.

"Yes, you know…the winner of Ms. Northern Nude takes home five thousand cash, plus you then get a show price raise of a hundred bucks from then on."

Val was shocked. Five thousand dollars would be enough for her and Ellie to find a new place to live. They could pay a deposit on a nice condo downtown plus a few months' rent. She quickly did the math in her head, thinking about the show price raise. It would triple her take home, before tips. Her mind buzzed. Would she be able to keep doing this work after what happened?

Frank looked intently at Val. "Of course, if you have an accusation to make about the other night, that would take precedence. There would be an investigation, and I would reluctantly have to take you off the playbill for at least a month.

You wouldn't be able to enter the contest." Frank tilted his head, giving Val a meaningful look. He must know what happened and needed to make sure it didn't get out.

Val was conflicted. She clenched her fists in her lap, thinking about Murph and what he would be getting away with. But nothing had happened to her thanks to Will. She decided to keep her cards close and make this a negotiation.

"I don't want to do private dances." Val said.

"Private dances are what bring in the most revenue at the club, you know that Val. I could hardly make concessions just for you."

"Well, I guess we don't have much more to talk about. I should probably go file a police report." Val made a move to get out of her chair, but Frank quickly waved his hand at her to stop.

"No, let's not be hasty. What if I reduce your quota?" Frank ran a hand through his greying hair. He obviously did not want the bad press that would come from an attempted rape accusation. There were a ton of rules about strip clubs, and the owners all stretched them to the extreme, with the authorities basically leaving them to do what they wanted. An actual investigation would bring in scrutiny that would throw a wrench into everything.

"Reduced quota of dances, *plus* I will only do them if Joey is watching the room," Val countered. She figured there was no way out of this without some concessions, but she knew she could trust Joey. There was no way he would sell her out to some asshole.

"Deal," Frank replied as he reached his meaty hand over to Val, which she shook, trying not to notice how greasy it was with lotion.

Frank rustled through some papers on his desk. "Oh, that guy, Will, left his number for you," he said, pulling a small slip of paper off his desk. "I figure you can call him or not; I'll leave it to you. I trust this guy isn't going to make any trouble for me either?" Frank held the slip of paper out for Val, looking at her intently.

"No, he won't be any problem." She took the slip and carefully tucked it into her pocket.

Val sat in her little Ford in the parking lot for a few moments, contemplating her decision. She felt guilty, letting Murph off the hook for his behavior, but also relieved she still had a job and the potential to make a big windfall. Just the thought of what she could do for the contest show filled her with excitement. She had loved planning the Black Swan routine, and she had countless other ideas to work on.

When Val went to start the Ford's engine, the little car gave a cough and died. It usually took a few times to get the engine going, so she tried again, pumping the gas repeatedly, but the little car wasn't going to give in. It sputtered to a stop like an anorexic marathon runner.

"Fuck!" Val wailed and slapped the steering wheel. She grabbed her cell and dialed Ellie. She didn't want to bother

her sister after having a night with Edward, but she didn't know what else she could do. When the call went to voicemail, she smashed the phone into the car seat next to her and gritted her teeth. Val reached into her pocket and pulled out the little slip of paper with Will's phone number on it. No, she couldn't call Will and ask him to rescue her again, especially since she hadn't seen him since the incident.

She leaned her head against the steering wheel and squeezed her eyes shut, trying to keep the angry tears from starting. This was the last thing she needed right now. As she sat with her head against the cold, hard plastic, she heard a light tapping on her side window.

"What?" Val groaned into the steering wheel.

When she raised her head, she was surprised to see Brandon's smiling face. He was back in his mechanic's gear, this time with a large, red flannel jacket over his white workshop T-shirt.

"Carburetor again?" Brandon asked when Val opened the door to the car.

"Why are you here?" Val asked, not able to keep the iciness from her voice, which she instantly regretted. She wasn't irritated with Brandon. In fact, he was likely the solution to her problem. Her irritation was with life in general.

"Oh, I was driving by, noticed an old Escort sitting here. There aren't any others of this vintage still running in town, so I figured it was you." Brandon didn't seem to be offended by her cold retort.

"Sorry, it's just that, you know, long day," Val said, giving Brandon a sheepish smile.

"And it's only 11:00 AM! Let me call my tow guy and get this car back to the shop. I can give you a ride home."

"Thanks, that would be…uh…really nice," Val said, stepping out of her little car and walked over to Brandon's truck, which sat idling next to hers in the empty lot.

The cab of Brandon's truck was warm and smelled of stale coffee, which was pleasing to Val. It reminded her of her dad's truck. He had always had a coffee on the go no matter the time of day or night. Val listened to Brandon on the phone with his tow truck guy.

She could tell that this guy was into her, and she really didn't want to give him the wrong impression. He was nice but just not her type. For one thing, he was way too old for her, and although he was in good shape, she could tell that his belly was getting a bit soft around the waistline. He had a full head of dark hair, but there were wisps of grey around his temple.

The drive back to her trailer was quick, and if it hadn't been for Brandon whistling what sounded like "She'll be coming 'round the mountain…," it would have been completely silent. Val didn't mind; she was in no mood for small talk. At least that was something positive that could be said for Brandon's character. Most guys when faced with a conversation lull filled it with boring talk about themselves.

As Brandon pulled the truck to a stop in front of Val's "new" home. There was smoke coming from the small chimney, meaning that Ellie must have got the stove going.

"Thanks for the ride," Val said, climbing out of the truck.

"Hey, can I ask you something?" Brandon asked, not turning to face Val, making her feel uneasy.

"Uhm, sure."

"Can I take you out to dinner this weekend?" Brandon continued to stare directly out the front window, not turning to look at Val at all. Val didn't know what to say. She felt indebted to Brandon but going on a date would definitely give him the wrong impression. Suddenly, she remembered she had an easy out.

"Ah, actually, this weekend is my dad's funeral."

"Right, I'm sorry," Brandon said. "Maybe I could come, you know, pay my respects?"

"I guess? It is a free country," Val responded, her last statement coming out harsher than she wanted.

"Great. It's a date!" Brandon said, smiling at Val.

Val couldn't think of anything to say as she climbed out of the truck. The end of the conversation had gone really weird. Did this guy now think they were going on a date...at her dad's funeral? As she watched Brandon turn his truck and head out, she could see that he had gone back to whistling.

fifteen

Ellie was sitting at the small kitchen table when Val walked into the trailer. The smell of the wood stove thankfully overwhelmed the cat-pee undertones. The extra pair of shoes was gone, so Val knew they were alone. Plus, it was hard to escape anyone in the tiny trailer.

"Was that Brandon who just dropped you off?" Ellie asked.

"Yes, the old shitbox finally gave up." Val shoved off her crocs and went to the kitchen, searching through an open box to find a coffee mug. "But whatever about Brandon, tell me what happened with Edward last night!" Val sat down with her full mug of coffee and began to doctor it with enough cream and sugar to make a cake.

Ellie smiled. "Yes, Edward stayed over."

"Duh, details…let's go."

"I'm not giving you the nitty gritty. I'll just say he is very attentive." Ellie hid her blushing face behind her coffee cup, trying to stem the barrage from Val she knew was coming.

"Oh Ellie, come on!"

"Look, Edward is really nice. And I like him." Ellie paused for a bit. "That's all."

"You like him. And he's nice. Why are you so boring?" Val rolled her eyes and blew across the top of her coffee.

"What about Brandon?" Ellie tried to turn the conversation back to Val.

"What about him? Yawn." Val made a patting motion over her mouth to indicate her non-interest.

"He is a really nice guy, and he has money you know. It couldn't hurt for you to be interested in a sensible guy for once. I'm pretty sure he likes you." Ellie finished her coffee and got up from the table, beginning to empty one of the large cardboard boxes that lined the kitchen countertops into the cupboards.

"There's this other guy." Val reached into her pocket and pulled out the slip of paper with Will's phone number on it.

"Oh, here we go. Some other Pompous Prick?"

"He is really hot, and I think we might have a lot in common," Val retorted.

"Where'd you meet him?" At her question, Ellie noticed a flash of concern cross her sister's face, like a bird flying in front of a window.

"Oh, he's a friend of a friend," Val murmured.

Ellie knew when her sister was hiding something from her, but she decided not to push it this time. When you were this close with someone, you had to give them privacy when they needed it.

"Well, give him a call then. I can see you staring at that phone number longingly."

Ellie went back to unpacking boxes and heard her sister move down the hall to her bedroom. The trailer was so small that she could hear the buttons on her sister's cell phone beeping. It was a good thing that they had been quiet last night as she thought back to the previous evenings activities with Edward. It took everything she had to not call out many times during the night. The thought made her body tingle. But once they'd heard Val leave in the morning, things had not been as quiet.

"Hi, it's Val."

Ellie could hear her sister's voice down the hall.

"Do you remember, from the other night?" There was a pause. "Yes, I'm fine, totally, thanks to you!"

Ellie stopped what she was doing to listen. Why was her sister thanking this stranger?

"I would love to! Yes, I'm not busy tonight…that would be great. Okay, bye!"

Val came running out of the bedroom, a gleeful look on her face that made her sister look like a schoolgirl that got a pony for her birthday.

"Will just asked me out to dinner! Tonight!"

"Wow! That's exciting." Ellie said, still concerned by the conversation she'd overheard. "Who is this guy?"

"Will Davis; he drives a Dodge Charger."

"So if you own a Charger, you can't be an axe murderer?"

"Look, you can meet him when he comes to pick me up okay? Judge for yourself. We are just going to Charlie's tonight. I need to unpack my clothes!"

Val ran back down the hall. Ellie realized there was no sense fighting this, even though they had a ton of unpacking to do. Val needed to have some fun to forget about all the shit that was going down in their life. She couldn't begrudge her sister that, especially now that she had her own outlet with Edward.

The rest of the day flew by in flash for Ellie. The unpacking was made bearable by the random text messages she received from Edward.

Edward: *Did you know you are kind of like dandruff? I can't get you out of my head no matter how hard I try.*

She realized she must be falling for the guy, as she kept laughing at his bad puns.

Ellie: *Maybe you should get that problem looked at. Dandruff is no laughing matter.*

Edward: *I know what is a laughing matter—you and your inability to breathe quietly. I didn't sleep a wink last night.*

Ellie: *I thought I felt someone staring at me all night. Creepy.*

Edward: *Consider it like Big Brother watching you.*

Ellie: *Is that supposed to make me feel less creeped out?*

Edward: *I couldn't sleep anyway. Your bathroom will haunt me until the end of my life.*

Ellie: *Right? The decor here must have come from a Catholic school girl's late '80s wet dream.*

Edward: *Careful, that's my aunt you're talking about.* Angry face.

Ellie worried that maybe she took the conversation too far. She tended to do that with her humour. It was fine for a bit, but then she'd cross a line and offend someone.

Ellie: *Ah, sorry?*

Edward: *You should be.*

Now she'd done it. The phone was silent for a while, which made her stomach turn. Had she really offended Edward? It was his aunt that was helping them out, and here she was insulting her. Suddenly her phone vibrated, and she grabbed it off the table.

Edward: *Sorry that you are living in my aunt's dirty sex dream!* LMFAO

Ellie breathed a sigh of relief. Maybe Edward's humour was more like her own. She vowed to be a bit more careful with her text messages.

Ellie: LOL. *Gross!*

Edward: *Can I rescue you from that shithole tonight? Dinner? My place? I'd like your opinion on the decor of my hotel room. I think this hotel might have used your shower curtain as inspiration for the bedspreads.*

Ellie: *Glad to help! As long as there's no 3-D religious art! I've had enough of that.*

Edward: *Pick you up at 7?*

Ellie: *Sounds good.*

Ellie was relieved. She really didn't want to be alone in the trailer tonight. Ellie was thinking about what she would wear, when Val came out of her bedroom, wearing a pair of tight-fitting jeans and a black T-shirt. Her hair was straightened to a glossy dark shine that framed her heart-shaped face perfectly. Ellie was amazed that Val could always make simple clothes look fashionable and sexy. It was a skill Ellie definitely didn't have.

"You look great!" Ellie said. "Are you going soon?"

"Yeah. He'll be here any minute, it is almost 6:30."

"Holy shit! I didn't realize it was that late. I've got to get ready!" Ellie ran off to her bedroom.

"Where are you going? You are still going to come meet Will, right?" Val called down the hallway.

"Yes! For sure. I'm having dinner with Edward. He's coming in half an hour."

They didn't have to wait any longer. Headlights flashed in the front window, and they heard a low rumble as a V8 engine purred to a stop in front of the trailer.

"He's here!" Val said.

Ellie scrambled to find a pair of jeans to put on, some that didn't have holes in the knees. She had to settle for the pair she'd worn for the last two days because there hadn't been time to go to the laundromat since moving in. She gave them a quick sniff and figured they smelled more like woodsmoke than cat pee, so they would have to do. When she came back to the kitchen, she was greeted by a tall blonde man with broad shoulders and a square jaw. Ellie could see instantly why Val was interested in this man. He was good looking to a fault, and his blonde curls looking like they'd been sculpted by Michelangelo. His smile was the kind of melt-your-heart type you see on the cover of *Teen Magazine*, complete with dimples.

"Hi. I'm Will," he said as he held out a hand to Ellie.

Will's hand was warm and smooth when she shook it.

"This is my sister, Ellie," Val said as she slid on her black boots. Ellie noticed Will's eyes intently on Val as she zipped the knee-high boots up her slender legs.

"Wow, two gorgeous sisters out here. It is like finding diamonds in a coal mine." Even though the compliment was meant for both of them, Will's eyes never left Val for an instant.

"Hmm…a charmer, I see," Ellie muttered under her breath. She was going to reserve her judgement of Will until later, not being a fan of over-complimenters.

Will and Val left in a flourish of spinning dirt beneath the tires of his Charger. Ellie wondered if this was supposed to impress his dates or just make them nauseous so he wouldn't have to buy much for dinner. But Ellie was not her sister. Men who drove sensibly did not suit Val.

Ellie was only able to throw some basic makeup on before she heard Edward's Beemer approaching. In contrast to Will, he was driving at a walking pace, which prevented the car's undercarriage from bouncing off the uneven ground. Ellie couldn't wipe the childlike grin off her face as she picked up her purse and ran out the door to meet him. The two Dashwood sisters were as predictable in their selection of men as the happy ending of a Hollywood rom-com.

CHAPTER
sixteen

Ellie and Val barely saw each other over the next week. If they weren't at work, they were with Edward or Will. Ellie was concerned about her sister spending so much time with a guy she barely knew, but she could hardly be a hypocrite, since Edward had only been around slightly longer. Perhaps it was the upcoming funeral for their dad that made them both want to hide in the sheets with a good-looking guy, but it didn't mean that the funeral didn't come anyway.

There was only one place for a funeral in Sober, The Resurrection Funeral Parlor, a name that struck Ellie as slightly over-promising, but the parlor was predictably full of quiet, sad-looking attendants and bouquets of plastic lilies. Dave Dashwood had only two requests in his will for the service. The first was that he would be cremated, and the second that there would be fireworks. Ellie had dealt with the service, and her half-brother John was supposed to take care of the fireworks and after party.

The small hall was almost full of people when Ellie arrived. Edward had insisted on coming and driving her to the event, stating that it wasn't safe to drive yourself to your own father's funeral. Ellie had accepted, but she was disappointed that her sister had obviously spent the night at Will's place and was not going to come with her to the funeral. She had received a text late the night before.

Don't wait up. I'll see you at Dad's thing tomorrow.

It was unlike her sister to be standoffish, especially concerning family. When Ellie found her way to one of the front seats with Edward, Val's chair was still empty.

The rest of the seats were predictably filled with her extended family and a few of their dad's friends. John and Fanny were there, and Ellie was relieved to see that they had left their son, Michael, at home with the nanny. (She liked the boy, but he would have been allowed to run amok.) Her hockey friend, Carrie Braun, sat in the second row, wearing a black suit jacket that looked uncomfortable by the way it stretched across her shoulders, giving the impression that Carrie wouldn't be able to lift her arms. Carrie smiled warmly at Ellie as she walked past, a look of sympathy in her eyes. Next to Carrie sat Ellie's old school buddy Joey Dawson. Ellie knew that Joey worked with Val at The Bush, so even though Ellie hadn't hung out with Joey since high school, she wasn't surprised to see him.

Of course Betsy and Jim Price were in attendance, for which Ellie was actually grateful because it helped to fill out the room. She didn't really believe in an afterlife, but if her father had some inkling of what was going on, at least he would see a full room. As Ellie was sitting down, she was surprised to see Brandon come into the room, dressed neatly in a suit and tie. He gave them a small wave before finding a seat at the back of the room. Ellie looked at Edward to see if he had invited his friend, but Edward shrugged, looking as surprised as she was.

It was already ten minutes past the start of the service, and her sister had still not arrived. Ellie pulled out her cell and sent a curt text.

Where are you??

The funeral parlor attendant had already gone to the front podium at a nod from her brother John. Ellie was stressed about her missing sister. What if Will was an axe murderer and had waited until the day of their dad's funeral to chop her to pieces just to be dramatic?

"Please be seated. The ceremony will be starting shortly," the attendant said. At this signal, John Dashwood got up from his seat and walked to the podium. The plan was for John to say a few words, followed by Ellie.

As John walked up to the front, he pulled a stack of cue cards out of his pocket. "Thank you everyone for coming. I'm John Dashwood, Dave's first-born son."

"Many may know that I am married to Fanny, of the Price family. My dear wife is sitting right here. Give a wave dear so everyone knows who you are." Fanny obligingly turned and waved at the seated congregation, her hand rotating like a royal, a fake looking smile plastered across her large lips. "Sadly, our son Michael could not be here today as he was having some issues…you know…of the toilet kind." John looked grim when he said the last part, as if his son shitting himself was the worst part of the day.

"I'm happy to say that Betsy and Jim Price are also in attendance, and we can thank them for the refreshments that will be served later." John paused. He appeared to be waiting for applause, but there were only a few awkward coughs.

Ellie looked pleadingly at her brother, attempting to urge him with her eyes to get on to talking about their father. "But we are here to talk about Dave Dashwood." At that moment, the door to the hall slammed open, and everyone swiveled to see who was coming in late. Of course, it was Val and Will that stumbled into the room together, barely able to keep each other upright, and planted themselves in the back row. Ellie sighed and looked down at her lap, embarrassed for her sister arriving late and obviously drunk.

"My father was a stand-up guy. Anyone who knew him would profess to his kindness and generosity." At this statement Ellie heard her sister give a loud snort of laughter. She could hear Will making a shushing noise at her. Maybe he wasn't as drunk as she was, but it didn't excuse the part he played in their actions.

"Dave Dashwood was a family man. He doted on his daughters, Ellie and Val. They were the world to him, and he went to any lengths to ensure their well-being."

"Bullshit!" came Val's voice from the back of the hall.

There was a scramble as Val stood up from her chair, Will attempting to keep her sitting, but she escaped his arms and strode up to the podium, careening off the seated people on either side of the aisle, like a ball bouncing off the targets on a pinball machine. Ellie tried to grab her sister as she went by, but it was no use. When her sister had it in her head to do something, it would be like trying to stop a train with a feather, especially when she was drunk.

Val shoved her brother away from the pulpit and clasped her hands on either side as if the very structure would keep the world from spinning.

"Sit down, John," she waved her brother away like she was brushing away an annoying gnat. John was never one to stand up to a strong-minded woman, so he skittered off to the chair beside his wife, who gave him a glare as if he were a disobedient child.

"Hi!" Val said overly loudly into the microphone, causing a buzz of feedback that made everyone in the hall cover their ears.

"I'm Val. His piece-of-shit daughter. Or maybe I am. I don't know." Val paused, her glazed eyes unable to focus as she glanced around the room.

"When he was drunk, Dave used to say that the black hole that birthed me had slept around, so who knew where I came from. He was referring to our mother. And of course, she couldn't be bothered to show up today." Val's eyes finally found Ellie, and she could tell even through her drunken haze that her sister was profoundly sad.

"That is something you could say about Dad; he stuck around." Val looked proud that she had come up with something nice to say about her father. "Until he died, of course. Oh hey! Bad news. Your dad's dead. You also lost your house, and he left you with crippling debt."

Like her brother, Val looked intently at the audience like she had just delivered a punchline, but again, all she got in response was a few coughs.

"Oh, and let's not forget about the Price family! To the rescue! Gave us some cat-pee-smelling trailer to live in that we are supposed to be happy and kiss their asses for."

Val looked pointedly at Fanny, who was glaring daggers at her sister-in-law, to which Val was utterly oblivious. There were a few shocked gasps and mumblings from the audience.

Ellie decided it was time to rescue her sister. She had been in a bit of a trance listening, part of her needing Val to let it all out. It was almost cathartic. She couldn't listen to her brother John saying a bunch of outright lies about Dave either. Ellie made her way to the podium and made to guide her sister back to her seat.

"Oh, my sister Ellie, the great protector!" Val warbled. "Wait! I have a story I need to tell. This one's about you, too." Val grabbed the microphone off the pulpit stand and moved deftly away from her sister's grasp, continuing her "eulogy."

"When I was in ballet class all the other kids used to make fun of me because I didn't have fancy pointe shoes like everyone else. I used to put a piece of cardboard into the end of my socks, and then I could almost go on pointe. But the other kids called me ghetto-sock girl. One day they stole my old socks, so I didn't even have the piece of shit crap that I needed to try and fit in. That day, good ol' Dave had actually been on time to pick me up from ballet. He was only a little bit drunk this time, and he saw I was crying. Stupid me told him the whole story. Dave promised me right then and there that he would buy me new pointe shoes. And you know what? I believed him."

Val moved towards the seated congregation, pausing for dramatic effect. One thing Val knew was how to captivate an audience.

"And whaddya know? The next week there was a brand new pair of pointe shoes sitting in their pink box waiting for me before my next class."

Val stopped, looking around the room slowly and then back at Ellie. Ellie remembered that day and how happy her sister had been when she got those pointe shoes. The crowd was murmuring and nodding, content that someone had actually told a nice thing about the deceased.

"The thing is, I heard my sister Ellie arguing with him that week. He had blown all his money; I think he bought stocks in Blockbuster. Ellie was pissed because she knew I was counting on getting those shoes. She was wrong though; I wasn't disappointed."

Val paused to look at Ellie. "Dad screwing up was the norm for us. So, when the shoes showed up the next week, I new it was Ellie who had bought them. I didn't know how she did it, but she pretended Dad had done it."

"So, there's my story. Goodbye, Dad. You were an asshole, and now you're dead."

With that comment, Val held out the mic in front of her and dropped it on the floor, causing another squeal of feedback. Val stumbled to the back of the room, grabbing Will on the way out the door.

Ellie picked the mic off the floor, but when she stood back up again, she found that her words were stuck in her throat. It was like she was back in grade one, and the teacher was calling her out in front of the class. Was there really anything left to say? The roomful of people stared at her with expectant eyes, but it was like any energy left in her body had drained out of her like a bucket with a hole.

She had good memories of her dad. They were there, in the back of her head like tiny gemstones. But if you looked too closely, the gems were dulled. She remembered when their dad would wash Val's hair in the kitchen sink. Ellie would stand on guard to keep the toddler from squirming off the countertop onto the floor. Dave would be half cut, singing "Yellow Submarine" at the top of his lungs. When he got to the end of the chorus he'd let out a giant fart, the sound echoing around their tiny kitchen like someone shuffling a deck of flapjacks. Val would forget she had soap in her eyes and break out in a fit of giggles. Ellie knew if she hadn't been there, Val would have fallen on the floor or been left in the sink to play with the kitchen knives. How do you tell stories like that at a funeral?

Finally, Ellie broke the silence. "There will be refreshments in the main hall. Join us afterwards for a short celebration on the lawn outside."

Ellie placed the mic back in the pulpit, and she walked off the stage and down the aisle. Edward stood as she passed, his eyes teary. At least someone felt bad about things. Ellie didn't have any tears these days. She was empty.

The refreshments were as tasteful as they could be in Sober. Plates of grocery store sandwiches and small miniquiches lined a table with various arrangements of flowers. Ellie was thankful that John had at least done his duty with that part. A plate of delicately decorated sugar cookies stood out amongst the store-bought hors d'oeuvres. It was only when she looked closer that she noticed each cookie had either a carefully drawn casket on it or a tombstone. They were beautiful, but perhaps not quite tasteful. She saw a small paper sign labelling them as "The Three Bisquiteers, by Joey Dawson." Ellie smiled, thinking that her old school buddy must have started his cookie business.

Ellie was only somewhat surprised to find a tray of Jell-O shooters in a variety of colours on one of the tables. Val and Will were there, attempting to hold each other's shooter cup while sucking it out. Ellie walked over to talk to Val, leaving Edward with his sister, Fanny.

"Val, what the hell?" Ellie said, trying to make eye contact with her sister as she sucked the last bits of Jell-O from the plastic cup in Will's hand. When Val finished, she gave her sister a quick smile before grabbing another Jell-O shooter off the table.

"Nice of Dad's drinking buddies to bring these, eh?" Val observed, clinking her plastic cup against Will's in salute and downing it as quickly as one can when dealing with Jell-O. Ellie shook her head. There was no use trying to get through to her sister in this state, so she just glared at Will. He at least looked contrite, although was likely too drunk to even know what was going on.

"Go easy on your sister, Ellie," Will said, his words slightly slurred. "It's been tough for her."

Ellie rolled her eyes at him. As if she didn't have to deal with their father's death as well.

Ellie noticed Brandon staring at them from the food table, a look of disgust on his face. She gave up trying to talk some sense into Val, and so Ellie walked over to see what had brought Brandon to her dad's funeral. She hoped he wasn't just there for the show.

"I'm very sorry for your loss, Ellie," Brandon said to Ellie as she approached.

"Thank you." Ellie noticed that Brandon was still glaring angrily at her sister and Will. "Did you know my dad?" Ellie asked, picking up a small cucumber sandwich off a plate and beginning to nibble on it.

"No, sorry, I didn't. Your sister said I could come, so I'm here to support her."

At that moment, Ellie spied Betsy at the other end of the food table. She opened her large designer purse and slid in a handful of mini quiches before stuffing a couple into her mouth.

At least someone's enjoying the food, Ellie thought.

"How long has your sister been dating William Davis?" Brandon asked, bringing Ellie's attention back from the food-stealing Betsy.

"Not long. Just a week now. Do you know him?"

"A bit," Brandon responded, the dark look on his face expressing his obvious dislike of her sister's new boyfriend.

Before Ellie could interrogate Brandon further about Will, John cleared his throat and announced that the final event would be taking place outside on the lawn. Everyone slowly made their way out the large double doors. As Ellie walked outside, she saw Edward and Fanny engaged in a heated conversation. She couldn't hear what they were discussing, but she could tell that they were unhappy with each other.

It was a brisk, late fall afternoon, the air smelling like snow was on the way. As most of the gathered company were wearing dressy funeral attire, people began to get cold almost immediately. Ellie looked around for her brother because he was supposed to be organizing the fireworks. She saw John questioning one of the funeral parlor attendants, who then quickly ran off into the hall. After what felt like an overly long wait, where many of the people standing around were starting to discuss whether they should just leave, the funeral attendant came running back. He was wearing oven mitts and carrying a smoking silver urn in his hands. He placed it down next to the area where John had set up the fireworks and passed the oven mitts to John.

"Is that Dad?" said Val loudly, as she hung off Will's shoulder, holding a Jell-O shooter in one hand.

Concerned murmurs rumbled from the people gathered, as John opened the urn with his oven mitts and poured the contents into a small box. Ellie had no idea what her brother was up to, but she had to put a stop to it. She walked up to John and said under her breath, "What the hell do you think you are doing?"

"Ellie, this is what Dad wanted," John said, as he put down the now empty urn and removed his oven mitts. "Do you have a lighter?"

"No!" Ellie said.

"Oh, hold on, I did remember it!" John patted his pockets and pulled out a small lighter. "You'd better get back, Ellie."

Ellie was about to protest, but her brother was already lowering the flame to the fireworks fuse, so she hustled back to the crowd. John was quick to follow, running backwards away from the sizzling fuse like a man who'd just snipped the wrong wires on a bomb, his long coattails flapping against his knees like a cape.

The fireworks went off in quick succession. They were no extravagant affair, being only what you could buy in a small, northern town. A series of appropriate "oohs and aahs" ensued from the gathered congregation. When the final one launched, it appeared to lift off slowly, like something was holding it down. It was then Ellie realized in horror what John had been doing with her father's ashes. In a split second, the firework exploded in a dazzling array of red and white sparks followed quickly by a puff of grey powder. The extra weight of the ashes had not allowed the firework to gain an appropriate height, making the explosion dangerously close to the crowd of people. Instantly, they were all covered in grey ashes, and since most were looking up into the sky, it was their faces that took the brunt of ash shower.

As realization struck, shrieks of dismay issued from everyone. Ellie's sister-in-law, Fanny, must have been one of the last to come to the understanding that her father-in-law's ashes were now all over her.

She screamed, "He's in my mouth!" and ran back into the funeral hall, losing a high heel on the way and tripping, barely able to see in front of her as she ran, her eyes coated with a dead man's ashes.

seventeen

Most of the people left the funeral quickly after the final event. At least being showered by her father's ashes had the effect of getting rid of everyone, so Ellie didn't have to deal with more condolences and awkward hugs from people she barely knew. When she went back inside, she found Edward cleaning up the random paper plates and plastic glasses left strewn around the small hall. Edward's face was covered with grey soot, except for his eyes, giving him a raccoon-like look. Ellie wondered what kind of disarray she was in, but her appearance was the least of her worries.

"I hope you don't mind, but Betsy already took home the leftover food," Edward said.

"Well, she paid for it." Her voice had an edge to it that Edward didn't missed. "Sorry," she said, immediately regretting her harshness.

"No, don't be. You've gone through a lot today." Edward paused. "Is your sister okay?"

"I don't know what's up with her. I think she left with Will after the fireworks." Ellie was grateful her sister was gone; she was in no mood for a fight right now.

"Ellie, I need to talk to you," Edward said. He put down the garbage bag he was holding and looked intently at Ellie. Ellie didn't respond. She had a sinking feeling in her gut, the kind you get when you've eaten bad funeral food or when your boyfriend is about to tell you something you don't want to hear.

"I'm going back to the city." Edward said.

Ellie's brain couldn't compute what Edward was saying. She stared at him blankly. "You're leaving? When?"

"Today. Fanny, says our mother really needs me at home right away." Edward looked stressed, his eyes flickering around the room like a man caught red-handed at a murder scene.

"You're leaving today?" Ellie repeated blankly. "Edward, I don't understand. Why?" Ellie continued putting paper plates into her garbage bag, just to keep her hands moving.

"It's complicated," Edward said, running his hand across his forehead. "There's something else I need to tell you about," he said, following Ellie as she continued to clean up the hall.

Ellie stopped and turned to face Edward. Whatever this was it couldn't be worse than Edward leaving her on the day of her dad's funeral, but she needed to brace herself regardless.

"A long time ago, I made a promise," Edward said, looking intently at Ellie.

"A promise for what?"

Edward sighed again, "It's complicated," he repeated.

Ellie didn't know what to say, so she continued to pick up leftover Jell-O shooters and slam them into her garbage bag. The last one she smashed with such force that orange-coloured Jell-O shot up and splashed all over the front of her white blouse, making her look like a drunken clown at an after party. Ellie closed her eyes in exasperation and sighed loudly. Things couldn't get much worse.

"I can explain," he continued, handing Ellie a napkin from the table so she could wipe her shirt. "I made the promise when I was young and stupid."

"Doesn't everyone," Ellie replied, swiping the Jell-O off her shirt, which only made larger orange streaks.

"Do you know the Martin family?" Edward asked.

"No. Should I?"

At that moment Fanny Price came up to Edward with John trailing her like a lost dog.

"Edward! Why are you delaying? Our mother is expecting you tonight!" Fanny's manicured hands were on her hips, her big head oscillating like a bobblehead doll.

"I know Fanny, just give me a minute!" Edward's voice went from compassionate to angry in a microsecond, making Ellie feel like she'd never want to be on his bad side.

"Edward! Now!" The stress in Fanny's voice was causing a vein to pop out of her neck.

"Look, Edward, I get it. You have to be somewhere. You have important things to do. And whatever it is, it's complicated." Ellie's voice remained calm and level, not giving away her carefully hidden emotions.

"Edward! We don't have time for this." Fanny was tapping her foot expectantly, hands on her hips and her soot-covered face looking like she was ready to "Step-in-Time" with Dick Van Dyke in *Mary Poppins*.

Edward sighed and ran his hands through his hair, which Ellie now recognized as his stress response.

"It's okay Edward. Just go." Ellie forced a smile at him. She wasn't sure she could keep her composure after the day's events.

"I'm sorry, Ellie," Edward said with a look of genuine concern.

Before she would have to listen to anything else, Ellie left, dragging the Jell-O shooter–filled garbage bag with her. She had no fight left in her.

As she exited the funeral hall into the crisp night air, her mind filled with self-pity. Her dad was dead; her sister was drunk; and her boyfriend was leaving for the city. Could it get any worse?

eighteen

Val woke the next morning with a splitting headache. Opening her eyes felt like needles were stabbing into her brain. She rolled over to see Will sleeping soundly beside her, his blonde, wavy hair crowning his face and giving him an almost angelic look. Despite the hangover, Val couldn't help but feel totally enamored by Will. He was everything she wanted in a man—good looking, passionate, honest and funny. She knew that she was falling hard for him, but she didn't care. It felt amazing and blurred over the pain of dealing with her father's death.

Hazy memories of the funeral flashed through her mind. Had she really given that speech? The angry and sad look on her sister's face stung in her mind. She felt guilty. Ellie did so much for her, but the thing with Ellie was that whatever Val did, she was always forgiven. Val worried that one day she would take things too far, and her sister would not be able to forgive her. But there was a side of her that wanted to find that limit, as crazy as it seemed.

Val pulled herself from the feather duvet that covered Will's king-sized bed. It was the coziest bed she had ever slept in and certainly beat the tiny single bed with the broken springs she had back at the trailer. Will's condo was in one of the new developments in Sober. No oilfield workers could afford to live there, so the place was mostly empty, unless as in Will's case, they had wealthy families.

Val walked out into the designer kitchen looking for coffee but was faced with a complicated espresso machine that looked like it was ready to launch into space. She made a few attempts at navigating the touchscreen and managed to find a selection that looked like just plain coffee, but when she selected it Val didn't realize she had to have a cup in place before pressing the "on" button. Val was rewarded with a spew of coffee that pooled out over the marble countertops and spilled onto the floor.

Val was hastily trying to clean up the coffee mess when Will came up to her, grabbed her in an embrace and kissed her. He was tall enough that Val was lifted off her toes, her arms wrapped around his bare neck. The kiss sent shivers through her body that immediately erased the hangover feeling in her head. He slowly lowered her to the floor, Val's hands running down his muscled chest.

"Making coffee, are you?" Will said as he glanced at the mess of coffee on the floor and counter.

"Yeah," Val said, still dazed from his kiss.

"Here, maybe let's start with getting out a cup."

Will opened the cupboard, revealing a stack of paper coffee cups. He grabbed two and placed them on the machine, quickly selecting a number of buttons on the screen, until the coffee began dispensing. Val was a bit surprised by the paper cups in such a fancy apartment, but she didn't think much of it. Maybe Will wasn't a fan of doing dishes, or the environment. Whatever. Val didn't care. The guy was perfect in her eyes.

"Are you working tonight?" Will asked as they sat at the breakfast bar. Val was thrilled that Will seemed content to hang out wearing only his Snoopy boxer briefs.

"Yeah, I'm going to have to go soon so I have time to get ready. That reminds me, I still have to go pick up my car from Brandon. Could you give me a ride?" Val asked, trying to give Will her best doe-eyed look.

"Sure, babe," Will said, flashing a gorgeous grin that lit up the dimples in his cheeks.

"Are you going to come by the club tonight?" She hadn't worked at the club since the infamous night, and even though Frank had made concessions for her, she was still nervous.

Will put down his coffee cup and put his hand on her bare thigh. "I have no interest in watching other men get their rocks off over your naked body."

Val smiled. Will must be really into her if he was this jealous. Part of her really wanted Will to be there for her. He felt like a security blanket. No other "Murphs" would dare come after her if Will was there. But if it made him jealous, she understood why he wouldn't want to be there.

Will's hand didn't leave her thigh but started moving slowly up her leg. "You don't have to leave right away, do you?" he asked, his blue eyes steely with lust.

Val glanced at the time on the stove, she had a good ten minutes before she had to leave.

"Nope." After that, the Snoopy boxers didn't stay on for long.

Val felt giddy riding in Will's Charger, the low purr of the engine emulated the cat-like contentment she felt at that moment. She must be more than just Will's fuck toy. Having coffee together and giving rides was real relationship-like behaviour.

Will let the wheels spit up gravel as he shot into the parking lot of Brandon's garage. The day was overcast and threatening flurries later, so Val sprinted inside, having not thought in her drunken haze the night before to bring an appropriate jacket. She was a bit surprised when Will blasted out of the lot the second she closed the Charger door, but she figured Will had already gone out of his way and was probably late for work.

Brandon stood at the side window of the garage shop, silently watching as the Charger disappeared down the road. His brows were furrowed when he turned to acknowledge Val, but he didn't say anything, just motioned her to the back desk, wiping his hands on a shop towel.

"Here's the invoice for the Ford. I did what I could to get the carburetor working again, but the reality is, that vehicle isn't long for this world."

Val looked down at the invoice and couldn't believe what she was seeing. It was like it was missing a few zeros after the number.

"Are you sure this is right, Brandon?" she asked, not wanting to cheat him, but also feeling a bit giddy that her bank account would not suffer much.

"Yup. That's right," he said, not elaborating. Val pulled her wallet out of her purse and handed him a few bills.

"Thank you, Brandon." As she passed him the money, she couldn't help but notice that his dark eyes locked intently on her face. It was an unsettling, since most men would make some sleazy comment or blatantly stare at her breasts. Brandon's stare felt more like he was trying to read her mind.

He finally looked away, appearing to busy himself with the papers on his desk. But as Val turned to leave the garage, keys of her Ford in hand, she was caught off guard by his quiet voice.

"Please be careful, Val," he said. "People aren't always what they seem."

Val paused and glanced back at Brandon. The comment was unusual, but then the guy was a bit weird. She didn't respond, just gave her head a small shake, rolling her eyes as she left the garage and strode through the brisk morning air to the ancient Ford. The car sputtered to life like it had been resurrected. Brandon may be weird, but he definitely was a miracle worker with automobiles.

nineteen

When Val returned to the Northern Bush Club for her first night of work after "the incident," she couldn't help but feel a nervous anxiety. What if something bad happened again? Will wouldn't be there to save her. But as she entered the club and let her eyes adjust to the dim lighting, the first face she saw was Joey's. His face switched from stern bouncer to smiling teddy bear the instant he saw her, and his reception eased Val's anxiety. Joey wasn't going to let anything happen to her.

"So, I hear I get to be your number one bouncer from now on?" Joey said, looking like a kid in a candy store, if a kid could be three hundred pounds and six foot three. "How did you wrangle that deal with Frank?"

"Oh, I have my ways." Val gave Joey a mischievous look. She wasn't going to burden her friend with her traumatizing incident. Better if Joey just thought she made some back-hand deal so she could hang out with him more.

"Goodie!" Joey whooped. "You are so much nicer than the other girls. Except Katrina or maybe Carmen. Oh, I guess Portia is nice, too." Joey was counting off his favourite girls on one hand.

"What? You like Katrina better than me?" Val pretended to look hurt.

"Oh no! Babe, you are my fave. I just mean that Katrina is also nice."

Val smiled and gave Joey a kiss on cheek. She had to stretch up on her tippy toes to reach, and even then, only got to his jawline. He blushed bright red in response. "You are my fave, too," she said.

"How goes the cookie business?" Val asked as the two of them made their way together through the club.

"Not great. I can't get a loan for the start-up. And I'm not going to borrow more money from my ma. I just gotta keep working and save up. I know I gotta get to the city and try to set up there. Not enough market here in Sober."

"I know how that is, buddy," Val said. It made Val realize that many of her friends were in the same space that she was, trying to figure their way out of this town.

Val left Joey to go and get ready. The club was filling up even though it was a Tuesday night. They had rotating deals on weeknights to keep clients coming in, and tonight they had extended happy hour. Sometimes a stripper could make more on a weeknight than a weekend if she played her cards right. Katrina LaRue was just finishing up a set on stage, and it looked like her money buckets were filling up. Val wasn't on for another hour, so she had time to get some of her private dance quota in.

When Val came back onto the floor, she was wearing a tight, leather skirt that was short enough that part of her butt cheeks showed out the bottom. Her top was constructed from white leather straps, strategically placed so that only her nipples were covered. The outfit accentuated her flat belly, which she had adorned with a few fake diamond piercings. Her four-inch stilettos helped with her vertically challenged stature. Val swallowed down her anxiety as she walked around the club, looking for an easy and innocent mark for her first dance. Before she had completed a round, a young couple sitting at one of the booths caught her eye. Val walked up and forced a sexy smile onto her face. She noticed matching wedding bands on their hands, which were clenched together on the table. Val did the math and decided on her approach.

"You guys celebrating something tonight?" Val asked.

"Yes, our third wedding anniversary," the woman replied. She had a small, pretty face, with short-cut, blonde hair. She reminded Val of a young Cameron Diaz.

"Congratulations!" Val said, pulling up a chair.

"Thanks," the wife said. The husband was awkwardly trying to look anywhere but at Val. It was hard to look at Val and not see something inappropriate. He looked like a business executive of some sort. He was wearing a nice suit, and Val noticed he had on an expensive watch. A sure sign there was some money here.

"This was my idea. You know, spice up our sex life!" The wife grinned at her husband, whose eyes widened in horror. Obviously, the husband was not as open about intimate relations as his wife.

"You should celebrate! Can I take you both for a dance?"

"Oh! Yes! I would love that." She turned to her husband. "Please sweetie, can we?"

The husband's frozen expression looked like he was going to go ostrich, as if he wouldn't have to deal with the situation if he buried his head in the sand and remained perfectly still. But eventually his head gave an almost imperceptible nod.

The wife clapped her hands in joy. "Oh boy! I'm so glad I brought the balloons!" She picked up her jacket and purse and pulled her husband by the hand out of the booth.

Val didn't give much thought to the balloon comment as she gave a wave to Joey, alerting him she was on her way to one of the private rooms. She felt pretty confident that nothing weird would happen with these two, but she wasn't going to take any chances. Val was relieved that the private room she had been in with Murph was already taken, so she didn't have to deal with the stress of going in there again. Val pulled the mauve curtain closed behind them and motioned for the couple to sit on the couch.

The husband sat petrified next to his wife as the music started, but before Val could even make one move, the wife handed Val a small bag.

"If you could just blow these up and pop them, that would be great." The wife looked at Val as if she was head of the PTA and used to people doing her bidding.

"I'm sorry, what?" asked Val, as she looked down at the small package in her hands. It was labelled "Party Time" and appeared to be filled with multi-coloured balloons, the type you might find at a five-year-old's birthday party.

"Oh, I know it might be a bit weird, but if you can, there's an extra twenty in it for you." The wife said, as her husband continued to sit motionless beside her.

"So, you just want me to blow up these balloons and pop them," confirmed Val, looking directly at the wife like she might have to call the insane asylum.

"Yes, would you? Please?" Her eyes were pleading as she stared up from the couch.

Val sighed. *Well, this would be one for the books,* she thought. She pulled a blue balloon out of the package and began to exhale into it, letting the balloon expand in front of her. As she did so, she noticed out of the corner of her eye the husband start to relax, as if every breath she emptied into the balloon was relieving some pent-up tension in him. When the balloon had reached max capacity, Val quickly tied it off then grasped it to her chest, squeezing hard, causing her breasts to push up against the rubber. Val realized that this balloon wasn't about to give in easily. But thankfully she always took good care of her nails, and with a quick poke of her finger, the balloon popped.

The husband let out a groan, his eyes relaxing as an expression of euphoria spread over his face. The wife watched him carefully, her hands on his thigh. Val began on her second balloon, but she decided to place this one between her thighs and squeeze them together until she got the resounding pop.

With each balloon the husband looked more relaxed and turned on, his wife swelling with lust as a result. When the song ended, Val still had half a package of balloons left, but she was beginning to feel a little light-headed from all the blowing. The husband eagerly asked for another dance, pulling a hundred out of his wallet. Val decided this wasn't a bad way to make money, and if this is what got some people off, who was she to judge. The wife asked her to pop some with her teeth, which resulted in an awkward moment of Val spitting out pieces of rubber that threatened to choke her, but otherwise the whole affair was strangely civilized.

Val left that private dance feeling much more relaxed. There was something cathartic about popping balloons. The next few private dances were business as usual. Lonely guys, just wanting some company. They were all regulars, oilfield workers who were interested in Val since she was the new girl. One of them choreographed her whole routine, right down to the direction she was to rotate her hips, which made the process very simple for Val. She didn't even have to think, although she felt a bit like a marionette.

Next was a burly guy with a handlebar mustache, wearing jean overalls and a John Deer baseball cap. He was at the club with a bunch of his buddies, who had all come in from a forestry camp. It was his birthday, so the group had bought him a private dance. When Val got him alone in the private room, she was surprised when he told her to stop dancing. Her heart fluttered in her chest for a moment before she reminded herself that Joey was watching out for her on the cameras. Even if this guy turned out to be creepy, Joey would be in there in a heartbeat and rip his arms off like a Wookie losing at space chess.

"Can we just sit and talk?" The guy asked, as he took off his John Deer cap to reveal a giant bald spot underneath.

"Sure." Val sat down on the couch next to him and immediately regretted it, the cold fake leather of the couch felt strangely sticky, and Val had to suppress her gag reflex at the thought of what must be on the surface.

The guy sighed loudly. "You're very pretty. Don't get me wrong; you just aren't my type," he said, looking at Val kindly.

"Oh, yeah?" Val said. "What's your type?"

"Dudes," he responded. "Preferably small dudes with kind hearts."

Val was shocked at his comment and sat silent before she caught herself. Why couldn't a big, burly forester be gay? She gave herself a careful check that she shouldn't stereotype.

"Do you have a boyfriend?" Val asked.

The big guy sighed again, looking down at his hands. "No. It is really hard to meet anyone, especially when you spend all your time out in the wilderness. Sure, I'm surrounded by men all day every day, but I can't be 'out' with them." He paused and looked over at Val. She at once noticed that his eyes were kind and soft, although his face was weathered from working outside in the cold, like an old piece of leather.

"That's why I let the guys buy me dances. It is just easier this way. You looked like the type that wouldn't go gossiping around. And it is even more awkward when I have to pretend to be into the girls."

Val smiled. "Don't worry, I won't say anything."

The two of them continued to chat for the rest of the song. Somehow, Val ended up telling the guy all about Will, and they chatted at length about what characteristics made the best boyfriend. The guy was more on the Ellie side, and in the end, he started to lecture Val that she should consider sensible guys as better prospects for long relationships. When Val made it back out onto the floor, she had another three dances off her quota (the mustache guy had bought two more just so he could chat a bit longer.)

Val's stage show that evening pulled in more than five hundred bucks in tips. She dressed as an astronaut, in a skintight space suit. The back was adorned in sequins with the phrase "URANUS—Boldly Going Where No Man Has Gone Before." It was a hit.

When Val came off the show floor, Joey was there to escort her to the change room.

"Love the astronaut, babe!" he said, giving Val a thumbs up with his meaty hand.

"Thanks, Joey." Val was breathing hard as she walked offstage. For the last part of the act, she had performed a launch sequence that involved climbing up the stripper's pole and landing naked on the floor in a graceful turn holding a Canadian flag which she ceremoniously placed on the ground.

"Oh, you should know, I noticed this guy at the back. He just came for your show and then left immediately when it was over."

Val looked at Joey's face with concern; she did not want some stalker after her. Joey was the good kind of bouncer that noticed unusual shit and did his best to keep the girls safe from weirdos.

"What did he look like?" Val asked, as they approached the strippers change room.

"I didn't get a good look at his face. He was sitting in the back booth wearing a baseball cap. The servers were pissed cuz he didn't order anything."

Val breathed a sigh of relief. It must be Will! Who else would come by to keep an eye on her? He must not have wanted her to know that he was there.

"Joey, I think this dude is okay."

"Are you sure?" Joey asked, his face looking like that of a concerned cabbage patch doll.

"Yeah, I'm sure. Don't worry, 'kay?" Val turned into the change room, leaving a bewildered Joey behind her. She couldn't wipe the grin off her face, knowing in her heart that Will had felt that he had to be there to watch over her.

Val was thankful that she didn't run into Ellie that week. Their work shifts were completely offset, and Val went back to Will's place after her shift was done. She'd sent a few text messages to her sister, from which she was receiving curt responses, so she knew Ellie was still pissed off.

Val: *Staying at Will's again tonight. I'm working a double.*

Ellie: *Your life. Do what you want.*

Val decided to leave well enough alone, but later that week, she received a message from Ellie.

Ellie: *Betsy has invited us to a dinner party this Saturday. You are expected to be there.*

Val: *Sure, I can be there. Can I bring Will?*

Ellie: *How the fuck should I know? Figure it out yourself.*

After the last message, Val thought that her behavior at the funeral might have finally pushed her sister too far. Her heart felt heavy with guilt. She would have to make it up to her somehow.

twenty

Getting back to work for Ellie after her dad's funeral felt somewhat cathartic. She was good at her job, and for the most part, people left her alone. She felt like she was in a daze, her head filled with cotton candy. It didn't help that she and Val had had a falling-out. Ellie's relationship with her sister was a cinderblock in her life, and being angry with Val felt like someone had pulled the bottom piece out of a sketchy Jenga tower. Val was avoiding her by staying at Will's every night, but Ellie knew things wouldn't feel right until they got their differences out in the open and pulled the scab right off.

The week went by fast, and Friday rolled around before Ellie knew it. When she walked out into the warehouse to pick up her welding kit, she was accosted by loud music playing across the bay speakers. She couldn't pick up the song at first because the sound was tinny, but it was definitely something from the '80s. As she rounded into the work area, she immediately recognized the song even as the scene before her gave the necessary context to clarify it in her mind. It was "Maniac," from the 1980s cult classic *Flashdance*.

A bunch of her work colleagues were gathered around Wayne Smith, who was perched on a chair, his toes delicately pointed into the floor. He wasn't wearing a shirt, which was not surprising to Ellie as Wayne often took any opportunity to be shirtless. Thankfully, he did have on a pair of black spandex bike shorts, the kind that were unforgiving to most people, with black knit leggings covering the bottoms of his thick legs. As Ellie approached, Wayne pulled off the classic *Flashdance* move on the chair, perfectly timed to the music, arching his back like a pro and pretending that water was cascading over his body. Ellie wondered how much time her boss had spent practicing this routine by himself. As he finished, the gathered crowd applauded and whooped.

Ellie gave Wayne a slow clap, "Ha ha! I get it…*Flashdance*… woman welder. Nice one."

Wayne was panting as he got off the chair, swooping his soaking wet dark hair off his face, obviously devised that way to finish out the scene.

"Glad you liked it, Ellie!" Wayne huffed, his pierced nipples pulsating on his large pecs. Ellie wondered if that was an effect of too many steroids or if he just had a twitch.

"I've got to get to work," Ellie said, unimpressed, as she turned to grab her welding kit and supplies. The gathered group began to disperse, deciding the show was likely over.

"When are we going to see the sister combo act?" Wayne asked Ellie's back.

Ellie froze. What did Wayne mean? She turned and glared at her boss, but all he did was wink back at her and walk out of the work bay, his ass like perky oscillating melons in his tight spandex bike shorts.

Ellie stood motionless for a moment, glancing around at her colleagues, many of whom were snickering as they went back to their work. Everyone knew something. No one would make eye contact with her. *What the hell is going on?*

She knew the truth in her heart. Ellie was going to have it out with Val tonight no matter what.

Ellie sat at the small kitchen table in their trailer, fists clenched. She had spent the whole day raging in her mind. Embarrassed by the scene at work with Wayne but mostly angry with Val for not telling her what was going on. She had sent an innocuous text to her sister to get her to come home that night, knowing that if she tried to confront her by text, her sister would use the avoidance technique and would just stay away.

Ellie: *Can we talk tonight? It's important.*

Val: *Sure sis. I'll be home around 7.*

Ellie: *Don't bring Will.*

Val: :-((sad face) *Are you sure?*

Ellie: *Please, this is serious!*

Val: *Okay!*

Ellie had to make sure her sister came alone, or she would just use her new boyfriend as an excuse not to talk. Ellie was tapping her fingers on the table. Val was late, as usual. Finally the predictable rattling of the Ford Escort filled the room. Val banged her way through the trailer screen door, letting in a blast of cold air and a few snowflakes that had started to fall.

"Holy shit, it's getting frosty out there!" Val said as she dropped her purse onto the floor and kicked off her brown faux fur boots. She didn't look at Ellie as she swooped into the room, trying to ignore the awkwardness that had formed between them like the jam between toes.

"Sit down, Val. We need to talk," Ellie said, her voice steely and quiet.

"Sure!" Val continued to bustle around the kitchen, filling the kettle up with water at the sink and still not making eye contact with Ellie.

"Val!" Ellie slammed her fist down on the table, causing the ancient piece of furniture to shake down to its vinyl core. Ellie rarely raised her voice, especially to Val, so the effect was immediate. Val stopped what she was doing and sat down.

"You need to tell me what's going on," Ellie said.

Val wouldn't look her in the eye, immediately reminding Ellie of when Val would get caught in a lie as a child. One time she hid their dad's porno magazines underneath the stairs and charged the neighbourhood boys fifty cents a page to come and get an eyeful. Their father had been almost proud of his daughter's business acumen, leaving Ellie with the dirty work of kicking out the lineup of boys at the bottom of the stairs and telling them, "No, you won't get your money back."

"What do you mean?" Val asked, blinking innocently at her sister. This was always her first level of response—denial.

"Let me paint you a picture. Today at work I got to witness a beautifully choreographed rendition of Jennifer Beals' "Maniac" routine from *Flashdance,* performed by my asshole boss, Wayne Smith." Ellie paused for effect, noticing a look of resignation in her sister's downturned eyes.

"He was doing a stripper routine. You know...when women take their clothes off for money. Like what they do at that club you work at."

Ellie's tactic when dealing with her sister's misdemeanors in the past was always to inject a bit of sarcasm into the lecture, layering on the guilt like icing on a cake.

"We actually prefer the term 'exotic dancer'," Val muttered, continuing to look at her hands like they were the most interesting appendages she had ever seen.

"A-HAH! So you have been stripping! I knew it."

Val shrugged in response. This really was not the way she wanted Ellie to find out.

"What are you thinking? You are only nineteen years old. Do you want to get labelled as 'one of those girls' for the rest of your life?"

"Ellie, what choice do I have? I can't keep bussing tables for the rest of my life." Val switched to defense mode, finally able to look at her sister.

Ellie sat calmly watching her sister. She knew now that everything would come out. It always did, you just had to press the right buttons with Val, and the flood gates opened.

"I'm not smart like you. I can't get a job at the oilfields, and there is no way I'll ever get into college. So how the hell am I supposed to get out of this town?" Val's eyes started to get misty around the edges, but Ellie could tell she was bringing some anger into her argument to keep the tears at bay.

"So what? The solution then is to show your pussy to a bunch of greasy oil workers? Sure, that works when you are nineteen, but what happens twenty years from now when your clit begins to sag and you get a bunch of ingrown hairs that won't come out?"

Ellie raised her eyebrows at Val, knowing that praying on her sister's insecurities about getting older and losing her youthful body was a good tactic.

"I am only going to do this until I can make enough money to get out of this town," Val responded. "And that might be soon." She paused for effect, wondering if she should let Ellie in on her plan.

"Why? Are you going to get Will to buy you butt implants? Because if anything, I would say your butt is the one feature of yours that could use a bit of emphasis." Ellie knew Val had some insecurities about her smaller backside.

"What? No. My butt is fine. Maybe a little flat..." Val instinctively lifted a butt cheek because the hard plastic chair was harsh against her tailbone. Her sister was right; her butt could use a little extra meat on it.

"There's a contest," Val said. "Ms. Northern Nude. The prize is five thousand bucks." Val was looking away from Ellie, resorting again to her avoidance technique. She needed to hook Ellie on her plan, and playing the little sister role was the best way to get that done.

"A stripping contest?" Ellie said. "So what...first person to get naked and flash their labia around the room wins? Do you need to answer a skill-testing question?"

Ellie wasn't going to let her sister off the hook quickly. She was playing dumb. She'd heard of Ms. Northern Nude; it was big talk at the oilfields amongst her colleagues. Even Carrie from hockey talked about it—who she'd picked as her favourite, what their best attributes were. Ellie had no idea the prize was that much money though.

"No. I have to do a routine, and there is a panel of judges, as well as patrons from the club who vote. Afterwards, I'll get a big raise as well."

Val leaned forward, looking directly at her sister.

"Ellie, with five grand we could move out of this shithole, maybe find a decent condo in the city. You know, something with central heating and a bathroom that doesn't invoke nightmares?"

Ellie's heart sank; this was not how things were supposed to be. She was the one who looked after Val, not the other way around. The idea that her baby sister had resorted to taking off her clothes for money to support them was depressing. Val must have noticed the look on her sister's face; she reached out and grabbed Ellie's hand.

"Look, it doesn't have to be forever. Let me do this contest. I think I have a good chance of winning. Then when we move out of here, I'll go back to bussing tables. I promise."

Ellie sighed. She knew there was no stopping her sister once Val had her mind made up. And the thought of being angry at her or keeping more secrets was worse than just letting her have her way. She didn't like it, but if Val promised she would quit the stripping gig after the contest, she would go along, for now.

"Okay," Ellie said. "But just make sure you don't do it half-assed."

"Oh, don't worry. I *always* show my full ass, even if it is a bit flat."

twenty-one

The sisters spent the next morning lounging around the trailer in their PJs. It was a relief for Ellie to be back on speaking terms with Val. She hated feeling stress in their relationship, especially after the double whammy of losing their dad and then Edward ditching her to go back to the city. Val was all she had. As tough as she was, Ellie still needed someone in her life.

After binge watching five episodes of *Fresh Prince*, Ellie decided it was time to go to the gym and get some exercise. She left Val curled in a ball on the corner of the couch, her hair tied in a floppy bun, looking like she could fit in a suitcase.

"Don't forget we have Betsy's dinner party tonight," Ellie said before walking out the door, gym bag in hand.

"Oh, fuck," Val grumbled, her head popping up from the fetus position. "Do I have to go?"

"Yes! You can't leave me alone with those people."

"Fine, but I'm bringing Will." Val's attention immediately reverted to the TV, where Carlton was performing his iconic dance.

Ellie sighed. She wasn't sure about Will, but if he was making her sister happy, then she was going to have to be content with the relationship.

"Fine. Just make sure you're ready to go by five."

"Omigod, why the hell do they eat so early?"

"I think that's just when the drinking starts. Better anyway, so we can have an excuse to leave early."

Ellie left the trailer to find the ground blanketed with a dusting of snow. For northerners, the first snow was a comfort, like putting whitewash on a pockmarked mall. It covered up all the garbage and frost-bitten plants, giving the town a newly painted look. She shivered in her truck as she made her way into town. The weather wasn't cold enough to merit warming up vehicles before driving but cold enough to make sitting motionless for fifteen minutes a painful affair.

The rec centre gym was busy. Ellie usually liked to go early in the morning to avoid the crowds, but she had needed the sleep-in and lazy time with her sister. She hoped she could get through her workout without being hampered by anyone, and as luck would have it, she almost made it to the end unhindered. Her last exercise was bench press, but a group of guys had been occupying the only bench for the last twenty minutes.

A stocky triangle-shaped dude stood behind the bench spotting for his buddy. He had a military style crew-cut, sported a pair of dark sunglasses that made it impossible to tell where he was looking, and the thickness of his neck seemed to prevent his head from moving. To complete the Cory Heart look, he wore a tight tank top that barely covered his nipples and a pair of tie-dyed Hammer pants. She assumed the baggy pants were meant to disguise the fact that he never took a leg day.

The guy on the bench was beefy and wearing a backwards baseball cap. She couldn't see his face because it was obscured by a Gym Bunny—a perfectly physiqued human wearing barely enough skin-tight clothes to cover disproportionately large breasts. The purpose of a Gym Bunny is to provide eye candy, comment on the lifts of the group and look at their own ass in the mirrors. A Gym Bunny could be of any gender; this particular one was female, red haired and tanned within an inch of her life.

"You got this! Come on! 'Atta boy...LIFT!" the Gym Bunny cheered. As the beefy guy hoisted an impressively large set of weights back onto the bench stands.

"Whoa, man, GAINS!" commented the sunglass-wearing spotter.

Ellie was about to ask them when they planned to get off the bench so she could finish her workout when the guy on the bench sat up. He was facing the gym bunny, so all Ellie could see was his broad back and backwards baseball cap. Something about him seemed familiar. He reached out a hand and smacked the ass of the Gym Bunny, sending her into a fit of giggles and causing her oversized breasts to oscillate in a manner that defied gravity.

"Oh, you bad boy!" the Gym Bunny squealed.

Sunglasses dude moved to take his turn on the bench, and Ellie decided that in her experience it wasn't worth waiting for this group. They could be there forever, and it was nearly 4:00 PM. She needed to get home and get ready for the party.

Ellie and Val entered the Price mansion five minutes late. They were greeted by Jim Price, his puffy face almost cracking into a smile as he took their coats. Val squatted to pet the Corgis, her coos sending them into fits of licks and scrabbling stubby legs. Their lateness was caused by Val's inability to choose the right outfit for the evening. She had finally settled on a navy-blue V-neck blouse that flattered Val's long neck and arms over a fitted pencil skirt. It was classy and sexy, a look Val could pull off without effort. Ellie, on the other hand, hadn't really tried, and at the last minute had thrown on basic black dress pants and a red cable knit sweater. She looked part grandma, part business professional, but Ellie didn't care. Who was she going to impress tonight? Edward was long gone, and she really didn't care if the Price family found her attractive.

"I hope the trailer is working well for you girls. Are you warm enough?" Jim asked, his voice raspy, like it was at war with a phlegm ball.

"The stove puts out a lot of heat," Ellie said. "Thanks for asking."

"Help yourself to as much wood as you need from the shed," he stated as he led them down the hallway to the sitting room, giving a quick whistle calling the Corgis to his heels.

As they entered the sitting room, Ellie was immediately accosted by Betsy, who wrapped her meaty arms around Ellie in an unwelcome squeeze. The smell of mothballs and perfume flooded Ellie's nostrils and made her eyes water.

"I'm so sorry for your loss. I never got to say as much at the funeral," Betsy said, and then quietly whispered into Ellie's ear. "I know how desperate things can get after a death in the family; I'll make sure to keep a close eye on that sister of yours." Ellie was shocked at her comment. Did Betsy know about Val stripping?

When Betsy finally released Ellie from her hug, a meaningful expression on her pursed face, she made a motion with her hand like she was taking an imaginary drink and then waggled her pointer finger like an upside-down pendulum. Ellie was instantly relieved. Betsy must be referring to Val's drunken scene at their father's funeral, her alcohol-laced breath adding a certain irony to her actions.

Val was oblivious to Betsy's comments as her eyes scanned the sitting room, quickly sweeping over Brandon who sat motionless on an antique flowered settee, obviously looking for the yet absent Will.

"Sit! Let's get you a drink," Betsy commanded as she placed her well-rounded bottom into a bulbous armchair. "What would you like?" As if on instinct, Silvie, their small neatly dressed maid, appeared at Ellie's side.

"I'll have red wine, thanks," Ellie said to Silvie.

"I'll have…"

Before Val could finish her sentence, Betsy interjected, "Silvie, bring the red for Ellie and a glass of Clamato for her sister." Betsy turned and winked at Ellie. This time, Val didn't miss it and was about to open her mouth to retort, but Ellie silenced her with a glare. Betsy may be out of line, but Ellie wasn't about to let Val bite the mouth that was currently housing them.

Val scowled but reluctantly collected her glass of juice when Silvie returned. Clamato had to be the worst possible virgin drink. If it wasn't bad enough that someone put clams in a beverage; they also gave it the texture of Pepto Bismol.

Ellie took a seat next to Brandon on the settee, feeling badly that he appeared to be ignored. But he didn't seem to mind; his focus was acutely on her sister, something that wasn't missed by their exuberant host.

"Val, dear, I heard that our Brandon fixed your little vehicle. Isn't he a gem?" she said, grinning at Val over the top of her wine glass, obviously attempting to get them into a conversation.

"Yes, the car is running better than ever. Thanks to Brandon," Val responded, barely looking up at Brandon. She attempted to take a sip of the red liquid in her glass, but Ellie noticed that she almost gagged, at which point she set it carefully on a side table.

At that moment the bell rang, sending the Corgis into fits of barking madness, like a small furball hurricane.

"Oh, that must be the rest of our guests!" Betsy clapped her hands exuberantly together as Jim slowly got up to answer the door, his jerky movements revealing the stiffness in his large form.

Val was on the edge of her seat, her eyes lit up with excitement. She flashed a grin at Ellie. She hadn't seen her sister this worked up since she got her first Cabbage Patch doll when she was eight. Ellie secretly hoped this guy was worth it.

Both sisters were surprised when Jim returned with two guests, Will Davis and a young woman they had never seen before.

"Who is that?" Val blurted out. Ellie glared at her sister, but she could see the shock and surprise on her face, obviously concerned that her boyfriend had showed up at a party with another woman.

"Oh, this is our dear Lucy Martin!" Betsy cooed. "She is a family friend from the city. I thought I would invite her as I know she'll have so much in common with you girls!"

Betsy was holding Lucy's hand in both of hers, like she was a precious stone.

"And this must be the dashing Will Davis. So nice to meet you! I have seen your car here at our property so many times, I thought you might be moving into the trailer as well!"

Betsy chuckled at her own joke as she reached out to shake Will's hand.

Ellie looked sideways at Brandon, who remained quiet, his face now knotted with concern, obviously displeased with the presence of Val's new boyfriend. She remembered his comments at their father's funeral about Will Davis and knew that there must be some history between them. Ellie wondered if the truth of that history would ever come to light.

Lucy Martin floated into the room like she was weightless and perched on the last foot of the settee next to Ellie. Physically she was a mystery. Lucy Martin had a pretty face, but her body was devoid of any shape, like it had been reluctantly dragged through puberty kicking and screaming. Ellie knew that being skinny was always considered a feature, but the thigh gap displayed by Lucy's skin-tight leggings was wide enough to store a family of small rodents. She had a dome of mousy brown hair that hung past her shoulders. Her teeth gleamed when she smiled, the lights reflecting off clear plastic teeth straighteners. When she finally spoke, Ellie detected a slight lisp.

"I've heard so much about you," she said, her eyes downcast but obviously directing the comment at Ellie.

"Really?" Ellie queried, not sure where this was going. Meanwhile, Betsy busied her maid with fetching drinks for the newcomers.

Val made room for Will next to her, and as soon as he sat down, his hand suctioned to her sister's thigh like a cleaner fish on a whale. As they were completely absorbed in each other, with Brandon glaring them down like a man possessed, this left Lucy and Ellie's conversation fairly private.

"Oh yes! Edward has told me all about you," Lucy said, a small smile pressed on her lips like it was painted on.

The shock of hearing Edward's name from this unknown woman was hard to hide.

"Edward Price?" Ellie said.

"Why yes, of course," she said. "Edward and I are very close." Lucy gave Ellie a meaningful look. "In fact, as I know you and he are friends, I was really hoping to talk to you about something."

Before Ellie could question Lucy about her comment, Betsy stood and rang a small bell, silencing the room.

"Dinner is ready! Please come sit. Silvie has made her famous duck legs with figs. It's a specialty from her country!"

Betsy nodded at Silvie as if her praise was likened to bestowing an Olympic medal.

Ellie's head swam as they made their way to the dining room. How did this woman know Edward? She wouldn't get a chance to question Lucy during dinner; she was seated next to Brandon, with Lucy, her sister and Will on the other side of the table.

Betsy rattled on about the quality of the duck they were eating.

"It is so difficult to get duck meat in Sober. Has to be special ordered; that's why it's a real treat! Jim has connections at the Happy Grocer, so he gets us an excellent deal, don't you dear!"

"Yes, dear," Jim said, not looking up from his plate.

What is it with the rich and obsessive bargain shopping? Ellie thought as she took a bite of the carefully grilled meat. If she didn't know better she would have thought this was grouse meat, something the local hunters sold at the market. And by the suspicious smile on Sylvie's face when Betsy was bragging about her husband's connections at the grocery, she thought maybe she was correct. Sylvie must have been passing the grouse meat off as duck to Betsy because it sounded a lot fancier than eating plain old game meat. Ellie didn't mind though; like most northerners, she enjoyed game meat.

Distracted by her meal, Ellie didn't notice that her sister and Will were oddly quiet. When she glanced across the table,

Will's face was contorted like he was holding back a sneeze, and her sister's hands were tucked below the table. Ellie shouldn't have let them sit next to each other. She looked over at Brandon, who was staring daggers at Will. It didn't make sense to Ellie that her sister had two guys vying for her, and Ellie couldn't even keep the one guy she had in the same town.

"Ellie, you certainly have become good friends with Edward. I see his car here quite often to visit," Betsy simpered, a mischievous look on her face. "Shame he had to run off to the city." She added between bites.

Lucy gave Ellie a hard stare at this comment, her angled face almost bird-like, accentuated by the way she was pecking at her food. Ellie told herself she didn't care what was going on with Edward. He'd left her and could do whatever he wanted, but inside, her heart was sinking in a green pool of jealousy. Ellie pushed the feelings aside, something she had been doing since she was a small girl.

At that moment, Val stood up from the table. "Betsy, where is your washroom?" Her face was flushed, highlighting that she and Will had been fooling around under the table.

"The guest powder room is down the hall on the right," Betsy said.

"Do you have to go?" asked Will as he grabbed Val's hand before she could leave. He looked longingly into her eyes. "I'll miss you." He pulled her hand to his lips, kissing her knuckles.

"Well, obviously the girl has to go; she just asked where the loo was." Betsy gave a small snort of a laugh.

Ellie felt bile rise up in her throat, but as much as the PDA grossed her out, she was more embarrassed at how smitten her sister looked. Val was eating up this crap. Ellie couldn't handle that kind of brazen sentimentality, but somehow Edward snuck into her mind, and she was reminded of the last night they spent together, his arms wrapped tightly around her body as she snuggled into his. It felt so wonderful to be held like that.

Val eventually left, her hand pulled behind her by Will's lingering grip, and he didn't turn back to the table until after she'd physically left the room.

Brandon broke the awkward silence with a comment, "So Will, do you have a job?"

"Uh, I have a few things on the go. I don't want to be tied down right now, with everything happening at the oilfields. Just keeping my options open."

"So you have a trade then?" Brandon continued.

"Trade? God, no. I was looking at some management positions, but nothing really seemed the right fit, you know?" Will said as he shoveled large bites of food into his mouth. His under-the-table activities with Val must have boosted his appetite.

Brandon nodded to himself, as if confirming what he already knew about Will. Ellie wasn't impressed either, but she wasn't about to comment.

"Oh, Will, you are right there!" Betsy said. "Young people these days are too quick to make decisions. They jump into something, and before you know it they are unmarried, alone and with a weathered and wrinkled body that wouldn't attract a sasquatch!"

If Ellie didn't know better, she might have thought Betsy was talking about her.

"I agree, Betsy," Lucy said in her mousy voice. "I plan to be married when I'm young. Women these days are so career focused; they forget our bodies weren't meant to have children in their late thirties."

"What if you don't want to have children?" Ellie queried, causing a silence to descend on the table like a blanket. Ellie's experience with parents, or lack thereof, was not something that inspired continuation of the process.

"Well dear, if you don't stop working in that terrible environment, it is quite possible your female parts won't work properly anyway. Why, even the men have problems!"

Betsy accentuated her last comment by holding up her pointer finger and allowing it to drop slowly to her hand.

The awkward silence was broken by Brandon receiving a call on his cell, which he hurried out of the room to take. Val returned, much to Will's excitement, as he fawned over her again. Ellie was thankful that the evening might end soon, as Silvie brought out the dessert, a flower-molded jelly, where you could see the berries suspended within the clear gelatin like eyeballs. Ellie wasn't sure she would be able to get it down without gagging.

Betsy leaned in closer to Ellie to catch her in a private conversation while Silvie plopped wiggling jelly piles into small bowls for each of them.

"You know, Brandon has a secret past," she said quietly, an edge of mischievousness to her voice.

Ellie raised her eyebrows at Betsy but was happy for the distraction to avoid eating the dessert.

"He was married when he was very young," said Betsy, "no more than seventeen years old, I believe. It was such a scandal for his parents because the woman he married was pregnant."

Ellie was surprised to hear the news but felt badly that Betsy was spilling the man's secrets behind his back, although she couldn't avoid the conversation. Teenage pregnancies were not uncommon, especially in small towns where there were no other options but to have the baby.

"Brandon stood by his wife and child, but eventually she ran off and filed for divorce. He has been dutifully paying the alimony for decades now but was barely allowed to see his child."

Betsy nodded approvingly as if to acknowledge the good character of her nephew's friend.

"Where are they now?" asked Ellie as she tried unsuccessfully to swallow a bite of clear jelly, the gummy consistency catching in her throat. She quickly took a large gulp of wine to force it down.

"Oh, we don't know. Brandon keeps that pretty close to his heart now and doesn't talk about it." Betsy touched the side of her nose as if to indicate that she was the modicum of discretion.

Brandon re-entered the room causing Betsy to sit up quickly and pretend to be fully absorbed in her dessert.

"I'm sorry," Brandon said. "I have just received an urgent call, and I have to leave immediately."

"You can't stay for dessert?" Jim asked.

"No, I'm sorry. I cannot. Thank you very much for the lovely dinner." His eyes moved around the table, settling on Val for a moment longer than the rest before he turned and left the room.

Ellie wondered about Brandon; he was a mystery. To find out he'd had a wife and child was a surprise for sure. Ellie tried to do the math in her head—paying alimony for decades gave the impression that he might be older than he looked.

Will stood up from his chair, not wanting to be the only man without something important to announce.

"We must be going as well. I mean, I must be going," he gave Val a shifty look, while adjusting his pants like there was something down there that was uncomfortable and needed attention.

"Oh dear! One leaves and then everyone else abandons me." Betsy looked genuinely upset. Ellie wondered if the woman was maybe a bit lonely living in this big house with her silent husband.

Jim must have recognized that his wife was upset as he stood up quickly from the table, announcing that it was time for his wife to retire. He said his goodbyes, stating unceremoniously that they could let themselves out. He was a man of few words.

Ellie was glad to have the evening over. She went to find Val, only to catch her and Will in the hallway in a sloppy embrace. The sound of their smacking tongues turned Ellie's stomach again.

"Val? Can we go, please?" Ellie asked as she stood awkwardly behind the romantic display.

"Oh! Sorry, Ellie. I'm going to go over to Will's, okay?" She looked sheepishly at Ellie, knowing her behavior that evening had left something to be desired.

"Sure, fine," Ellie said, trying to smile at her sister but finding only a strange feeling of loneliness.

As Will and Val left, Ellie realized that she was not alone in the entryway. Ellie jumped when she turned around to find a motionless Lucy Martin staring at her with the wide eyes of a lemur. She had put on her white fur jacket, which ballooned over her thin legs, giving the impression of a marshmallow on a stick.

"Would you walk me to my car?" Lucy asked.

Lucy grabbed Ellie's arm before she had a chance to respond.

"The sidewalk is slippery, and these heels are murder out there."

Ellie hadn't noticed that Lucy was wearing shiny, black, high-heel shoes, which would make walking on any surface difficult. As a result, the walk to Lucy's rental car was slow and tedious. Ellie was hoping this adventure would be quiet after the evening's conversations, but she was not surprised when Lucy broke the silence.

"I am so glad we have this time to talk," Lucy said.

When Ellie didn't respond Lucy continued, "I need to talk to you about Edward since you two are good friends."

Now Ellie's curiosity was piqued; however, she was concerned about where this was going.

"I'm not sure I know Edward as well as you think," Ellie said, trying to downplay any connection with Lucy.

"Oh, I know that's not true. Edward speaks so highly of you!"

Ellie felt her heart swell at these comments, but she quickly pushed the feeling away, thinking of how Edward had left her.

"Before I tell you, you have to promise me that you will not say a word to anyone!"

Ellie wasn't sure where this was going, but she nodded without looking at Lucy.

"Promise?"

Ellie sighed. Whatever this was, she needed to get to the bottom of it, even if that meant making a promise to this woman she barely knew.

"I promise," Ellie replied.

"You see, Edward and I have an arrangement," Lucy said. "And I was hoping you could help us."

"What do you mean, 'an arrangement'?" She didn't like the way Lucy said "us."

"Edward and I are secretly engaged to be married!"

Lucy's declaration caused Ellie to stop in her tracks, nearly toppling Lucy into the snow.

"What?" Ellie almost yelped before she managed to regain her composure and continue their slow march.

"We've been engaged for many years, but Edward couldn't tell his family about us, so it had to be a secret. I'm so tired of keeping it inside! When I heard that you two were friends, I knew I could confide in you!"

Ellie was silent for a moment, digesting the information. She felt betrayed. A hollow pit sliced open inside her from the same scar that was created all those years ago, the day her mother had walked out on them. But she swallowed that feeling, pushing it down deep and locking it away, a process so familiar to her it was almost unconsciously done.

"I don't see how I can be of help to you, Lucy," Ellie responded, her voice level with no hint of emotion.

"Oh, but you can! You are friends with Edward. You can talk to him and convince him we don't need to keep this secret anymore!"

Lucy looked at Ellie with pleading eyes, her bird-like face cocked to one side, emphasizing what Ellie assumed was an empty head.

"Why are you keeping your engagement a secret anyway? It isn't the 1800s," Ellie asked.

They had finally reached Lucy's car, but Lucy wouldn't let go of Ellie's arm. She was tempted to pry her off like you would a leach, but that might have come across as unfriendly.

"It's complicated," Lucy responded.

Funny Lucy should say that; those were Edward's exact words when he told Ellie he was leaving.

"I'm sure you know that Edward's family is very wealthy. His mother has very specific ideas about who he should marry. She's threatened to write him out of her will!"

"Well, that's just dumb," Ellie said.

"Isn't it?" Lucy looked wide-eyed at Ellie like she had found the only sensible person on the planet.

She let go of Ellie's arm and opened the door of her car.

"I'm so glad you are willing to help us. I knew it would be a good idea to confide in you."

She sat down without ceremony and shut the door before Ellie had time to respond. Ellie stood transfixed to the spot as the little rental car purred to life, and Lucy raised a small, gloved hand and blew Ellie a kiss, her tires slipping in the snow as she accelerated out of the driveway.

Did Ellie just get roped into helping Edward marry some tart she barely knew?

CHAPTER
twenty-two

November roared into Sober like a rabid polar bear, snowy white, cranky and just desperate to be put to sleep for the winter. The Tim Hortons morning line-ups grew as more and more wouldn't step outside their warmed truck cabs, exhaust circling above the town and framed in by snow clouds. Even Ellie couldn't be bothered to get out of her truck in the morning, choosing instead to sit moodily for the extra half hour and listen to the radio. On this particular morning, Ellie was listening to an interview with Richard Branch, CEO of the Sober Oilfields.

"Mr. Branch, how are the negotiations with Excon over the ownership of the oilfields progressing?" the interviewer queried.

"They are progressing slowly," came his calm response. "Our team is working hard to ensure a fair and equitable deal."

"But Mr. Branch, with the impending take over, how can you reassure your employees that they will have jobs in another month?"

"It is my number one priority to ensure that every Sober Oil employee has a job for Christmastime and going forward."

"Can you give us some details on how the deal will work?"

"Unfortunately, we are still in negotiations, so I can't go into detail."

Ellie switched off the radio. Mr. Branch sounded sincere, but she was as nervous about her job security as everyone else. Ellie wondered how much Edward had to do with this deal. Was he on their side? She doubted it. The Price family wanted a bigger piece of the pie, and if that meant getting Excon to cut out Richard Branch and the other board members, then that is what they would do.

On top of her job worries, she couldn't stop thinking about Lucy Martin and the dreaded secret she had laid on her, as thick as cream cheese on a hot bagel. The thought of Edward with that woman made her stomach turn. On one hand, Ellie would keep the secret because that is what Ellie did when she made a promise, but on the other hand, she was embarrassed that she'd been so blindsided by Edward. She had honestly believed that he was really into her. Part of her even felt something that might be like love. She had trained herself for her whole life to keep those feelings pushed down deep, but this time she had slipped, letting Edward in, and for that she was angry and ashamed of herself. Ellie was tougher than this; there was no way she would let another man into her life like that again.

There was one person she could talk to, and that was Carrie. Thankfully, they were meeting up tonight at the Northern Bush Club. It was the Ms. Northern Nude Contest, and Carrie was coming with Ellie to support Val. (Or so she said. Ellie was pretty sure Carrie was a yearly attendee.) Ellie had not seen her sister strip yet, and she was nervous. Not that she hadn't seen her sister naked a thousand times, but she just didn't like thinking of her baby sister as a sex object.

Ellie's thoughts rolled around in her head all day during work. She barely noticed when Wayne Smith came by her station, dressed in a pressed white suit, and asked her if she could see his underwear through his pants. She had replied, "Nope," even though she could clearly see the batman symbols, obviously a planned display, and gone back to work.

By the time Ellie got home from work, she had just enough time to get changed and head over to The Bush. She decided on a low-key look of jeans and her favourite T-shirt; plain black with "No Flux Given" written on the front. No one but welders got the joke, which is what made it so funny to Ellie. Carrie had texted her that she was already at the club and had saved her a seat.

Ellie had never been in the Northern Bush Club, but she was not surprised by the decor and atmosphere. A musty smell hung in the air, like the place had flooded once and never completely dried out. The lighting included just enough seizure-inducing neon lighting that you didn't run into things but not enough that Ellie could make out people's faces, so she had to walk around a while before she found Carrie. Of course, her friend had found a seat right in gyno-row, close enough to the stage that you were in danger of getting a spiked heel in the face when a stripper went round a pole.

Carrie's eyes were glued to the stage where a tiny blonde was warming up the crowd with an Alice in Wonderland routine. The dancer was riding a giant stuffed bunny (which must have been the White Rabbit) around the stage wearing only a frilly blue G-string. Ellie felt like she would never be able to look at one of her favourite childhood characters the same way again. She had to punch Carrie in the shoulder before she noticed Ellie was there.

"Hi!" said Ellie, having to lean into Carrie's ear to be heard over the blaring dance beat.

"Oh hey, Ellie!" Carrie turned and wrapped Ellie in a giant bear hug. Her friend's embrace felt really good right now. Ellie didn't realize how much she was missing physical touch. She wasn't much of a hugger, but since Val was spending all her time with Will, and with Edward gone, her only source of comfort was Elmer, her twenty-year-old teddy bear.

Carrie wore a backwards baseball cap over her short brown hair, looking the gym teacher part. She had a sloppy grin on her face that Ellie assumed must be from the few empty beer glasses in front of her, or the fact that a scantily clad blonde was thrusting her butt towards their table.

"It's been a while," Carrie said. "You haven't been at hockey." As she raised a hand to call over the server. "What's your poison?"

"Something cold, wet and frothy," replied Ellie as the server girl came by, a tray balanced perfectly on her outstretched hand.

"You know, I prefer them warm, wet and frothy," Carrie smiled as she handed a twenty to the server, ordering them a round of beers. Somehow Ellie figured Carrie wasn't talking about beers.

"I'll get back out to hockey," Ellie said, "just been busy, you know."

It was a lie because Ellie had just been sitting at home when she wasn't at work. She couldn't really put her finger on why she wasn't getting out to hockey. It was like something was constantly weighing her down.

"How have you been?" Ellie asked as their beers arrived.

The Alice and Wonderland girl had ended her routine and was going around to the front row patrons, soliciting people to throw loonies to try and knock a queen of hearts playing card off her bare breast. Ellie was wondering how it stayed put because Carrie managed to hit the card a number of times, and it didn't budge, causing Alice the Stripper to give Carrie a frowny face.

"Oh Ellie, I've got something important to tell you," Carrie responded as Alice moved away from their table.

"What's going on?" Ellie asked. "You finally snipe that goalie that's had your number all year?"

"Nope, I wish. It's better than that." Carrie leaned in towards Ellie, her breath a mixture of beer and mint.

She must be chewing gum, thought Ellie.

"I've met someone." Carrie said.

"Oh yeah? Who?" Ellie asked.

"Oh man, she's dreamy. Tall, red hair. You know how I love red hair. Super smart. Ellie, I swear, I think I might be in love." Even in the dim atmosphere of the club, Ellie could see Carrie's eyes light up; she looked happier than Ellie had seen her in a long while.

"That's awesome, Carrie. What's her name?" Ellie asked, taking a few big gulps of beer.

Carrie sighed, "That's the thing. Can't say. Not yet anyway. She isn't 'out' to her family, so we have to keep things on the down low. But this is the real deal, Ellie. I'm telling you."

Carrie paused, her attention drifting away and obviously thinking about her new girlfriend.

"Her tits, Ellie, oh my god!" Carrie held out her hands in front of her chest like she was testing melons at the market.

Ellie smiled. "I'm happy for you, Carrie. Really I am." She raised her beer glass, "To big tits and love."

"Here, here," Carrie responded, clunking her glass hard enough against Ellie's beer and causing a small geyser to erupt onto the table.

Ellie was waiting for the chance to talk to Carrie about her problems with Edward and the mysterious Lucy problem, but her friend looked so happy she wasn't going to be the one to put a damper on their evening. She resigned herself to suppressing her jealousy and sadness for what felt like the thousandth time.

There wasn't much time left to chat anyway because the DJ's voice came over the speaker announcing the start of the Ms. Northern Nude competition. Val had told Ellie that she was first, being a novice dancer she didn't get the luxury of the later show times. Those were saved for the veterans. The club patrons all rushed to get good seats, and the tables quickly filled.

As Ellie looked around the room, she noticed a man standing behind one of the booths, arms crossed, wearing dark sunglasses and a baseball cap that hid his face. He looked familiar to Ellie, but she couldn't quite place him. In contrast to all the other men (the club was filled mostly with men) this man was stoic and obviously alone. Before she could ponder the identity of the strange man any longer, the DJ drew her attention back to the stage.

"And now, for the first competitor for Ms. Northern Nude, please draw your attention to the main stage...for our own... STACEY BUBBLES!"

The crowd cheered, hooting and clapping, the anticipation of the contest hung in the air like the smell of old Chinese food. A few servers were picking through the crowd, handing out umbrellas to various tables. Ellie was completely in the dark about Val's performance. Her sister had spent weeks preparing, holed up in her bedroom. Strange things had come and gone in their little trailer, but none of it had made any sense to Ellie. Val had wanted the first time her sister came to see her to be a total surprise.

A hush descended on the crowd as they all pondered the umbrellas. Carrie and Ellie had been given a see-through umbrella with a ducky face on one side. Ellie immediately recognized it as one from their childhood. Val must have been digging deep to find enough umbrellas for her performance.

Before the crowd got impatient, the voice of Jaimie Foxx came over the speakers, starting the classic Kanye West version of Gold Digger. At the sound of the drumbeat, Val appeared on stage, her tiny form perched in the front seat of a child-sized Cadillac Escalade, the Hot Wheels version you can actually drive. Only her upper body was visible above the roof of the mini-SUV. She was fully outfitted as a pimp, complete with a money-print suit, matching fedora and gold chains. Her face was mostly obscured by outlandish white striped Kayne West glasses, but as she slowly circled the stage Ellie could see a flash of gold teeth from her grin.

Val grabbed a stripper pole, lifting herself out of the small car, her naked legs lifting up into the air. As Kayne rapped, "git down girl," she slid down the pole, ripping her suit top off as she landed. Ellie now realized the reason for the umbrellas, as the DJ seamlessly switched the song to "make it rain" and Val grabbed a bag from her Cadillac, emptying it out in front of a blowing fan, shooting dollar bills all through the club. Ellie grabbed one out of the air and saw that her sister had printed up fake money, complete with a pin-up picture of herself. She wondered how her sister had paid for all this promo.

Carrie must have seen her looking curiously at the bills. "The club gives the performers a promo budget for their shows; otherwise things would be pretty boring," she yelled into Ellie's ear. "Val is *so* good!"

Ellie nodded back. Her sister *was* good. Ellie felt her heart swell with pride as she watched the club patrons hooting and whistling for her sister. Val was meant to be a performer. So what if she wasn't doing ballet. If she could use her talent to make money, and as long as she was safe, why not?

Val was now down to just her G-string and fedora as she moved around the stage for the closing of her performance. The song switched again, and Val grabbed a large bag hidden on the side of the stage. She ripped it open, and hundreds of gold, silver and black balloons launched into the air. Val swung around a pole, kicking her sharp heel into one of the balloons, exploding it in a hail of gold glitter. Pretty soon the audience got the idea, as guys jumped in the air to pop the balloons, each one raining glitter. Soon the sound of popping balloons filled the air. Val finished up her act, ripping her G-string off and sliding onto her back, as the crowd rained down cash over her naked body.

Everyone was on their feet clapping and cheering.

"Give it up for Stacy Bubbles! That will be a hard act to follow!" the DJ roared as Val collected her money from the stage. She gave a small wave to Ellie as the bouncer came and escorted her off.

"I don't think anyone is going to beat her," said Carrie as they both sat back down from cheering Val off the stage.

"You really think she'll win?" asked Ellie.

"I haven't seen an act like that ever," Carrie responded. "I mean, this is Sober, and that had a Vegas-like quality."

Ellie looked around at the crowd, and she could hear people commenting on her sister's performance. She glanced at the back of the bar and noticed that the stoic-looking man was gone.

"Are you looking for someone?" Carrie asked.

"It's weird. I saw this guy I thought I knew, but he's gone now," Ellie replied. "It's like he only came to watch Val and then took off."

"Oh, if you're a dancer, you're going to have some weird, obsessed fans; that just comes with the territory."

"For a high school gym teacher you sure know a lot about strippers," Ellie cocked her head at Carrie. "What would your new girlfriend think if she knew you were here?"

Carrie grinned, "Oh, she knows. She desperately wanted to come with me. You see, buddy," Carrie put an arm around

Ellie, dwarfing her with her broad shoulders, "us lesbos know how to party, and we aren't so hoity-toity that we care if our partners go out and look at a bit of pussy. If you ever came to play on the *right* team, then you'd find this out."

Ellie laughed, "Sorry, not my game, but I'll let you buy me another beer."

"Fine. Be that way." Carrie looked mock hurt, but she waved the server over and bought Ellie another beer. Her friend must really be in a good mood if she'd already got two free beers out of her.

Before the next act came out, Val strode up to their table. She had put back on her skimpy bikini top and G-string bottom and had kept the fedora.

"Hey sis," said Val as she sat down on an empty stool.

"You were awesome!" crowed Ellie.

"Fucking awesome, actually," added Carrie.

"Thanks guys. Man, I was nervous as hell." Val said, glancing around the bar. She leaned in close to Ellie. "Did you see Will here?" she asked quietly.

"Uhm, not that I noticed," Ellie paused, "but there was this guy at the back. I don't think it was Will, but he was just here for your set and then left."

Val looked relieved. "That must have been Will. I think he has been secretly coming to watch my shows."

Ellie was doubtful. The guy didn't have the right body type for Will. But she didn't want to stress her sister out, not tonight, so she didn't say anything.

"Okay, I gotta go promote! Make sure you vote for me!" Val said, as she stood up, getting ready to do the rounds to convince the crowd she was the best bet for the big prize.

"I'll think about it," said Ellie, winking at her sister. As her sister waved and walked away, her long legs gliding gracefully around the club, Ellie thought about the mystery guy. He definitely wasn't Will. She just hoped he wasn't some creepy stalker.

twenty-three

The last show of the contest wasn't until after midnight. Val was anxious about the outcome, but after talking to the audience, she felt a surge of confidence. Everyone she spoke to said her performance was the best so far. She hoped it wasn't just talk. Winning this contest could change everything for her and Ellie. It wasn't just money; it was their ticket out of this town.

As the returning champion of Ms. Northern Nude, Candy had the final show time. Val and Joey stood at the back of the club, watching as Candy strode out onto the stage. She wore her classic Mini Mouse costume, fully equipped with bulbous head, ears and red polka-dot dress. The set started with "It's a Small World," her dance moves reminiscent of the small, waving robotic dolls from classic Disneyland ride.

"I don't get it," Joey said. "She has been doing this same routine for years; you'd think she would come up with something new." He stood in his bouncer pose, arms crossed over his massive chest and glaring like a silverback gorilla.

"Hopefully the audience will pick something they haven't seen before," Val replied. But she didn't feel as confident anymore because the crowd was picking up their cheers and cat-calls. Candy had moved on to the "dirty-mouse" part of her routine, where all she had on was the giant head and small pasties on her nipples, her body gyrating to Deadmau5s' "Ghosts 'n Stuff."

Joey looked sideways at Val, his eyes apologetic. "Babe, you don't need to win this contest to know you are the best. To me, anyway." Val wondered if Joey knew something she didn't. She smiled back at him as his form reverted to brick-wall mode.

Candy's set ended to raucous applause as the crowd showered her with paper money and coins. It took so long to clean up all the money, Val was beginning to wonder if people would stick around to see the awards because a few were already leaving. Joey was up at the stage now, escorting Candy off to the stripper's area and helping her carry the buckets of money.

"You see how the pros get it done, newbie?" Candy said as she strode by Val to the strippers' area, her long legs giving the impression of a naughty stick insect. She was almost as tall as Joey and didn't even bother glancing down at Val.

"Well, if by "pro" you mean "old," then I guess you qualify," Val said.

Candy swung around, nearly running into Joey and knocking a bucket out of his hands. "I'm surprised you're old enough to grow hair on that pussy." Candy glared down at Val like a woman who'd discovered gum on her shoe.

"At least my hair is on my pussy and not coming out of my nose!"

"You may think your little pimp dance was cute and funny, but there's no chance you'll win this. The judges know where their bread is buttered." Candy spun on her heel and marched off to the change room, leaving Val to wipe Candy's spittle off her face. Joey gave Val an apologetic look as he followed Candy down the hall carrying her money buckets.

Val wondered what Candy meant by that comment, but she didn't have long to wait as the line of judges walked up onto the main stage led by the DJ, who was holding a microphone.

"And now, the moment you've all been waiting for... the crowning of Ms. Northern Nude! Can I get a drum roll, please?" The crowd began to thump and pound on the tables and floors, the sound rising like thunder.

"And the winner is...Candy!" As the crowd erupted into applause, Val felt her heart sink, like she was being pulled underwater. The sound of the crowd was deafening, although through the buzz, she could hear some boos. Ellie and Carrie were on their feet, along many others in the crowd, booing and yelling, "FIX!" as Candy walked onto the stage wearing a skimpy gold bikini reminiscent of Princess Leia, fully equipped with a metal chain around her neck. The DJ placed a gold crown on her head that looked like it had been bought at Burger King and then handed Candy an oversized cheque. Candy proceeded to grab the cheque, mount it and ride it around the stage like a horse, whipping the back end with her neck chain. Candy must have been pretty confident about winning to choreograph her victory dance.

Val couldn't handle it anymore. She ran down the hall-way to the strippers' room, holding in hot tears. There was no way that bitch was going to see her cry. When she entered the dressing room, Sarah, aka Katrina LaRue, was packing up her stuff. She saw the look on Val's face and stopped.

"Hey, don't stress about the contest." Sarah came over to Val, putting a hand on her bare shoulder "It's fixed, you know."

"What?" Val said.

"Yeah. Candy is sleeping with most of the judges. She blackmailed them to make sure she wins. You know, threaten to tell their wives and employers, shit like that," Sarah said. "And she has lots of supporters in the audience, guys she's wrapped around her fingers for years. Sorry kid, but you didn't stand a chance."

"Fuck," Val said. "This town is so goddamn fucked." She began to walk around the room, collecting her costume and slamming items into her large suitcase.

"Yeah, tell me about it," Sarah agreed and went back to sorting out her stuff.

"Someone should give Candy what she deserves," Val said, as she picked up her money print suit and was about to slam it into her suitcase, thought better of it and then folded it carefully and place it inside.

"Sure, if you have a death wish. I got a kid to feed. I don't mess with the way things are. Fucking with Candy would be like pulling the wings off the queen bee while you're standing in the hive."

Val nodded. She respected that Sarah had bigger stuff to deal with, but that didn't mean Val wasn't still pissed off. Right now, she needed someone to talk to. She needed to find Will. She picked up her phone and saw a message from Ellie.

Ellie: *Sorry, kiddo, about the contest. We both thought you were the sure winner.*

Val replied: *Yeah, this shit stinks. Don't wait for me. I'm going over to Will's.*

Ellie: *'Kay, love you.*

Val finished packing and gathered her things. At least she'd made some good tips that night. She sighed. Not five grand, though. She quickly slipped out down the hall and out the side entrance, avoiding running into any other strippers. The club was emptying out fast. Now that the contest was over, everyone was eager to get home.

Val heaved her giant suitcase into the back of the Escort, having to slam the trunk down multiple times to get it to latch. Val was parked at the back of the lot, away from the other vehicles, but there was one lone truck nearby with a man sitting by himself. It was weird, but she felt like he was watching her. She hurried inside the little car, partly because of the icy cold wind that was blowing but mostly because she was concerned about the guy watching her.

She had to blow on her hands to warm the numbness away enough that she could grip the steering wheel. She was wishing she had her mitts today as she started up the engine. She was still surprised every time it started on the first try. Ever since Brandon had worked on it, it was like he had given the car another life.

As Val left the parking lot and drove down the road, she noticed the large truck spring to life and leave, going in the opposite direction. She breathed a sigh of relief. On top of everything else, the last thing she needed was a stalker.

Ten minutes later Val pulled up in front of Will's condo building downtown. As it was nearly 3:00 AM, there was lots of street parking. She decided to leave the car running and text him, not wanting to stand out in the cold in front of the buzzer.

Val: *I'm out front. Can I come up? Need a friendly face. :-(*

Val waited for a response. Even though Will had apparently only stayed for her routine, he must be wanting to hear what happened in the contest. She hoped he wasn't already asleep.

After what felt like an eternity, Val felt her phone buzz where she had tucked between her legs with her hands, trying to keep them warm.

Will: *Hey babe, it is really late. Can I take a rain check?*

Val: *I really need you right now! Let me up, please!*

There was a long pause while Val waited for his response. What was going on with him? This wasn't the first time Val had shown up after work in the early morning hours, and she was usually greeted with excitement and desire. This felt like the cold shoulder.

Will: *Okay, just give me a minute to get dressed.*

Val: *Better you stay undressed! Just need to see you. Hurry! Please!*

Val waited again. At least the little Escort was warming up now, but Val was starting to smell gasoline. The little car still had a small exhaust leak that Brandon said was not fixable. She would have to stop the engine and freeze or risk suffocation. Val decided it was better to stay warm. Her mood was dark after the night's events, and she figured getting stoned on some gas fumes might improve things. Eventually, Will texted back.

Will: *Come on up. I'll buzz the door in a minute.*

Val turned off the car and ran to the condo entrance. Her head spun as she got out, realizing she was just shy of her attempts at gas huffing. The door made a buzz and clicking noise, and Val raced inside, happy to feel the warmth of the entryway. She let self-pity flood back into her mind as she waited in the elevator. Val wanted to dump out all her feelings on Will. She needed his big shoulders to cry on right now more than she needed anything. When she got off the elevator, he was already opening his door as she came down the hall. Val tried to wrap her arms around his neck as she stepped inside, but Will dodged her like an experienced quarterback.

"Will, what's wrong?" Val asked as she closed the door behind her. His perfect face was knit with a frown.

"It's just really late. I was sleeping." Will walked away from Val into the living area.

Val kicked off her boots and followed him, feeling a surge of dread inside her. Why was he being so cold?

"Will, I just really need to talk to you after everything that happened tonight," Val said, her voice beginning to crack.

"Look, it's just not a good time for me. I've been really busy, and you showing up anytime you want just doesn't work for me."

Will stood in the kitchen next to the island, looking anywhere but at Val's face.

Val walked up to him, trying to put her arms around him again, pleading with her eyes.

"Will, what's going on?"

He brushed her away and walked over to the counter. Val noticed two paper cups sitting next to his coffee machine. She pushed a terrible thought out of her mind, taking a deep breath to keep her emotions in check, but Val had never had much luck with that in her life. Her emotions had a mind of their own, and Val had never been able to keep them inside, unlike her sister. Where Ellie was a calm lake, Val was a raging river.

She looked at the cups and then directly at Will, "Did you come see my show?"

Will sighed, looking like he was going to try and make something up, but then shrugged his shoulders.

"I wanted to. I really did. It's just…things are moving too quickly for me, Val. I need some space."

He turned back to face Val, finally settling his blue eyes on her.

"I've been meaning to tell you for a while. I'm leaving."

"Where?"

"I need to go stay at my place in the city for a while."

"How long is 'a while'?" Val felt her voice crack. Her hand reached out involuntarily for Will, but she let it drop to her side, knowing he would just evade her touch.

"It might be indefinitely. I don't know, Val. That's why I think we should take a break. Slow things down a bit. You don't want to be tied down to some guy off in the city!"

He smiled at his last comment as if he was offering the best deal in the world.

"I don't want to take a break." Val's tears were flowing now, causing her mascara to run and making her face look like a delusional clown's.

Will came up to Val and took her hands in his.

"It is for the best."

He gave her hand a quick pat then let her go like she had cooties.

Val started sobbing. She put a hand on the counter to keep herself from falling. What did this mean? She felt empty and alone.

"I think you had better go," Will said. "I'm leaving for the city first thing tomorrow."

Will began to usher the crying Val down the hallway.

"You need to pull yourself together. It is just a break. This is why things are moving too quickly. It will be better for you if you can get some time alone."

He sounded like he was building a case for his abandonment. Val hiccupped, trying to stop her tears. She swallowed, feeling a giant lump in her throat, but it quieted her sobs.

"You see? You're already feeling better."

Will smiled at her as he opened the door to his apartment and gave her a gentle shove out into the hallway.

"I'll text you once I get there. I promise!" he said, handing Val her boots and closing the door to his apartment in her face.

Val stood motionless for a minute, staring at the closed door as if she could will it open with her eyes. Giving up, she turned and ran, not stopping until she got to her car, still holding her boots in her arms like they were the last thing on earth she owned. The frozen ground was cold on her bare feet, but she didn't care. She slumped into the driver's seat and broke down in giant, chest-heaving sobs, leaning her head on the cold steering wheel.

Val sat and cried in her car until the first rays of light appeared over the horizon, flooding the sky with bright orange and purple hues. If she had any awareness left in her, she would have noticed the same truck from The Bush parking lot across the street, the man in the driver's seat watching her, his brown eyes filled with both menace and concern.

twenty-four

Ellie didn't see Val until early the next morning. She went out of the trailer to get more wood for the stove and found her sister sitting in the Ford Escort, half frozen to death in a catatonic state. Ellie plucked Val out of the car (thankful for her gym-acquired strength) and dragged her inside, plopping her on the chesterfield and immediately wrapping her in a Snuggie. It was some time before the colour returned to her sister's ghost-white face, and she began to fill Ellie in on the situation.

"Will is leaving," she said, staring blankly at the wall.

Ellie passed Val a coffee, and she wrapped her hands around it like it was the Golden Idol from *Raiders of the Lost Ark*.

"Where is he going?"

Ellie stuffed another log into the potbellied stove, causing a flurry of flames to erupt before she jammed the metal door and squeaked the lever shut. It wasn't a super-efficient stove, as evidenced by the haze of smoke that constantly floated around the ceiling. Ellie took a mental note that the smoke detector had likely been disconnected, something else she would have to look after.

"He says he is going to stay in the city."

"That doesn't sound all that bad."

Val began to cry, nearly spilling her coffee all over her Hello Kitty Snuggie. Ellie grabbed the cup and pulled her sister into her arms.

"I don't know Ellie; he was just so cold. And last night, I really thought I would win that money." Val buried her face in Ellie's sweater, leaving black streaks and gold glitter as Val's performance makeup finally relieved itself of her face.

"Don't worry about the money, Val. We'll be fine," Ellie stated, sounding more confident than she really felt. "Did Will break up with you?" she asked, knowing the hard question could risk an explosion of emotion. Val obliged, her tears escalating.

"He said we are on a break."

"A break is just that, a break. I think you are reading too much into this." Ellie was attempting to pull her sister back from the depths.

"Yeah, you remember what happened to Ross and Rachel on their 'break,'" Val said, bringing up one of their favourite TV shows.

"Kinda," Ellie said, searching her memories, but all she could come up with was Ross Geller yelling, "We are on a break!" She figured it didn't end well for Rachel.

"Ross cheated on Rachel; that's what happened. And Will is going to go sleep around on me. I know it."

"You don't know that. Besides, how do you know you want to be with Will anyway? We barely know anything about him," Ellie countered as she smoothed her sister's dark hair out of her eyes. Somehow it had come out of its carefully constructed 'do from last night's performance and was launching an all-out assault.

"We are perfect for each other, Ellie. He used to be a dancer; he's passionate and caring. The sex is great. I felt like I'd found my soulmate." Val sat up and looked Ellie in the eyes. Her face was puffy and red from crying, but somehow she still looked beautiful. When Ellie cried, she looked like she could be suffering from anaphylaxis.

"How long have you known him? A few months? We don't really know that much about his character."

"I'm not like you, Ellie; it doesn't take me years to figure out if I like someone. When I bond with someone, I know. I mean, don't you feel that way about Edward?"

Ellie stiffened at the mention of Edward's name, but Val didn't notice. Not waiting for Ellie to respond, she carried on, "When you're passionate about someone, you just have to go with it. What if that is the only time you'll have true love?"

"If Will is your 'true love' don't you think your relationship will survive a break?" Ellie asked. Val's expression softened, and her eyes lit up.

"You're right, Ellie! Maybe our love can survive this." Val leaned her head back against Ellie's chest and squeezed her tightly.

"You always know how to make me feel better," she said, her voice muffled as she spoke into Ellie's sweater, depositing even more gold glitter and mascara streaks. Ellie was going to have to soak the sweater in bleach to get it clean.

Ellie sighed and wrapped her arms around her sister. She felt content that Val was feeling better, but it didn't change the empty pit inside her.

"You'd better go get some sleep. You look like you've been up all night," Ellie said, concerned.

"'Kay, sis." Val got up from the couch. "Shower first." She stopped and turned back to Ellie, "Can you check the bathroom for spiders for me?"

Ellie smiled, "Of course, Kiddo."

Once Val was safely in a spider-free shower, Ellie sat back on the couch to check her messages.

Betsy: *Dear Ellie, Brandon is here at the house waiting to check in on you girls. He didn't want to bother you, but he wanted to make sure you were both home safe. I said both your cars were at the trailer, so he needn't worry, but you know how these men are! Is your sister getting into trouble? Jim and I would be very upset if anything were to happen to you girls.*

Warm Regards, Betsy Price

Sure they would be upset. Ellie found it entertaining how some people treated text messages like they were scripting a handwritten letter. But at least the meaning came directly across. Betsy was a busybody and was sticking her nose in where it didn't belong. Maybe her concern was genuine, but Ellie sensed not.

Her reply to Betsy took some thought, so she busied herself with stoking up the fire with another log before responding. Was Brandon aware that they were both at the Ms. Northern Nude contest? Was he just hanging out at the Price mansion waiting for them to wake up? Suddenly, her sleep-deprived brain put the pieces together in her brain like a puzzle clicking together—Brandon was the mysterious man that had watched Val's performance!

Ellie: *Dear Betsy,* (She decided the formality of the first message required an equal level in response.) *Thank you for your message. My sister and I are both well and not partaking in any nefarious activities. My sister is still asleep, but I will come up to the house if Brandon would like to talk. Dearest regards, Ellie Dashwood.*

Ellie lied about Val being asleep, but she was pretty certain she wouldn't want to talk to Brandon this morning. She didn't have to wait long for a response from Betsy.

Betsy: *Dear Ellie, Brandon says he awaits your visit with deepest anticipation! I will put the kettle on. Most Sincerely Yours, Betsy Price*

Great, thought Ellie, *now I'll have to talk to Betsy, too.*

She threw her parka on and shoved her feet into her faux fur-lined Uggs, stepping outside into the cold November morning. The walk up to the Price mansion was refreshing, the crisp air felt like it was washing away the remnants of her mild hangover. Ellie didn't often drink more than two beers, but somehow she had let Carrie talk her into two more rounds. Her tolerance was not what it used to be.

When Ellie got to the main door, she was surprised to find Brandon outside on the front step. Seeing him there wearing a baseball cap confirmed that he was the man she saw last night at the club.

"I told Betsy I wanted a quick chat with you in private. I'll leave you to figure out how to avoid tea after I'm gone," Brandon said, his face a blank slate, but somehow his eyes conveyed an understanding that there were some days you just didn't have the energy to deal with Betsy.

"Nice to see you again, Brandon." Ellie eyed Brandon with her comment, wondering if he would understand that she had seen him last night at the club.

Brandon almost looked like he blushed, but he carried on, pretending like he didn't understand.

"Is Val okay?"

"Yes, she is fine. Just tired and sleeping now."

"I wanted to do something nice for her. And I need your opinion. I know your sister is a dancer," Brandon paused before continuing. "Ballet dancer, I mean."

"Well, she was. That was a while ago now."

"I thought she might like to go to the ballet. In the city. I have four tickets." Brandon was rambling. He was slightly nervous, which Ellie found endearing. Unfortunately, it was a characteristic that would not be attractive to Val.

"Val would love that. Brandon, you are very kind. But you don't have to do this," Ellie said. Her ears were beginning to freeze, making her regret not throwing on her toque before she left the trailer.

"Yes I do. I have to," Brandon said with an emphasis that indicated he would brook no argument.

"Thank you. I think Val could use a little distraction right now," Ellie said. "You'll be joining us?"

Brandon shook his head, "Oh, no. The other two tickets can go to…" he paused, "whomever you would like," he finished, a knowing look on his face that said he really wanted to come but didn't want to impose himself.

"You will be missed," Ellie said, smiling.

"I hope that things are not going badly with that Will Davis?"

Ellie noticed a flash of anger in his otherwise serene face. She wasn't about to give details on her sister's relationships, but she could sense that her face was likely giving away her feelings.

"I'm sure things will be fine," Ellie replied, she began to stomp her feet to keep her toes from going numb, and Brandon noticed. Although he was wearing only a basic leather jacket that might be comfortable in mid-summer, not November, he didn't seem phased by the cold wind.

"I'm sorry. I've kept you out in the cold for too long. I won't keep you. I'll send over the ballet tickets tomorrow."

"Thank you again, Brandon. We really owe you." Ellie and Brandon walked down the front steps together. As they separated, and Brandon walked towards his truck, he called out to Ellie.

"Ellie, please do me a favor. Keep an eye on that Will Davis," he said. "Your sister deserves better."

Ellie nodded. Part of her felt like this was just a jealous man trying to undermine his competition for her sister, but alternatively, what if there was something he wasn't telling them about Will?

She walked slowly back to the trailer, letting the movement of walking bring some needed blood back into her numb toes. Ellie couldn't help her mind slip towards thoughts of Edward. He was in the city, and if they went there for the ballet, would she be able to see him? She cursed herself for letting these silly thoughts flood her brain. Edward was gone, and there was nothing she could do about it.

The dark thoughts about Edward were further cemented in her mind when she checked her phone messages back at the trailer. They hadn't even received the ballet tickets yet from Brandon and already Betsy was attempting to derail their trip.

Betsy: *Dear Ellie, Brandon is such a dear for getting you tickets to the ballet! I know what good friends you are with Lucy Martin, so I went ahead and invited her along! I know you will all have such fun together. And don't worry about your accommodations. You can't stay at my condo in the city!*

Yours always, Betsy Price

Ellie sighed. She couldn't really say no to Lucy coming if they were going to get to stay at Betsy's for free. Ellie's phone pinged again, and this time it was from Carrie.

Carrie: *Bad news. GF has left for the city! I think she is breaking up with me.*

Ellie: *Sorry to hear that Carrie. I'm sure she'll come around. Give her some time?*

Carrie: *I don't know Ellie. I'm really stressed. She says she isn't sure she is gay anymore. WTF!*

Ellie thought about how to respond but then remembered the last ticket she had to the ballet and wondered if it might help cheer her friend up.

Ellie: *Why don't you come to the ballet with me and Val? It will take your mind off things.*

There was a pause while Ellie saw the little bubble flashing next to Carrie's name.

Carrie: *Yeah. Thanks. Maybe I could do with watching some little tarts prance around a stage in tiny skirts.*

Ellie: *Not to mention men in tights, am I right?*

Carrie: *Gross! Nope. Last thing I want to see is their junk all tied up like the face of a pug wrapped in spandex.*

Ellie was happy her friend was back to making jokes. Not that she needed someone else in her life burdened with the loss of their relationship, but maybe helping her sister and Carrie would lessen her own pain.

twenty-five

Brandon was as good as his word on the ballet tickets. They showed up in Ellie's email the next day. The ballet wasn't for a couple weeks, but when Ellie informed Val about the tickets, her eyes lit up.

"Ellie, this is fantastic! Maybe I'll get to see Will! And isn't Edward in the city, too? Why don't you try and get in touch?" Val asked excitedly. She had managed to get herself out of her PJs this morning but was still in lazy mode, sitting on the couch and watching TV.

Ellie smiled at Val but didn't respond, pretending to be busy putting dishes away in the kitchen. There was no way she would reach out to Edward. Especially since they would be dragging along Lucy Martin. Val must have read Ellie's thoughts, something she was known to do.

"Why do we have to bring that Lucy chick with us? What a drag. She seemed a little annoying, don't you think?"

Ellie stopped for a moment, pondering whether she should tell Val about Lucy and the secret engagement, but before she could say anything, Val continued.

"Oh Ellie, I'm sure Will is going to want to see me, especially since we'll have been apart for over two weeks. That has to be enough of a break for him."

Ellie sighed quietly and went back to putting the dishes away. She did make a promise to Lucy anyway, even if she didn't really like the woman. She just wasn't the type to go blabbing other people's secrets around.

"And at least you'll have Carrie there. She's fun to hang out with. Might counteract the Lucy factor," Val said. Ellie couldn't agree more. If Lucy was the disease, Carrie could certainly be the antidote.

The next two weeks went by in a blur. It was already the end of November, and winter had hit Sober hard. The plan was for Ellie and Val to drive into Fort George, the bustling northern metropolis that was busy enough to get the title of "city" mostly because a Costco was located there. When Betsy Price heard the girls were going to drive down in Ellie's truck, she swore up and down that in no way would she allow them to take such a risk. Normally Ellie would have fought harder, but as Betsy offered to pay airfare for all four of them, and they could avoid a six-hour drive on a northern two-lane highway, she let her arm be twisted easily. Busybody though Betsy was, her heart was in the right place.

Thankfully, the small twin turbo plane they took from Sober to Fort George had only single seats on either side of the aircraft, so Ellie was not forced to sit next to Lucy and hear more about her secret engagement to Edward. Ellie put on her noise-cancelling headphones and enjoyed thirty minutes of bumpy, turbulent bliss. Adding to her enjoyment was watching Lucy, sitting across the aisle and obviously not enjoying the bumpy ride. It was impressive that Lucy's already alabaster-coloured hands could actually appear even whiter when clutching an armrest with primal ferocity.

Val didn't mind the bumpy ride either; she appeared to be watching the snowstorm out the window with curious intensity. The two sisters didn't get the opportunity to fly all that often, so the novelty won over any fear at the danger of being many thousands of feet up in a small aircraft. Carrie didn't look like she was enjoying the bumpy ride either. Ellie noticed a sheen of sweat across her friend's brow and a look of resigned terror on her face for most of the flight.

The landing was worse than the flight. The wind was blowing in the wrong direction, and the small plane had to come down at an angle, sweeping the nose over at the last second before hitting the runway. It was the kind of landing where the passengers erupted into applause for the pilot once they were safely on the ground. Lucy burst into tears of relief, which made Ellie suppress a smile. Why did this woman get under her skin?

Compared to Sober, the airport at Fort George was a bustling hub. They even had the privilege of walking in a covered jetway extending from the plane to the terminal, keeping them sheltered from the elements. In Sober, the walk to the plane was directly across the snow-swept tarmac, making a person feel like they were leaving on an Arctic expedition.

The four women gathered around the one luggage carousel in the Fort George terminal, having to wait for Lucy's overnight bag, which was too large to be a carry-on. Val rolled her eyes at Ellie as Lucy struggled to haul a giant pink paisley suitcase off the rotating rack before Carrie stepped in and grabbed it for her. Ellie was pretty sure the display was a carefully choreographed act, which was cemented in her mind as she witnessed Lucy tittering her thanks at Carrie like she had just saved Lucy from being eaten by a grizzly.

Carrie blushed bright pink at the attention Lucy was giving her. She smiled shyly at Ellie as they made their way through the airport, and Ellie glared back at her friend.

"What?" queried Carrie quietly. "She needed help, and who am I not to aid a damsel in distress?"

Ellie shook her head at her friend but was happy that Carrie was at least enjoying herself, even if she had to haul both her backpack and Lucy's giant suitcase through the airport terminal.

It was already dark when they stepped outside, even though it was just 5:00 PM. The northern sun didn't stick around long once it was anywhere near December. Ellie waved at a cabby that sat idling nearby, and the four of them clambered inside.

"Oh my gosh, it's so cold out," Lucy squeaked once she was sitting in the back seat squished between Carrie and Val. "Can you turn up the heat?" she asked the driver.

It didn't help that the jacket Lucy was wearing looked as if it had no zipper or buttons to do it up and was made from veil-like material that was almost translucent.

"Sorry, it's warm as it's gonna get," responded the driver. Ellie was sitting in the front seat and found it to be quite comfortable.

"Do you think he knows how to use the thermostat?" Lucy asked Val.

Ellie looked sideways at the driver, hoping he hadn't heard Lucy's comment.

"Excuse me," Lucy leaned forward to stick her small head between the front two seats as the little cab rolled slowly through the snow-covered streets of Fort George.

"Can. You. Turn. Up. The. Heat?" Lucy was accentuating the syllables like she was talking to a toddler.

"Lucy," said Ellie as she turned her head to face the back seat, "he already said it's turned up as high as it will go."

"Well, I just didn't know if he understood me or not, being he's foreign and all," Lucy grumbled, sitting back down like a sullen child.

"You know, I was an engineer in my home country. Here, I have to drive taxi because your government won't accept my master's degree," the cab driver said.

"I'm sorry," replied Ellie, apologizing for the cabbie's situation and for Lucy's behavior.

"If he is so smart, why can't he fix the thermostat," Lucy said under her breath, although it was obvious everyone had heard. The driver began to accelerate through the streets, obviously wanting this ride to be over before he considered more drastic measures.

When they arrived at Betsy's rowhouse Ellie made sure to tip the driver well, hoping it would make up for Lucy's comments. But by the way he sped off without helping get their luggage out, she was pretty sure the tip hadn't helped.

"Why did you tip him?" Lucy griped as she struggled to get her suitcase up the front steps to the townhouse. "He didn't even help with the luggage." After Lucy's behavior in the cab, Ellie was not surprised to see that Carrie wasn't eager to help her with the luggage again.

Ellie decided to keep her mouth shut. She had to spend the next couple days with this woman, and she didn't want to get off to a bad start. Surprisingly, Val was quiet, her mind obviously off on another planet.

Betsy's rowhouse was spacious, the large entryway led to a sitting room, meticulously decorated in a 1970s Danish style. An intricate twisted metal railing lined a set of stairs curving to the upper level. As a welder, Ellie could recognize custom work, and this particular railing must have taken weeks to construct. Each step was adorned with small metal leaves placed in perfect symmetry at the end of a curled metal branch, giving the impression the railing had sprung from the ground like a live plant. Ellie walked slowly up the stairs admiring the handiwork. Her sister, Lucy and Carrie had already found empty rooms in which to dump their belongings and start to prepare for their evening out. Ellie and Val were to share the large master bedroom, which thankfully had a king-sized bed, piled with enough throw pillows to equip a sorority of fights.

Ellie found Val sitting on the bed, holding her phone in her hands. She had immediately plugged her phone in when they arrived, having killed the battery during their travel.

"He hasn't texted back," she said, staring intently at her phone.

Ellie sighed, "I'm sure he will. Why don't you get ready for the ballet? This weekend is supposed to take your mind off him."

"He has to want to see me. It's been weeks since we were together." Val looked up at her sister, worry etched across her face.

Ellie started getting ready for the night out, hoping her sister would come around and eventually enjoy the evening. Ellie had decided on a sparkly navy-blue dress that swept down to her ankles. It had long sleeves that would keep her warm, but the front neckline dipped down low enough to show considerable cleavage. It was sophisticated enough to wear to the ballet but also made Ellie feel sexy, something she really needed these days.

Carrie was already downstairs digging into the pizza she had ordered for the group as a pre-show snack. She had dressed up as well, wearing a perfectly fitted pinstripe suit with a bright red bowtie, her short, cropped hair slicked back Rat-Pack style. Ellie smiled at her friend as she came downstairs and helped herself to a piece of Hawaiian, before almost gagging on the first bite.

"Why does this taste like fish?" Ellie said, her slice of pizza drooping off the end of her hand.

"Anchovies, the potato chip of the sea," Carrie crooned. Ellie's friend was moving a bit stiffly, and Ellie wondered if the suit jacket didn't quite fit Carrie's broad shoulders.

"Wow. As if pineapple on pizza wasn't weird enough, you had to go and make it taste and smell like pussy. But I guess I shouldn't be surprised."

Ellie managed to keep eating her slice, not willing to admit that the salty and sweet combination of flavors was beginning to grow on her.

Carrie grinned, "You know how I like it."

The two friends perched themselves on bar stools at the edge of a large kitchen island, each finishing off a second slice. Betsy's city home looked like it was rarely used, as evidenced by the brand-new pans on a pot rack hanging from the ceiling.

"Have you heard anything from your girlfriend?" asked Ellie, not wanting to bring her friend down but knowing that Carrie likely had it on her mind.

"Yeah, it's over," Carrie sighed. "I don't get it, Ellie; she is most certainly not straight. I don't know why she can't admit that to herself." Ellie regretted bringing up the subject after watching the sadness creep across her friend's face.

"She is getting married. To a dude. It's a total lie. Just so she can make her parents happy." Carrie grabbed another slice of pizza, digging in like she was drowning her sorrows in cheese and salty fish.

"I'm really sorry, Carrie." Ellie reached out a hand to comfort her friend after unsuccessfully trying to reach around her friend's wide shoulders. Carrie gave Ellie a small smile. Like Ellie, Carrie wasn't one to show her emotions. Where Ellie just pushed her emotions away, Carrie hid behind a false wall of bravado.

Thankfully, Val provided some needed distraction as she entered the room wearing a short red dress that emphasized her long legs. Val was never afraid to show some skin, even when the weather threatened to make her uncomfortably cold.

Carrie whistled. "Smokin' hot, Val."

"Thanks!" she replied as she pulled up another bar stool and grabbed a slice of pizza.

"Oh yum!" said Val. I love pineapple and anchovy!" Carrie grinned mischievously at Ellie behind Val's back and raised her two fingers to her mouth, darting her tongue between them like she was licking a lollipop. Ellie shook her head and stifled a laugh. At least Carrie was up to her usual antics again.

The three of them waited another twenty minutes for Lucy to get ready, and Ellie was beginning to worry they would be late for the show. Eventually, just as the cabby was pulling up, Lucy clomped down the stairs wearing what looked like a pink cupcake fully loaded with white bows and frills. It was a bit overkill for the ballet in Fort George. Her hair was swept up into a tight bun, giving her face a stretched balloon look.

"Do you like it?" Lucy asked, fanning her pink-gloved hands over the cupcake as if she was ready to get into her Pumpkin Carriage and meet Prince Charming.

"Yes, it's very...frilly," said Ellie slowly, choosing her words carefully. Carrie looked like she had just witnessed a train wreck, which wasn't far from the truth. Val was staring at her phone, but when she finally looked up she jumped and shuddered. Val lifted her eyebrows at Ellie but didn't say anything.

Lucy was the last to climb into the backseat of the cab and then was unable to close the door because of the puffiness of her dress. Ellie had to stuff the dress inside, like she was packing a sleeping bag, slamming the door multiple times to get it to latch. When Ellie finally got into the front seat of the cab, she was relieved to see that they had a different driver, a large middle-aged woman who spoke like she smoked a few packs a day.

"Where're ya going?" came the raspy voice of their driver.

"Fort George Hall," said Ellie.

"Oh, Swan Lake!" said the driver. "It's amazing. Went last night. You girls will love it," and she sped off.

The driver was right. Ellie was mesmerized by the ballet. She had never seen anything so intricate and graceful. The Royal Winnipeg Ballet was world renown, and even though Fort George Hall was a small northern city venue, the ballet company had brought their big city sets and costumes. The northerners felt like a little piece of big town life had been brought to their small community. Ellie was only slightly distracted by the tights the men wore, remembering the comment from Carrie about their spandex-clad package.

Ellie was surprised that her sister remained distracted. She kept looking at her phone, the bright light distracting to those around them. When they went out to the lobby for the first act intermission, Ellie pulled her sister aside.

"You have to stop looking at your phone, Val. It's really rude for everyone around you," she reprimanded.

"I know. I'm sorry. It's just that I can't miss a message from Will. What if he wants to see me tonight?" Val looked pleadingly at her sister.

"Val, just try and enjoy the show. You love the ballet." Val nodded slowly and put her phone into her purse.

"I'll go get us some drinks," Val said.

"Let me help," said Carrie, and the two of them walked off together, leaving Lucy and Ellie to stand in the crowded lobby together.

Lucy didn't waste any time. "Finally! I have been waiting to talk to you for so long," came Lucy's small voice. She wasn't lisping anymore, so Ellie assumed she had removed her plastic teeth straighteners. She grasped Ellie's arm like they were long lost friends. Lucy's sharp fingernails felt like talons through her pink silky gloves.

"I am so hoping to see Edward while we are in town," Lucy said. "We haven't spoken in months, but I know he's anxious to see me."

Ellie kept looking around the room, hoping Val and Carrie would come back soon so she could be freed from this conversation.

"I know most people would be so jealous to have their boyfriend away for so long, but Edward is very devoted. He never speaks of anyone else. I do have a jealous nature."

"Are you going to tell his family about your engagement?" Ellie asked, but she was saved from any answer as Val came back, gracefully balancing three drinks in her hand. She hadn't worked tables for years to not obtain server skills. Carrie held a large mug of beer in one hand, surprising Ellie that they served anything but wine and cocktails, but fancy ballet none-theless, they were still in a northern town. Ellie gladly reached for her drink, wresting her arm away from Lucy's grip, so she didn't notice the excited look in her sister's eyes.

"Ellie, Edward is here." Val said, directing her com-ment at her sister.

"Edward?" Lucy said.

Val didn't pay any attention to Lucy as she pointed with her finger to the far side of the room. There stood a tall man with his back to them. He was wearing a dark, neatly tailored suit.

"Come! Let's go say hi!" Val said as she grabbed her sister's hand and dragged her across the room, Lucy and Carrie trailing behind them.

"Val, wait!" But Ellie couldn't stop her sister when Val had a plan in mind. "How do you know that's Edward?"

Her question was answered as Edward turned around, his eyes lighting up when he saw Ellie. He looked so hand-some it nearly melted the cold spot in Ellie's heart. Standing next to him was a large, elderly lady dressed in a flowing, black sequined dress, her hair swept up in a chignon and adorned with a matching black feather. She had a pinched look to her face as if she was trying to hold in a fart.

"Ellie!" Edward exclaimed, "it's so nice to see you." His eyes were glued to Ellie, so he didn't notice Lucy immediately. When his eyes flickered over to Lucy, he gave a start like he'd been stabbed with a hot poker.

"Lucy! What are you doing here?" he asked, the shock in his voice more than apparent. Lucy batted her eyelashes and looked demurely at the ground.

"Edward, aren't you going to introduce me to your friends?" asked the elderly woman. Somehow words were able to escape her mouth without her lips moving. Ellie wondered if she was a ventriloquist in a former life.

"Oh, yes." Edward was fumbling in a way Ellie had never seen him do before. He was obviously caught off guard by the presence of Ellie and Lucy together.

"This is Ellie and Val Dashwood, friends from Sober, and this is Lucy Martin. And I haven't been formally introduced to your friend," he paused as he gestured to each of the women, ending with Carrie.

"Carrie Braun," Carrie said as she reached for the elderly lady's hand, gave a slight bow and lifted the woman's fingers to her lips.

"This is my mother, Isabella Price." Edward looked a bit puzzled by Carrie's formal greeting, but it seemed to please his mother as she smiled brightly at Carrie.

"Nice to meet you, Mrs. Price," Ellie said.

"Oh, you can call me Isabella," replied Edward's mother. "Such a nice young gentleman," she said, gesturing to Carrie. "So many men these days do not treat their elders with respect." She turned a sharp eye on her son.

Ellie snuck a look at Carrie, but her friend appeared to be taking her gender misidentification in stride, just nodding appreciatively at Isabella.

"Edward, where have you been?" Val said. "You've been gone so long!"

Ellie couldn't help but notice Isabella's eyes looking disapprovingly at Val's short dress. She shifted uncomfortably, attempting to pull the V-neck of her gown up to cover more cleavage, an action that wasn't missed by Edward's mother. At least one thing could be said for Lucy, her pink cupcake gown covered every inch of skin like it was meant for the 1800s. Maybe Lucy would meet with Edward's mother's approval in that regard.

Edward ran his hand through his hair, looking tired and drawn, but before he could respond his mother spoke up, "I need Edward here right now. He is indispensable to me."

They were saved from any more awkward conversation by the flashing of lights in the hall, signaling the end of intermission. As they all made their way back to their seats, Lucy grabbed Ellie's arm and whispered in her ear.

"Did you see the way Edward was looking at me? And his mother…such a lovely woman! Oh, I'm so excited! I'm sure we will be able to see each other again soon!" Lucy tittered, and Ellie gritted her teeth to hold in her feelings. She shouldn't care that Edward was with someone else, but it still cut into her like a knife through butter.

Val grabbed her phone out of her purse as they sat down, checking one last time for a message from Will.

Carrie leaned into Val. "Why are you so desperate to hear from him anyway?" Carrie asked, her eyes flickering down to the brightly lit screen. Carrie's face faltered into recognition as she read Val's phone screen.

"Will Davis?" Carrie said.

"Do you know him?" Val looked hopefully at Carrie.

"Yeah, I do." Carrie said. "That's the guy who's marrying my ex."

"WHAT?" Val blurted out and was greeted with a chorus of shushing from the guests around them, including Lucy, whose expression was a mixture of disgust and annoyance.

"I'm sorry, Val," Carrie said. "Believe me, I'm pretty pissed about it, too. I think his stag is tonight."

Val stood up and grabbed her purse, causing everyone in the row to shuffle uncomfortably. The orchestra was already beginning to play, and the stage curtains were rising.

"Val, what are you doing?" Ellie whispered, trying not to disturb the other guests. "Sit down! Can't this wait until later?"

"No, it can't," Val said firmly as she made her way out to the aisle. Ellie made to get up and follow her sister, but Lucy grabbed her arm.

"You can't leave me here alone!" Lucy cried, which produced another round of shushing and a few "keep it downs!"

Ellie stared at her sister as she stomped down the aisle and then down at Lucy, her mousy face with a pleading look that was completely self-serving. But Ellie knew where her allegiance lay, and there was no way she was letting her sister go through this alone.

Carrie looked up at her friend, "I'll stay here with the Cupcake. You go help your sister." Ellie nodded a thanks to Carrie, knowing she would owe her one.

"Oh! We can ask Edward to take us home," came Lucy's squeaky voice, a mischievous look on her face as she went back to watching the ballet.

Ellie rolled her eyes at Carrie as she made to follow her sister. She wondered what she had done, leaving Lucy Martin to spend more time with Edward. She resigned herself that it didn't matter anyway. She had to help Val.

CHAPTER
twenty-six

As the theatre doors swung shut behind her, Val looked down again at her phone, seeing the dozens of messages she had sent to Will still unanswered. She decided on a more direct approach. If he was just going to ignore her virtually, she was going to find him and confront him somewhere he couldn't hide. Carrie had said the stag was tonight, and that made things pretty easy for her. Fort George was much bigger than Sober but not so big that it had more than one decent strip club. Chances are that a stag would be held at the French Maid.

The French Maid was affiliated with the Northern Bush Club. If you got a good reputation as a dancer at The Bush, you could get some gigs down at the French Maid. Val heard that the money was good, but the place was teaming with blow, so you had to watch you didn't get wrapped up in the cocaine business. Just as Val was asking the theatre maître d' to hail her a cab, Ellie exited the theatre.

"Val! Wait!" Ellie called, moving as fast as she could in four-inch heels.

"You can't stop me," Val said.

Ellie sighed, catching her breath from the awkward running.

"I'm not going to."

Val gave her sister a confused look. She was expecting a lecture on how she was being silly, should calm down and stay for the show.

Ellie put a hand on her sister's bare shoulder. "Let's go find this asshole," she said.

Val smiled. She was still very emotional, but somehow having Ellie with her gave her a sense of calm and purpose.

"Yeah. Let's do it. But what about Lucy and Carrie?" Val asked, as they made their way outside into the icy winter night for another cab ride.

"They're big girls. I'm sure they'll figure things out."

"I feel bad for Carrie, being left with that woman," Val said, looking sympathetically at her sister as they climbed into the cab.

Val told the driver to take them to the French Maid but didn't notice his raised eyebrows in the rearview mirror. Obviously, taking two young women dressed for the theatre to a strip club was an unusual fare for him, but he didn't say anything.

The neon sign of the French Maid club glowed in the hazy night air like the Holy Grail beacon. It was a Saturday night, so the parking lot was packed. Many cars were still idling, pumping exhaust into the atmosphere, a northern practice that allowed you to return to your vehicle at any time and have it be toasty warm. Environmental concerns were a low priority when you worked at an oil refinery.

Val and Ellie ran quickly to the club entrance through the cold and were admitted without paying the cover, as pretty, young women were always welcomed into a club where most patrons were middle-aged men. Val scanned the club quickly, getting the layout, which was much like The Bush but with more neon. To add to the sophistication, the French Maid also boasted a fog machine that added to the haze. Val took them directly to the DJ booth, where a skinny guy wearing head-phones and a T-shirt branded with "Osama Spin Laden" in gold sequin letters was spinning beats. He looked like if he even stepped foot in the Middle East, his pasty skin would melt like raspberry sorbet on a barbeque.

Val handed the guy a twenty and leaned in, yelling in his ear. Ellie couldn't hear what they were saying over the pound-ing beat of the music, but she guessed it had something to do with finding out where the stag parties were because Osama then pointed to a booth on the far side of the main stage.

Ellie had to move fast to keep up to her sister, who could stride with purpose in heels of any height, even the red-strapped circus stilts she was wearing tonight. The booth was filled with a half dozen men all in various stages of drunken-ness. Will Davis sat at the centre, wearing inflatable boobs and a purple feather boa around his neck. Val stopped short when she saw who else was at the table, causing Ellie to run into her back. At the edge of the booth sat Murph, with Candy sand-wiched between himself and Will. It was like someone took all

Val's fears and insecurities and wrapped them up like a bad burrito. It was her worst nightmare played out in real life.

The set ended causing a lull in the music, and Val's voice brought the attention of the whole group to her.

"Will!" She felt tears at the corners of her eyes, but Ellie grabbed her arm, holding her steady and helping to keep the tears suppressed.

"What are you doing here?" Will asked. His voice had a trace of concern that Ellie thought might be genuine.

"Well now, if it isn't the little ballet dancer!" Murph sneered.

His arm was draped around Candy, who Val was surprised to see did not have her usual venomous look but appeared almost browbeaten and upset.

"You just couldn't get enough Murph, could you?"

He let his hand slip down Candy's shoulder, and she gave an almost imperceptible shudder. A flash of anger passed through Val as she thought about what must have happened to Candy. Even though Candy had been a super-bitch to her, Val wouldn't wish Murph on her worst enemy.

"You lied to me," Val directed her comments back at Will. Will's eyes were blurry with booze, but he still managed to look embarrassed as he tried to look anywhere but at Val.

"Were you with this little tart?" Murph asked, and then he broke into laughter, which was echoed by their drunken buddies at the table.

"Maybe she just wants in on a piece of the action, eh?" Murph pulled a wad of cash out of his wallet. "I'd even include that meaty friend of yours for an extra fiver."

He grinned at Ellie, which made her stomach turn. Ellie gripped her sister's arm and felt Val's fists clench at her sides. She knew when her sister was angry, and this asshole was really getting under her skin.

"Murph, just let them go," Candy said, and Val noticed her usually perfect mascara was smudged like she'd been crying.

Hearing Candy try and protect her was enough to push Val over the edge. She leaned into Murph, who had turned towards Val and spread his legs like he was inviting her in. Val knew how to play the game, and she smiled her best sexy smile and stepped towards him as if she was going to take the money. At the last second, Val drove her knee up into Murph's crotch with the force of a quarterback kicking the conversion field goal. Murph grabbed his balls and fell to the floor, whimpering in pain. But Val wasn't done; she lifted her heeled foot and cracked it down into his nut sack just as he rolled towards her.

Ellie stood stunned next to Val who was panting from the adrenaline. Before she turned to leave, Val looked up at Candy and saw a flash of admiration across her mascara smeared face, but it passed so quickly that she couldn't be sure. Val grabbed her sister's hand and turned to leave, striding quickly away from the group.

Their scene had drawn considerable attention, not the least of which was from a two bouncers who were making their way across the room. Just as they got to the DJ booth, a greasy little man stepped in front of them. He barely came up to Ellie's shoulder, making the shiny bald spot on his head glow under the neon lights.

"Hey," the man said, "do you remember me?" He was talking directly to Val, and as she looked down at him her memory flashed back. It was the guy she had kicked in the balls for five hundred bucks in what felt like a lifetime ago.

The little man licked his lips, his beady eyes shining with lust from behind his round glasses. He must have witnessed the Murph ball-kicking scene moments before and was looking to get in on the action. Val's adrenaline was racing, and she wasted no time nailing the small man in the groin with a swift upward knee jerk that knocked him sideways onto the floor.

"What the hell?" Ellie said as Val grabbed her arm again to lead her away. As Ellie stepped over the body of the shaking small man, she heard his squeaky voice. "Thanks for the freebie!"

The two sisters made it back to the door just as the bouncers were bearing down on them. As they ran outside into the snowy night, Ellie heard one of them say to his counterpart, "Let the crazy bitches go. No way I'm getting sacked!"

twenty-seven

The cab ride back to the rowhouse was slow because snow had begun to fall in earnest. The streaming snow against the windshield looked deceptively like they were in the *Millennium Falcon* travelling at light speed, even though the cab was moving at a snail's pace. Ellie didn't notice; her attention was on Val, who lay in her lap sobbing. The tidal wave of emotions from the evening, which had been barely contained up until now, were literally flooding out onto Ellie's dress. Ellie stroked her sister's hair back from her wet face, not saying anything. What could she say? That Will is a lying ass-wipe who didn't deserve her? That he is marrying a woman who is likely gay? None of this would make Val feel any better. Only time would heal her sister, and maybe booze. Copious amounts of booze.

Ellie was happy to find that Betsy's liquor cabinet was decently stocked, albeit with what would be considered a pre-legal teenager's wet dream. She quickly scanned through, dismissing the peppermint schnapps and bottles of baby duck, finally settling on a bottle of strawberry lemonade vodka. Potent and fruity. She poured two drinks on ice and carried them up to the master bedroom, where Val lay on the bed, having ejected the throw pillows in a wild frenzy like a Boston terrier digging for bones and finally collapsing, an empty shell. Ellie noted that her sister appeared to be cried out as she lay quietly on her side, staring at the wall and sniffing occasionally.

"Hey, you! Brought you something," Ellie said, as she brought the double-shot drink to her sister's bedside table.

"Thanks."

Val sat up and picked up the pale pink drink, downing it in a couple gulps and shaking her head from the blast of alcohol. Val held out her hand to Ellie, looking expectantly at her sister, who obligingly passed the second drink to her sister.

She needs it more anyway, Ellie thought. At least the second one was going down at a reasonable pace.

"Go easy, kiddo," Ellie cautioned. Just then she was interrupted by a loud banging on the front door.

"That must be Carrie and Lucy. They don't have a key."

"Don't let them come up here, but bring me another drink." Val held out her glass to Ellie, before adding, "Please?" Ellie smiled and took the glass from her sister.

"Only a single this time," Ellie said over her shoulder as she left to go let Carrie and Lucy inside.

When Ellie opened the door, a flurry of snowflakes flooded into the front entryway.

"Holy shit! It's like a dandruff party at a Head and Shoulder's convention out there," Carrie said, stomping the snow from her black leather shoes as she closed the door behind them.

Before Ellie could reply, Lucy scampered away from them and up the stairs, crying loudly. Unfortunately for her, a bow of her cupcake dress caught on one of the leaves of the metal railing tearing a strip off the dress like someone peeling an onion. It didn't stop her; however, and as she continued her ascent, layer upon layer of the dress was stripped away until by the time she got to the top all that remained was her beige Spanx, her torso like a tube of toothpaste squeezed in the middle. There immediately followed a loud slamming of a door and sobbing yelps. Ellie couldn't understand why someone so skinny would force themselves into Spanx, but she didn't understand women's couture at the best of times.

"What the hell happened?" Ellie asked, as she followed Carrie into the kitchen.

"Oh, I'll tell you, but first I need a drink," Carrie said, sitting down on the Danish-style barstool and brushing snowflakes from her dark hair.

"Gotcha! We've a choice of fruity-themed liquors or cheap bubbly wine," Ellie replied as she swung open the liquor cabinet door above the fridge for Carrie's perusal.

"Um, wow, okay. I'll take a very large glass of the champibble."

"Fantastic choice," Ellie tittered in a French accent as she poured the fake champagne into a tall water glass. Carrie held her finger on the edge of the glass right at the top to indicate how much Ellie should pour. It was full enough that Carrie had to lean over and sip from the glass while it remained on the countertop, much like a toddler learning to drink juice from a cup for the first time.

Carrie didn't begin her story until the glass was half empty.

"So, we got a ride home with Edward and his mother. Wow, that woman would not give up on the whole 'I'm a dude thing.' It was cute in the beginning but really began to wear on me when she started asking if Carrie was short for Carlton or Carlyle. Anyway, did you know that Lucy is actually engaged to Edward?"

Ellie nodded, not looking her friend in the eyes.

"Sorry to hear that, buddy. I know you two were a thing."

Carrie took another long drink of her champibble before continuing. "Edward's mother was also not aware that her dear little boy was engaged to that overstuffed cream puff either, and she was none too pleased."

"So what happened? Did Lucy just blurt out that they were engaged?" Ellie asked, not sure why Lucy would choose that particular moment after keeping her secret for so long.

"During the ride, the mother was commending our little Lucy on what a 'lovely thing' she was, and how she would 'make some lucky man a perfect wife.' You know the ingratiating bullshit you hear from rich people sometimes. I'll be honest; I think she assumed that the two of us were a couple."

"Ahh," Ellie said, "so Lucy figured she had an opportunity with the mother and went for it."

"I guess so, but to the detriment of the rest of us. The old bat ordered her driver to dump us at the side of the road, in the middle of this bloody storm no less."

"Holy shit!" Ellie replied, trying to hide her joy at the treatment Lucy received. She immediately felt guilty. Why did she hate that woman so much?

"Yeah, but to give Edward some credit, he got out with us and refused to get back in unless his mother relented. He is one stubborn bastard, that's for sure. The family shit doesn't fall far from the asshole if you know what I mean."

"So what happened?" Ellie refilled Carrie's glass as she tapped on the side again.

"Eventually, Mother proved the most stubborn, and she drove off, leaving me, the Cupcake and Edward to freeze in the storm. Thankfully, Edward had some connection with a local cab company, and after he called someone, we were picked up in under five minutes. It was enough time for Lucy to complain bitterly that she was getting hypothermia and convinced poor Edward to give her his suit jacket." Carrie paused, gulping down some more bubbly, "It wouldn't even fit over that stupid dress of hers anyway. What a waste of chivalry."

There was a long pause while the two friends sipped on their drinks, contemplating the evening's activities.

"What happened on the hunt for my ex-girlfriend's new fiancé?" Carrie asked. Ellie couldn't help but notice a hint of sadness flash across her friend's face, but it was gone as soon as she downed the rest of her drink.

Ellie filled Carrie in on the adventures at the French Maid, sparing no details on the number of balls her sister had damaged.

"I knew your sister was a ball cracker," she said. "Didn't nail that bastard Will Davis though, huh?"

"No, he was pretty protected behind all his cronies."

"Too bad. Maybe if his dick wasn't working, Victoria might leave him." Carrie let an edge of sadness creep into her voice.

"So Victoria is her name?"

"Yeah, I guess it doesn't matter anymore. Not like she is going to come out of the closet if she is going to marry that asshole. Victoria Lane. Beautiful, gorgeous, heavenly Victoria Lane. Her boobs, Ellie, man." Carrie exhaled and shook her head, looking down at the floor, remembering. "And red hair. Like real red hair. You know, where the carpet matches the drapes. I've always dreamed I'd have a girl like that."

Ellie paused, something in her memory flashed through the haze of night. She remembered the group that was hogging the bench press at the local gym more than a month ago now. She knew the guy had looked familiar. It must have been Will Davis. And he had that gorgeous, busty, redhead gym bunny with him. She wondered if that was the Victoria Lane. She shook her head; it didn't matter now anyway.

Carrie didn't seem to notice Ellie's reverie; she was in her own little world, half cut from two glasses of fake champagne and deep in thought about her lost girlfriend.

"I promised I'd bring Val another drink. Then I'm going to bed. Don't drink too much," Ellie said, but she noticed her friend was already picking up the bottle of champibble and moving to go up to her room. She sighed, *What harm would it do?*

When Ellie got back upstairs, all was silent. Lucy must have cried herself to sleep; there was no sound from her room. She almost felt a flash of pity for the woman, and she wondered what would happen between her and Edward now. When Ellie walked into the bedroom, she was thankful to find her sister sound asleep. Somehow her tiny one hundred ten-pound body was taking up almost the entire king-sized bed. Ellie took one last look out the window at the blowing snowstorm and quietly finished off the rest of the strawberry lemonade vodka. The apocalyptic weather was poetic given the experience of the evening; however, watching the snow blow and swirl had a calming effect on Ellie. When she finally went to bed, first pushing her sister out of the way to make a small corner to sleep on, she fell asleep the instant her head hit the pillow, exhaustion overwhelming her churning mind.

twenty-eight

Ellie woke the next morning to a loud banging. It felt like someone was hammering in her head, and she realized that she must have imbibed more than her fair share of the strawberry lemonade vodka. Or the champibble. Or likely both. Whatever happened, she just wanted the banging to stop and for someone to wash the giant caterpillar out of her mouth.

Eventually, Ellie realized that the banging was actually at the front door (did this place not have a working doorbell?), and since there appeared to be no movement from anyone else in the townhouse, the duty of finding out who was there fell to her. She quickly put on a fluffy pink bathrobe she'd found hanging on the back of the bathroom door, stuffed her frozen feet into matching slippers and wobbled downstairs, trying to keep the room from spinning out of control.

She was somewhat surprised to find a snow-covered Brandon Turner at the front door, dressed warmer than she had ever seen him in a large down parka, Sorel boots and hunting cap. The piles of white snow were blinding to Ellie's hungover eyes. To get to the door, Brandon had to push through a good four-foot thick embankment. She waved him in and shut the door, shivering.

"Brandon! What are you doing here?"

The snow Brandon stomped off his boots was making a large pile, some of which was falling onto Ellie's slippers as she backed away.

"Get that gear off and come into the kitchen. I'll make some coffee," Ellie said before Brandon could reply.

"I'm sorry to disturb you," he said as he hung his thick parka on one of the woven metal coat hooks, which Ellie noticed exactly matched the intricate stair railing.

Ellie busied herself with preparing coffee. Thankfully, Betsy's kitchen was equipped with a regular drip machine, something she was familiar with, and her hungover brain was able to handle the process with ease. Brandon sat down at the bar, pushing aside the empty glasses and bottles of vodka, about which he made no comment.

"Betsy contacted me," Brandon started. "She knew I was in town and wanted me to check in on you."

"We're fine," Ellie said as she pulled a couple mugs out of the cupboard and placed one in front of Brandon. She really didn't want Betsy sticking her nose into their affairs, even if it was well meaning.

"I know what happened to Val."

Ellie paused in the coffee preparations to turn and look at Brandon.

"How?"

"Lucy messaged Betsy while you were at the ballet," Brandon said.

"Of course she did."

She was not surprised that Lucy would want to share that juicy tidbit of gossip.

"I know Betsy can be intrusive, but she does mean well." Brandon paused. "Lucy also told her about getting dumped at the side of the road by Betsy's sister-in-law. She's furious."

Ellie nodded, thinking about the family connection between Betsy and Edward's family, Edward's pinched-looking mother was Betsy's sister by marriage.

"I'm afraid I haven't been honest about something with you and your sister," Brandon said as Ellie poured him a coffee and offered cream and sugar, which he refused.

"I wanted to come by and set things straight because I think at some point it might make Val feel better."

Ellie was all ears now, wondering if she was finally going to hear the details of Brandon's apparent dark feelings towards Will Davis.

"No doubt Betsy has filled you in on details of my past," he paused, looking at Ellie's face and when she nodded, he continued. "As you know, I was married before, and I have a young daughter named Alisa."

"I've been looking after my former wife and daughter for many years now. I wish I could be more a part of Alisa's life, but my ex, Sarah, won't let me in." Brandon looked down at the kitchen island, his face a mix of worry and resignation.

"I was young, and I didn't fight the custody battle with Sarah, which I regret to this day. I don't agree with the way she has raised Alisa, and the girl has grown into a very headstrong young woman." He paused, his large hands wrapped around his mug of coffee, which he stared into but was not drinking.

"It was my fault, too. Whenever I see Alisa, I indulge her."

Ellie shook her head at Brandon, but he continued before she could dispute him.

"Alisa left home when she was eighteen, and both my ex and I lost track of her for months. On the night of the dinner party at Betsy's, I finally received a call from her."

Ellie remembered the concern in Brandon's face that night but had not considered what might have been at stake for him.

"She was nine months pregnant. And the man she said was the father, who had left her as soon as he found out her state, was Will Davis."

Ellie was in shock. She already thought Will Davis to be the lowliest of the low on account of his treatment of her sister, but abandoning a child put him on par with politicians in Ellie's eyes.

"I had heard rumours that Will had been hanging around Alisa, so I had my suspicions early on. I regret that I never said anything to you and your sister."

"Will should be made to look after the baby. He can't marry this Victoria woman," Ellie said.

It just didn't make any sense to her. It was like a story out of the 1800s, when men never had to live up to their responsibilities.

"What can I do? He claims the baby isn't his. My daughter doesn't want to force a paternity test. It's her decision, really." Brandon shrugged his shoulders.

Ellie was watching Brandon intently, so she hadn't noticed that Val had been standing at the entrance to the kitchen, listening to the whole story. When Brandon saw Ellie's eyes flicker over, he turned on the stool, taking a sharp intake of breath at the site of Val. Her face was drawn and pale, with giant bags under her eyes like she'd been crying recently. She gave a small half smile at Brandon.

"I'm sorry you had to hear that," Brandon said. "I hope I was right to tell you."

"Yes, you were." Val looked completely forlorn.

"Val, come, sit and have a coffee," Ellie said, reaching to grab a cup from the shelf.

"No, I'm going back to bed," she said, turning and walking back up the stairs.

Brandon turned back to Ellie. "I think I should go. I've done enough damage here." He got up, leaving his untouched coffee on the counter.

"Brandon, you did the right thing," Ellie called out after him, but he didn't respond. There was a flurry of snow as he left through the front door and then silence again.

Ellie poured a coffee for her sister and went to take the mug upstairs. She found her sister at the front of Lucy's bedroom door, staring intently. As Ellie approached, she noticed a small handwritten note taped there, the loopy script like that of someone who had just learned handwriting.

Dear Ellie et al,

I'm writing this note to inform you that I will not be returning with you to Sober. Edward came by early this morning to pick me up and take me back to my home with my parents in the south. As I know you are all aware, Edward and I are to be married, and despite his mother's cruel treatment, he is a gentleman and will not go back on his promise.

As a testament of my friendship, I insist that you all be at my side for the wedding. There will be at least six bridesmaids, so consider yourselves some of the lucky few. Your manly friend is unfortunately excluded, unless she would be comfortable in a seafoam gown, of which I doubt.

Yours,

The Soon to Be Mrs. Edward Price

Val turned to Ellie with shock on her face. "How long have you known?" she demanded. Ellie pulled her sister into their bedroom and shut the door.

"Ever since the first night we met Lucy," Ellie said.

"Why didn't you tell me?" Val was indignant.

"She made me promise not to tell anyone," Ellie shrugged, but she knew in her heart that Ellie had assumed her sister was too absorbed in her own problems to want to support her. Although from the hurt look on Val's face, she knew instantly that her assumptions were false.

"What bullshit," Val said. "I can't believe that Edward would treat you that way."

"Would you have him treat Lucy as poorly as you've been treated by Will? At least he is keeping his promises."

Ellie paced around the bedroom, still holding the coffee she had brought up for Val, which she realized was splashing all over the pink bathrobe and making large brown stains. She carefully placed the cup down on the dresser.

"Why are you so calm? For once spill some coffee, get angry, break some shit!" She picked up a pillow and threw it at the dresser, smashing the cup and spraying coffee all over the mirror and floor.

Ellie sighed and shook her head. "There is no fairy-tale ending for us, Val. You had better accept that."

She got down on her hands and knees and began to pick up the broken shards of the cup.

"Edward will marry Lucy; Will will marry Victoria; and we will go back to Sober."

Ellie sat up, feeling the sharp pieces of ceramic in her hands. How easy it would be to clench her fist and feel the sharp cut. For once she wanted to feel something, but her sensible mind stopped her. It would just mean more mess for her to clean up.

A tiny tap at their door, caused both sisters to look up. Carrie stuck her head in. "Everything okay in here?"

"Yes. According to my heartless sister, everything is just hunky-dory," Val said through gritted teeth as she pushed past Carrie and left the room.

Carrie came in and began to help Ellie clean up.

"I'm sorry," Ellie said.

Carrie shrugged. "Family."

"Did you check your phone yet?" Carrie asked.

"No?"

"Our flight is cancelled. There's another winter storm coming through, and no small planes are leaving." Carrie stood up and dropped a few shards of mug into the small waste basket.

"Oh great," Ellie said. At this point, she just wanted to get home, even if it was to their cat-pee smelling trailer.

"Yeah, I'm going to have to get a sub in for school on Monday," Carrie said. "I'd better go call the school and let them know."

"I read that letter from Lucy," she said as she was leaving the room. "Damn, the Cupcake moves pretty fast if she is already planning her bridesmaids."

Carrie paused, looking at her friend to gauge her emotion, but Ellie's face was as unreadable as an accounting textbook.

"And she is right about the seafoam," Carrie continued. "It doesn't work with my eyes. I'm more of an emerald green kinda gal."

Carrie smiled at her friend, the joke having the desired effect as Ellie's face cracked into a smile. At least if they were going to be stuck in Fort George, she would have Carrie here for support.

CHAPTER
twenty-nine

Now that Val was off sulking, Ellie found the once spacious rowhouse very cramped. The living room boasted a giant flat screen TV, which Val had occupied in coup style, stretching her tiny body across the chaise lounge, preventing anyone else from joining her. Carrie didn't appear to be affected by Val's state and sauntered in, shoving Val's skinny legs out of the way and grabbing the remote out of her hand. Val was about to make a sulky retort as Carrie switched the TV from reruns of *Antique Roadshow* to the CFL semi-finals, but Val was a pseudo-Canadian football fan, or she just didn't mind watching big men in tights run around a snowy field. Either way, she kept her mouth shut.

Ellie decided to hide away in the bedroom, busying herself with ensuring they were rebooked on the next available flight out of Fort George. She spent a couple hours on hold with the airline company, who rerouted her to someone named Sarbjeet, who turned out to be extremely helpful. By the end of the call, Ellie was consoling Sarbjeet because the love of *his* life had been promised to another man, and he felt he would be single forever. Ellie was unfortunately able to relate.

Thankfully, the next flight out would get them home early Monday morning, and Ellie would be able to get to her shift at the oilfields although slightly late. She sent a text to her boss, Wayne Smith, letting him know she would be late for work the next day. He felt that emails were too impersonal and insisted that his employees communicate in the modern medium of instant messaging. She received a reply back almost instantly.

Wayne Smith: *Stuck in Fort George? Likely story, Dashwood! I know about your loose and dirty lifestyle LOL.*

Ellie decided she wasn't going to reply, but unfortunately, Wayne wasn't going to let the opportunity pass.

Wayne Smith: *Quite the scene you and that* Flashdance *sister of yours made last night. I didn't know you had a side job....*

Ellie watched the screen of her phone, wondering how she was supposed to respond. What was he hinting at? Did he know someone that was at the French Maid? It was almost unavoidable in a small town to get away from gossip.

Ellie: *I can assure you that I have no other job.*

Wayne Smith: *Tell you what. You go on a date with me, and I won't make a big deal about your little stripping side job 'kay?*

Ellie decided to ignore the last text and just hope that he went away. Thankfully, her phone rang almost immediately. It was her half-brother, John. He never called, so she immediately wondered if there was a tragedy in the family. He launched into the conversation without preamble.

"What a travesty last night! Fanny is up in arms. She had no idea about this Lucy woman. How could she be so presumptuous as to assume she could get into the Price family this easily?" John said, his voice squeaky with concern.

Ellie paused, not sure where her brother was going with the conversation. "Well, Edward made a promise to her, and he is following through."

"My mother-in-law nearly had a heart attack! Did Lucy not think of her health?" John asked querulously.

"John, why are you calling?" Ellie asked, thinking she'd better get to the bottom of what was on John's mind.

"Well, Fanny and I wanted to make sure you two girls were both all right, what with everything going on and the storm." He paused, and Ellie remained silent, sure her brother had another purpose for the call. Finally he continued, "Also, Fanny would like to know if either of you was in cahoots with this Lucy character about her apparent engagement to Edward."

Ahh, so that was the rub. Fanny was assuming they were somehow involved. Maybe she thought that Ellie and Val were trying to take down the Price family by shoving overgrown tarts into their ranks like landmines, ready to go off at a later point and dismantle the family hierarchy.

"John, I only just met Lucy. How could we have anything to do with the situation? Lucy and Edward have been engaged for years," Ellie said emphatically.

"So they say," John replied. "Fanny believes this Lucy girl is just in it for the money. She even went so far as to say that she would have rather Edward marry one of you two, if you can believe it."

Ellie took a few deep breaths to calm herself before replying.

"John, I'm sure if Edward says he cares for Lucy, then it is for real. Your wife's family is just going to have to accept it."

Before John could continue, Ellie hung up, which was quite out of character for her, and she immediately felt bad. But then again, upon watching the falling snow out the window increasing, she felt better, consoled in the fact that John would assume their line had been cut.

Having slept in late and spent most of the day on the phone, when Ellie finally went downstairs, it was getting dark outside. She found Carrie and Val curled up on the couch, watching football. Carrie had pulled the leftover pizza out of the fridge and was eating it cold while nursing a glass of peppermint schnapps.

"The alcohol pickings are getting slim," Carrie commented when Ellie came into the room. Her sister appeared to be not eating or drinking (for the latter she was thankful).

"I'm not sure I can drink that," Ellie said. "It tastes like toothpaste." Carrie raised her glass to Ellie and took another sip.

"Val, you should eat something," Ellie said as she sat down on the couch and picked up a cold slice of anchovy Hawaiian.

"No thanks," Val replied, her voice quiet and sad.

The football game was almost over, but as was typical, the last few minutes went on for almost a half an hour. When it finished, Val got up and stretched, looking back at Ellie and Carrie as she walked out of the room.

"I'm going to go for a little walk," Val said.

"What?" Ellie replied. "Have you seen what it's like out there?"

"Yeah, snow, I saw," she said, leaving the room and grabbing her parka from the coat hooks.

Ellie got up and followed her sister. "I don't think this is a good idea."

"Ellie, I'll be fine. I just need some air and time to think. It is snowing, but it's no worse than the weather we had to walk through to school for all the time we were growing up." Val smiled at her sister.

Ellie sighed but was somewhat reassured by her sister's comments. They were northern girls after all, and a little winter weather never stopped anyone with ice in their blood. She wouldn't be able to stop her sister anyway because when Val had it in her mind to do something, there was no stopping her.

Val left in a cloud of blowing snow. Ellie was happy that she had at least dressed warmly, finding a toque and mitts to go with the parka, so Ellie went back to watching the post-game analysis with Carrie. The television flowed into reruns of *Grey's Anatomy,* and Carrie and Ellie fell into a sloth-like state, perhaps owing to the fact that she had been convinced to imbibe in some of the schnapps, which was tasting better and better with every sip.

It was only after two back-to-back episodes that Ellie looked at her phone, realizing that it was after 9:00 PM and Val still wasn't back. She texted Val but got no response.

"Call her. She might not hear the notification of the phone out there in the wind," Carrie said, noticing the growing look of concern on her friend's face.

Ellie called her sister, and as they sat in the living room she heard a faint ringing. Getting up from the couch Ellie followed the sound. It was coming from upstairs, and when she opened the master bedroom door the sound increased. Val had left her cell behind. Panic began to set on Ellie, a cold shiver running through her body. She ran back downstairs to find Carrie.

"She left her phone here," Ellie said, her face white.

"I'm sure she is okay."

"I'm going out after her." Ellie turned to get her coat from the entryway.

"What? On foot? And then you'll be lost out there, too? That makes zero sense."

"Well, we don't have a car. What else can I do? I can't just leave her out there in this weather," Ellie said, the distress in her voice evident.

Carrie paused, "Why don't you call that Brandon guy? He must have a four-wheel drive truck if he came by the house this morning."

Ellie nodded, pulling her cell phone out and dialing Brandon's number. He answered before the second ring.

"Brandon, I'm sorry to bother you." Ellie said. "It's Val."

"What happened?"

"She went for a walk in the storm and hasn't come back."

"I'm on my way."

CHAPTER
thirty

Val always loved the sound her boots made in newly fallen snow. Ellie had told her once that the crunching noise was from the snow molecules breaking apart under her steps, and as a child, she imagined herself a giant with the strength to break apart the very structure of life. Now the crunching noise was comforting, filling her mind with nostalgia.

She didn't even notice the cold anymore. The moisture of her breath was causing small icicles to form on her eyelashes, so that they stuck to her forehead. She blinked a few times to clear them away. Val let her feet guide her, not really knowing where she was going. There were no cars on the roads and no snowplows either, so her trudging was slow. Her face was numb from the wind and the snow. Val didn't realize how long she'd been walking before she found herself in front of the French Maid, the last place she had seen Will. It was closed because of the storm, but the neon sign continued to glow, lighting the snow-filled parking lot with an eerie purple hue.

Val let her butt fall into a snowbank, forming a small ledge to sit on. It was comforting to sit and rest, letting the falling snow collect on her body. Nothing else ever stayed with Val—her mother, her father and now Will. For a brief moment, her mind drifted to Ellie, but that thought just filled her with guilt. She was a burden to her sister and always had been. If it wasn't for Val, Ellie would be off at university. She wished she could be more like Ellie, stoic and sensible. But it wasn't her nature.

Like every northerner, Val knew the danger of the cold. Freezing to death was an easy way out. It was painful at the start, but your body systems eventually shut down, numbing your limbs so you felt nothing. Eventually, you felt the pull of sleep, and when you finally succumbed, you never woke again. Val thought it was strange that the harshness of living in the north could provide such a simple and easy way out with no pain. It was poetic in a way. Wouldn't Ellie be better off if she didn't have Val to look after?

Val thought about her funeral. Would Will come? Would he be upset that she was dead, or would he be too busy with his new wife? She hoped Ellie would get lilies for the flower arrangements; they were Val's favourite. Thinking again about Ellie and imagining her at the funeral, she could imagine the pain on her sister's face and the loneliness. Val couldn't hurt Ellie like that. She stood up from the snowbank, barely feeling her toes in her boots, but she forced herself to take one step forward and then another.

Val made her way back to the road, trudging along. Her fingers and toes were burning. If you tried to fight the numbness of frostbite your body would punish you; that was a fact. When blood returned to your extremities, it was painful enough to make you want to vomit. Val squeezed her eyes against the burning pain in her hands and feet but forced herself to keep moving.

She didn't notice the noise of the snowplow approaching over the howl of the wind. The driver, high up in the truck cab, didn't see the small person in dark clothing on the side of the road, nor was he expecting pedestrians late at night in the storm. The plow rocketed along the road, its giant shovel pressed flush against the side where Val was walking. Eventually, she heard the scrape of the shovel and turned to see the blinding headlights of the plow. She had only a second before the shovel was on top of her, so she jumped headfirst onto a steep embankment.

She tumbled through the snow, her body sinking into the drifts like she had jumped into a pool. Once she stopped sliding, the once fluffy white stuff hardened around her buried body like concrete. Val was awake long enough to remember that the worst way to die in the north was to be buried in snow; it was a painful, suffocating experience, and she felt a fear engulf her mind like a virus before she lost consciousness.

Brandon drove his truck as fast as possible around the streets of Fort George, his high beams on as he searched for any trace of Val. His heart was beating fast in his chest, but he remained calm, not wanting to think the worst. Ellie didn't know where her sister had gone, but she had mentioned to Brandon about their interaction with Will Davis at the French

Maid, so on a hunch Brandon drove by the club in case Val had walked that way.

There was no sign of her in the parking lot, so he continued back along the main road, following the recently plowed street. As Brandon scanned the sides of the road, he saw what he thought was a piece of clothing sticking out of the embankment. Brandon stopped his truck immediately, jumping out and running down the snowbank. He saw a tip of a boot sticking out of the snow. Brandon began to dig with his bare hands, scooping out the snow around the boot, which led to legs and a torso. Val was buried face down in the snow, and as Brandon scooped the snow away from her body, he was finally able to turn her around.

"Val!"

She was silent and not breathing.

Brandon pulled open her mouth, finding it full of snow. He pulled a bloody chunk of snow from her mouth and pressed his lips over her, breathing air into her lungs. On the second breath into her, Val coughed, her eyes fluttering.

Brandon scooped her limp body into his arms and carried her up the snowbank. He placed her on the seat of his truck cab and drove off, heading straight for the hospital.

thirty-one

Ellie ran through the front doors of the hospital with Carrie trailing behind her. As soon as she got the call from Brandon that he had found Val, Ellie had called a cab. Thankfully, the snow had slowed, and most of the roads were plowed, so the wait for the cab was short. She wanted Brandon to stay with her sister, so she would know if her condition changed.

The front desk directed Ellie and Carrie to the ER, where they found Val lying on a bed in the back behind a blue curtain, Brandon at her side. The dull fluorescent lights were flickering in the corner, giving a post-apocalyptic feel to the situation. Val was sleeping, but her breathing was raspy.

"Has the doctor seen her yet?" Ellie asked.

"Yes, she was assessed when we arrived, and they said she is not in danger. They treated her for frostbite and that's all. But she needs to remain overnight so they can monitor her because she nearly suffocated," Brandon said, his eyes never moving from Val.

Ellie put a hand gently on her sister's forehead like she had done so many times when Val was a child. She was clammy and warm, her body obviously kicking into overdrive to reverse the near freezing to death.

"Val, what were you thinking?" Ellie asked.

At that moment, the curtain was yanked back, and a young, very good-looking, Asian doctor walked in. He was staring a clipboard like it held the answers to the universe. Ellie noted that her sister would be devastated if she was awake and realized how this man was seeing her. It's funny the things your brain comes up with in stressful situations.

The doctor looked up from his clipboard, seeing the small group gathered around Val's bed. There was no room to move in the tiny space.

"Are you all family?" he asked. "If not, you'll have to leave."

Ellie was going to dispute this because, other than Val, Carrie felt as close as family, and after what Brandon had done to rescue her sister, he deserved to be there. Brandon spoke up first.

"Of course, I was just leaving." He stood, glancing back at Val. "Ellie, please keep me updated."

"I will."

"I'll get a ride home with Brandon," Carrie said, giving Ellie a hug before she turned to leave as well.

As soon as they left, the doctor moved in to look at Val.

"What was she doing out on a night like this?" he asked, as he lifted her eyelids, pointing a small pen light at each of her eyes in turn.

Ellie sighed, "It's a long story."

"Probably had something to do with a man. Always does with girls like this."

Ellie was affronted, what did he mean "girls like this"? "I'm sorry, I didn't get your name, Doctor...?"

The doctor ignored her and kept examining Val. "I'm going to move her out of Emergency. We should have a bed ready soon. She needs to be monitored for twenty-four hours for signs of secondary drowning."

"What does that mean?" Ellie asked.

The doctor stood up and looked at Ellie. "It means your sister was dumb. She inhaled a bunch of snow. When snow melts, it turns to water. Water in your lungs is bad." He inhaled in a stiff manner like treating patients was a great inconvenience.

"Is she going to be okay?"

"Do I look like a fortune teller?" The doctor slammed Val's chart back onto the end of the bed, storming out of the curtained area like a child having a tantrum.

Ellie sighed and grabbed the chart, looking for the name of the doctor. At the bottom she found his signature, and she thought it read "Hardick." The name certainly fit his personality.

Val's breathing was labored, and Ellie wondered if she was fighting the water in her lungs. She didn't have much time to think about it as a small, rotund nurse came into the area, smiling and humming to herself.

"Don't mind Doctor 'Hard-Dick,'" she said. "He has been grumpy ever since his wife left him last month."

She began to disconnect Val from the various devices around her.

"We have a bed for Ms. Dashwood ready. It's in the extended care area, unfortunately, so she'll have to share, but she will be in good hands there."

Ellie was happy that the new room had a chair next to Val's bed that she could sit in. It was not a peaceful room; the co-habitant was an extremely large elderly man whose snores echoed through the room like an idling chainsaw. Val had a fitful sleep. Occasionally she would wake in a fever-induced delirium, not really aware of where she was. Ellie would hold her sister's hand until she became calm. Eventually, Ellie drifted off to sleep next to her sister, only to be awakened in the early morning hours by the alarm from Val's oxygen monitor.

Nurses hustled into the room, pushing Ellie aside and checking her breathing. Everyone was moving quickly, and Ellie, having just woken, felt like she was in a dream.

"Get the doctor," said one of the nurses. "She needs to be intubated." More people bustled into the room, and Val was rushed out.

"Where are you taking her?" Ellie asked frantically, finally coming to her senses.

"She needs to be in the ICU," replied the nurse, but Ellie got no further information.

Ellie made her way down the elevator to the ICU, panic settling in her chest like a stone. She went up to the closed doors where her sister was taken, but she was stopped by the same nurse she'd met in Emergency.

"You can't go in there while they're intubating. Just wait until she is stable."

The nurse had put a firm hand on Ellie, knowing that family sometimes do desperate things when they are scared. Through the small window on the door to the room, Ellie could see the doctors prepping her sister for the procedure. A tube would be forced down her throat, so that a machine could breathe for her.

"Is she going to be okay?" Ellie asked the nurse, whose face gave her all the answers she required.

"When patients are intubated it is very serious," the nurse responded, not unkindly. "But she's in very good hands."

Eventually, Ellie was allowed into the room, and she hurried to Val's side. It was a disturbing sight. A tube was protruding from Val's mouth, secured with tape on either side, which connected to an oscillating machine and a monitor displaying Val's vital functions. Ellie held her sister's hand, listening to the slow beep of the heart monitor and rustle of the hospital staff as they collected their tools and instruments.

She looked at her sister's sedated face and felt the tears well up for the first time since this terrible evening began. The prospect of losing the most important person in her life filled Ellie with dread.

"I can't do it," Ellie whispered, "I can't live without you."

She kissed Val's hand, letting her tears fall.

"Please."

Ellie's mind flooded with all the loss in her life. Their mother leaving. Their father's death. Edward's abandonment. Any of those were insignificant compared to what she was facing now. Ellie wasn't sure she could carry on without Val in her life.

thirty-two

Ellie was at her sister's side for days, watching the mechanical breathing machine and pleading for everything to be okay. Brandon was a near constant fixture at the hospital as well, bringing food for Ellie that she had a hard time eating. She had to endure the presence of Dr. Hardick who, despite his continued snarky remarks, actually cared and watched over Val very closely. After Val had been on the ventilator for six days, he came by with good news.

"We are going to take your sister off the ventilator today. Her oxygen levels have significantly improved."

Ellie's heart leapt. "Thank you, Doctor!"

Doctor Hardick grimaced at Ellie, "It is a good thing, too, because it is not like this hospital has ventilators to spare." He left the room without further comment.

Later that day, Ellie was happy to be invited into Val's recovery room, where her sister sat upright in bed, looking very pale and worn but otherwise okay. Ellie ran to her sister and gave her a hug.

"Careful!" Val said in a raspy voice. Brandon was in the room as well, but he stood by the door quietly watching the two sisters. As he was turning to leave, Val called out in a small voice, her throat damaged from almost a week suffering with a ventilator tube.

"Brandon," she said. Brandon stopped and turned, his eyes looking tired but content.

"Thank you."

Brandon nodded at Val, his eyes lighting up at her acknowledgement.

thirty-three

Never had the cat-pee-smelling trailer felt so welcoming as upon the return of the two Dashwood sisters to their humble home. Even the persistence of Betsy insisting they come by to visit for tea could not alter their positive feelings. Thankfully, they could respectfully decline the invitation on account of Val's health. She was still weak and spent most of her days curled up on the couch. Ellie was happy to see her sister's spirits somewhat restored and even more so when Brandon came by to visit, which was often.

The two of them had taken to watching TV together, which Ellie thought was cute. Brandon would sit on the small loveseat with Val, doing his best not to come in contact with her, his body upright and proper. Val would eventually stretch her woolly-socked feet out onto his lap, which he accepted with a contented look.

With things returning to normal, Ellie had to return to work. She'd used up all her sick leave while at Val's side in the hospital, and it was with great reluctance that she conceded to going back to work. As Ellie was getting ready to leave, she overheard Brandon and Val from the living room chatting. It was hard to keep secrets in their tiny trailer.

"I know it was you who came to watch all my shows at The Bush," Val said. Ellie did not hear any response from Brandon, but then Val continued. "I'm not sure Ellie wants me to continue stripping."

"What do you want?" Brandon asked. "Because if you want to keep dancing, I'll support you, and I think your sister would too."

Ellie's thought about Brandon's comments, not wanting to leave her bedroom and disturb their conversation, but she had to get on the road or be late for work. When she walked out into the kitchen, the two of them sat up straight on the couch like two teenagers caught snuggling a little too close by their parents.

"Hey Ellie, you off to work?"

"Yeah, you sure you are okay?"

"Absolutely. Besides, I have Brandon here looking after me." She smiled at Brandon, who looked as pleased as a kid on Christmas morning.

Ellie was relieved that Brandon was there, she hoped that Val wasn't leading the poor man on. She seemed genuinely happy to have him around, but it was quite out of character for her to fall for a man like him. She resolved to have a heart-to-heart with her sister later on and make sure she was up front with Brandon.

Ellie had a message when she arrived at work to see Wayne Smith. She wasn't surprised. Having put in for the extended leave last week, she knew he would want to dig into her story. When she got to his office, his back was turned and he was talking on his headset with the door wide open. His voice was strained in a way that Ellie had never heard from him before, his usual overconfidence was overrun with concern.

"I don't believe you," he said into his headset.

Ellie moved to the side of the doorway, not wanting to listen in, but some part of her thought a little background on her asshole boss couldn't be a bad thing.

"The baby can't be mine." He ran his hand through his wavy dark hair. "It was only the one night. How can you be sure?"

At that moment, Wayne turned around and saw Ellie standing in the doorway. He nearly jumped out of his tight-fitting dress shirt.

"Oh, yes, so as I was saying…we need you to be sure of those reports. Get them to me right away." His voice had returned to his usual confident tones as he hung up on the mystery woman. Ellie smiled inside. Somehow it felt better that other people also had chaos to deal with in their lives.

"Ellie Dashwood, nice of you to finally come to work," he said as he sat down on his leather-backed steno chair.

"I used my sick leave, which the union allows us to use for family."

"Don't mention the "U" word around here, please."

Even though he had his confidence back, his usual sexual harassment tone was gone, replaced with a stressed business-like approach. Maybe pressure from the union about the potential takeover was stressing him out.

"You've been away, so I wanted to let you know that there will be an all-company meeting this week with the Excon executives."

"Oh, okay."

She wasn't sure why that meeting required her to have a personal meeting with her boss. Surely she would have seen the notice when she checked her emails.

"It has come to my attention that you have a connection with the Price family," he continued.

Ah, thought Ellie, *this must be why he wanted to talk to me.*

Ellie nodded, not sure where his line of questioning was going.

"That's why I've been trying to see you in private. I need you to talk to Edward Price. He seems to have some kind of personal connection with your family, and he has a lot of pull with the Excon board."

"I don't know what you expect me to do," Ellie replied briskly. This interaction with Wayne was awkward. She was used to the sexual innuendo, not the outright frankness and business-like approach he was using now.

"I'd like you to convince Edward to go ahead with the takeover," he paused, looking directly at Ellie to gauge her reaction. "If you are successful, I am willing to offer you a deal."

Ellie didn't respond, waiting to hear what Wayne was willing to put on the table. He looked at her sideways, in a way that sensed he was considering how much he would have to offer to entice Ellie.

"I'm willing to make you Site Manager," he said. "You wouldn't be union anymore, so no more overtime, but the Site Manager position would result in a doubling of your salary." Wayne watched Ellie intently.

"So, does this mean that Excon is considering pulling out of the takeover deal?" Ellie asked, putting together the pieces with what Wayne was offering.

Wayne sighed, "It doesn't look good. Edward Price spends more time with that geriatric Richard Branch than he does with the rest of the board. Something is going down, and he is going to leave all the rest of us with nothing!" He slammed his palm down on his desk, causing the Newton's Cradle on his desk to click into motion.

"So what do you say, Ellie? Can you help me out here? This could be a big ticket for you. Maybe your sister won't have to take her clothes off for a living anymore? Might be a chance at a decent life." Wayne had saved this dig until the end, trying to capitalize on Ellie's weakness—her family.

Ellie's mind ticked through the options. Sure, the idea of being a manager and making double her salary was tempting. Wayne was right; it would mean Val wouldn't have to strip anymore. But what chance would she have of convincing Edward anyway? And there was a good chance that a total takeover by Excon would result in many of her colleagues losing their jobs.

There was just no way she could do it. She stood up, resigned in her decision.

"Sorry Wayne, I can't help you." She turned to leave his office, fairly certain he wouldn't have anything else to say to her.

"Don't be too sure you'll still have a job on the other side of this, Dashwood."

Ellie paused before leaving Wayne's office, her back turned to Wayne so he couldn't see the look of hatred on her face. But she kept her mouth shut and walked away.

Conflicting thoughts swirled in her head that week. She didn't know what was going to be announced at the all-company meeting, but from her discussion with Wayne, she felt like things weren't going the way he wanted. She couldn't help but hoped that perhaps Edward had something to do with it. She didn't have long to find out; the all-company meeting was scheduled for the next day.

As Ellie gathered in the main warehouse room with her colleagues, there was a general rumble from everyone about what might be happening. On an elevated platform at the front of the warehouse, she could see the board of directors assembled along with the executives from Excon, including Edward. As Ellie expected, Edward was neatly dressed, looking handsome in his business suit, chatting with the tight-bun lady Ellie remembered from their tour months ago.

Richard Branch got up to the microphone to start the meeting.

"Thank you all for coming." The elderly man stood tall at the microphone, his body showing no signs of his advanced age. Ellie had calculated that he must be nearing eighty years old, but he still looked spry.

"I know it has been a stressful time for all of you," he continued, "but I will say immediately so as to not draw this out that we have come to a mutual agreement with Excon." He glanced back at the table behind him where Edward and the other executives were sitting. Ellie thought she saw his eyes rest on Edward slightly longer, but she could have been mistaken.

"Excon will take over forty-nine percent of the shares, leaving the controlling fifty-one percent with myself and the remaining board members."

Applause erupted from the assembled workers. They all trusted Richard Branch, and the news that he would remain at the helm of the company was reassuring.

"Further to that," he continued, "as we all know, I'm no spring chicken," he paused, letting the few laughs from the crowd die down. "I realize that a succession plan must be put in place. I'm happy to say that we have come to an almost unanimous agreement that my shares shall be distributed to the employees of Sober Oil in a profit-sharing initiative that is unprecedented in this industry. In this way, we will ensure that you, the heart and soul of this operation, will drive the company forward while continuing to bring wealth, prosperity and economic growth to the community of Sober. You will all be shareholders in Sober Oil."

With that he raised his arms out to the crowd to the thunderous applause that echoed around the room.

Ellie was cheering along with everyone else. She couldn't have hoped for a better outcome, and she was certainly relieved. Ellie's job was secure, and she was content with her decision to decline Wayne's offer. She looked up at the stage and saw that Wayne's face looked even more stressed than when she had seen him earlier that week.

Her eyes drifted down the table to Edward, and she could swear that he was looking right at her even though she was in a crowd of hundreds. She felt her heart warm at his look, even though she knew their relationship would never be rekindled; at least she now knew that he was indeed a good person.

CHAPTER
thirty-four

Val and Ellie couldn't avoid a visit with Betsy for much longer. Eventually, Val felt better and said she could walk up to the mansion with Ellie, saying that she would enjoy the cold winter walk. As it was into December, the winter had shifted from snowy, to just plain cold. The thermometer dipped into the range where it didn't matter if it was Fahrenheit or Celsius, the number was the same. Ellie made sure Val was bundled up like a Jet-Puffed marshmallow, wearing a full snowsuit and looking like she was ready for an Arctic expedition.

"I think this is a bit overkill, Ellie," Val complained as they finally left the trailer, Val holding onto Ellie's arm for support. She was better, but her body was still weak, and she had bouts of dizziness when walking around.

"No, not overkill at all." Ellie patted her sisters mittened hand as they slowly made their way through the snow to the Price Mansion. The afternoon was clear and crisp, and despite the cold, it felt good to see the sun although it was already low on the horizon.

"Isn't it strange how quiet it is when the weather is cold," Ellie said. Her sister was not nearly as talkative as she used to be, and it bothered Ellie to see Val so reserved.

"Yes, it is very peaceful," Val said.

"I hope you don't still feel bad about Will," Ellie had avoided talking to her sister about Will, but she worried that Betsy would ask questions, and she wanted to gauge her sister's feelings.

"No, not at all," she replied. "My only regret is about my behaviour."

"Val, don't feel bad about that." Ellie looked over at her sister. Val's eyelashes were frosted on the tips, looking like a crystalline halo, even though they had only been outside for a few moments.

"No, Ellie. I mean it. I should have been more like you. And to think what could have happened if Brandon hadn't found me. I'm sorry."

Ellie smiled at her sister, giving her arm a reassuring squeeze, but the compliments felt good to Ellie, like all her stress hadn't been for nothing.

"Also, I've decided you're right. I should quit stripping." Val was staring down at her feet as they crunched across the frozen ground.

"Is that what you want?" Ellie asked, thinking of the conversation she'd overheard between her sister and Brandon.

Val paused and looked over at her sister through the faux fur of her parka hood.

"No. But I want to do what's right. I don't want to stress you anymore."

Ellie pulled them up short on their walk, turning to face her sister directly.

"Kiddo, you are good at performing. When I watched you in the contest, I couldn't believe your talent and creativity. I was so proud of you. If you want to keep doing it, then I will support you. Besides, someone has to beat that bitch, Candy!"

Val's face lit up at her sister's acceptance. As they continued their walk to the Price mansion, she began to talk excitedly.

"I have some amazing ideas for my next show! We should work on it together. I'm thinking of re-enacting *Gladiator,* the scene where Russel Crowe gets the sign from the king to execute, except I'll get the thumbs up from the crowd to remove layers of clothing!"

"Sounds like fun, but maybe let's not discuss your stripping routines in front of Betsy Price? That would be more excitement than she's had in decades."

The Price house was comfortably warm with a brightly burning fire in the front sitting area. Betsy fussed about Val, making sure she was as close to the fire as possible and ordering Silvie to bring hot tea for everyone.

"I told you Jim could have picked you girls up. You shouldn't have walked in this cold, not with your condition." Betsy was placing a blanket on Val's legs. Even though she was refusing, Betsy would not have it, so Val eventually relented.

"We needed the fresh air," Ellie said.

"Oh, speaking of condition, do I some have news for you girls!" Betsy looked like she was ready to explode out of her seat as she waved at Silvie to get out of the room. Obviously it must be good gossip if she didn't want her maid to hear.

"I got a message from Lucy Martin this morning. I was not surprised, what with her upcoming wedding. I knew she would consult with me on the preparations, but I was surprised by the content of this particular message."

Betsy leaned in towards the two sisters sitting side by side on the love seat. "She said she was happy to inform me that she is expecting!"

Val looked at her sister, who looked drawn and shocked. For once it was Val who responded.

"Did she say who the father was?" Val asked.

"Well, it must be our dear Edward! I know I should be shocked given that it is out of wedlock, but I am not such an old-fashioned toddy. I, too, can be a modernist."

She lowered her voice and looked carefully around the room, even though they were obviously alone. "I have even been known to read *Ms. Magazine.*" She nodded in a knowing way, sitting back against her paisley chair like she was the next Gloria Steinem.

Val smiled at Betsy. "Please wish Lucy the best from us." Val grabbed her sister's hand as Ellie still remained frozen in place. The realization that Edward was absolutely bound to Lucy Martin was difficult to accept.

"I'm sorry, Betsy," Val said, putting a hand to her forehead, "I'm feeling weak again. I think my sister and I need to be going."

Ellie looked over at her sister, knowing full well that she was giving an excuse to get them out of there, and she was extremely grateful.

"Of course, of course!" Betsy tittered, as she rang a small bell calling again for Silvie to come and remove the tea.

The two girls were silent on the walk home. Val knew her sister needed time to process Edward having a baby with Lucy and that Val wouldn't be able to help. As they approached the trailer, they heard the low rumbling of a diesel truck.

"Oh! Brandon is here!" Val smiled at her sister.

Ellie remembered her vow to talk to Val about Brandon.

"Val, I hope you know what you are doing with this man. He is really into you."

Val smiled back at Ellie. "I have a secret."

For the first time in a long while Ellie noticed a glow in her sister's eyes, that or the cold was freezing them into ice cubes.

"I think I'm falling for Brandon."

Ellie raised her eyebrows at her sister.

"Don't worry. I have no intention of rushing into anything," Val continued.

"I like Brandon," replied Ellie. "It is just..."

"You are happy it is just the two of us right now. And we don't really need anyone messing things up again," Val added.

"Yeah," Ellie gave Val a small smile. "Something like that."

"Sis, I couldn't agree more."

They had almost arrived at the trailer, and Brandon was waiting in his idling truck.

"Brandon is coming over today to talk with me about Joey's cookie business. He says he is going to help him out with some start-up cash."

Ellie smiled, wondering if Brandon's intentions were exclusively to help Joey or if he was still trying to get on Val's good side. In her books, the guy had done enough good deeds to get him past the Pearly Gates, but who was she to question.

CHAPTER
thirty-five

The cold spell continued in Sober as the year advanced further into December. The sisters made plans for Christmas. Betsy was arranging a big Christmas 'do at her place, inviting the entire Price family, including their half-brother John and his wife, Fanny. Ellie was actually looking forward to being around family, albeit her half relations. Brandon was invited as well, which meant that Val was happy with the arrangement.

Ellie felt better being around her sister-in-law, Fanny, knowing that Sober Oil would remain partially owned by the employees, and that the Price family would remain on the sidelines. She still thought about Edward, not having heard any word about him. She hoped that his new situation would bring him some contentment in life.

Ellie was deep in reverie that morning as she approached the long line of trucks for the Tim's drive-thru. She had reverted to her old habit of braving the cold weather and going inside the coffee shop. Given it was still minus forty, she thought even fewer people would risk leaving their vehicles for coffee.

There was no one in line when she went inside, and she was immediately called to the till by a kid with enough zits to build a small puss farm. As she was about to place her order, another voice came from behind her.

"I'll get her bill and add another double-double to that please."

Ellie turned around to see Edward standing behind her, smiling, his hair slightly tousled from his walk outside. She noticed immediately that he again was not wearing a jacket, just like the first time they met, and she wondered how on earth he had survived the run from the car.

"Hi," Ellie gulped, her shock at seeing Edward very apparent. "I didn't think you were in town anymore."

"I had something I needed to look after."

"Oh, congratulations by the way."

"Congratulations?" Edward looked confused.

"I hear Lucy is expecting."

"Oh. Right. I guess you haven't heard."

Ellie froze, but Edward wouldn't look her in the eye. He remained speechless for what felt like ages.

"The baby isn't mine." Edward paused with a look on his face that could only be pure relief.

"In fact, Lucy felt that she needed to be with the father, so we ended the engagement...for the child's sake."

Edward was rambling, looking awkwardly anywhere but at Ellie's face. If he had, he would have seen a crack in her usual emotionless mask.

"So, you aren't marrying Lucy?"

"Ah, no. She is marrying this guy…" Edward paused and ran his hand through his hair, a look of surprised disbelief on his face. "From Sober Oil…Wayne Smith."

Ellie broke. She emitted a strange squeak and then a sob that sounded something like a donkey being strangled. Not the most attractive of noises, but for the first time in her life she felt completely out of control.

"Uhm…is someone going to take these coffees or what?" asked the guy at the till, who was staring at the strange interaction with a look of boredom only a teenager can convey.

Edward continued, ignoring the cashier.

"The promise I made to Lucy was so long ago. We were both young. I knew then that we didn't work together, but when I tried to leave her, she threatened to hurt herself. I should have gone for help, but I was young and didn't know any better. So I proposed to keep her safe, and then hoped she would get over her infatuation with time. It was cowardly of me, I know."

Edward paused, his expression contrite. "On the plus side, she seems really happy now that she is engaged to Wayne Smith."

"They are perfect for each other," Ellie squeaked through gritted teeth, as she attempted to maintain her composure. For some reason her normally compassionate brain was not filtering out her nasty thoughts. She envisioned Lucy and Wayne together, an image of his erect nipple piercings prominently on display in their wedding photos. She gave a small shudder. Nope. She actually felt sorry for Lucy.

"I'm sorry Ellie, for everything. I never would have left you if I knew how much it would hurt you, but I had convinced myself that you didn't care for me that way."

Ellie gave another snort and held her arm up to her nose to try and hold back her tears, but it was no use. Edward quickly moved forward and grabbed her in his arms. She collapsed into wet tears against his clean, pressed dress shirt.

She choked back a sob. Although she was wearing a giant parka Ellie could feel the warmth of his arms wrapped around her. It was the embrace she had been needing for a very long time.

"Why aren't you wearing a jacket?" she asked into his thin shirt. She could feel the wonderful shape of his muscled pecs under her face.

Edward pulled away slightly, looking down at her tear-streaked face.

"Less to take off later," he whispered into her ear as he pulled her mouth to his. Edward's lips were cold but felt wonderful against hers. She kissed him for what felt like an eternity.

thirty-six

Ellie was back at hockey the following week. It felt great to be back. She didn't even mind when Edward showed up to watch, sporting a giant foam finger that he waved like a lunatic every time she scored a goal.

Carrie was playing tonight and smiling like a Cheshire cat.

"What's flown up your butt and hatched a smiley egg?" Ellie asked when the two of them were on the bench together, sipping water and trying to avoid the giant snot loogies on the floor that the men deposited, thinking if they spat like an NHL player that would make them play better.

Carrie grinned, "Victoria came back to me."

"No kidding." Ellie thought about the ramifications.

Carrie finished her thought before Ellie could continue. "She dumped that Will Fucktard. Left him standing at the altar no less."

Ellie was stunned. This was news. But she didn't hear the end of the story until after their next shift, during which Ellie scored another goal for a hat trick. Edward was waving his foam finger and cheering exuberantly from the sidelines.

"Yup! Victoria walked up the aisle with her father and everything. And when the priest asked if there was any reason these two shouldn't be married, she turned around a shouted, 'I'm gay!' to the entire congregation and then ran out. She's been hiding out at my place ever since. The makeup sex is great." Carrie winked at Ellie before heading back out onto the ice.

Ellie thought about the ramifications of what Carrie had told her. She couldn't wait to tell Brandon. Perhaps he could finally arrange some support for his grandchild from that loser.

During Ellie's final shift she almost scored her fourth goal of the game but got a little close to the other goalie. Number 69 was there again, and he took offense to Ellie dancing around him. As Ellie was about to skate away, he caught his stick between her legs and gave her a can opener, sending her sprawling to the ground. Ellie was quick to jump to her feet, and she saw Carrie move to step in and defend her, but this time Ellie didn't back down. She skated between Carrie and Number 69 and punched him straight in the face. It felt so good to release her pent-up aggression. She vowed to do let fly more often.

Ellie spent the rest of the game in the penalty box, listening to Number 69 chirping away at her from the opposing box. But nothing could take away the feeling. For once she didn't feel trapped, not in her own emotions or in this town. Edward may not be her ticket out of here, nor may Brandon be for her sister, but they would find their own way.

About the Author

Emily Kirkham grew up in Prince George, BC, where the air always smelled of wood pulp from the pulp mill—so when she moved to Whitehorse, YT, she thought the "clean" air smelled funny. After earning a BSc in chemistry from McGill University, she worked as a chemist for twenty-two years.

Her short story, "Tales from the Tube," was published in the Winter 2020 edition of the *MS Shared Voices* newsletter, and her radio show, "My Sister is a Stripper," aired on the CBC Radio show *Outfront* in April 2009.

Emily now lives in Port Moody, BC, with her husband and children, where she spends her time playing hockey, coaching soccer, driving her children around, picking up dog poop and occasionally doing chemistry and writing.